Ruinous Notion

A Prevalent Notion Novel

Linnea March

To Rusty

for being my first love and last kiss

A Very Short Song

Once, when I was young and true,
Someone left me sad-
Broke my brittle heart in two;
And that is very bad.

Love is for unlucky folk,
Love is but a curse.
Once there was a heart I broke;
And that, I think, is worse.

-Dorothy Parker, 1926

PROLOGUE

TWELVE YEARS AGO

THEO BLAKE WAS NEVER a smart man. As much as his teachers tried with him, the best he could do was middling grades. He had little patience for algebra, his knowledge of American history was atrocious, and he had read only one book over the span of a year. But he had his three truths. He had a talent others only dreamed of. While classic literature held no interest, he could place his fingers on the strings of his guitar, open his mouth, and out came songs that brought people to tears. This came with a second truth, he would never achieve his dreams if he didn't leave the small town of Cape Rose on the Oregon Coast.

And most importantly, he knew he loved Matilda Lewis the second he saw her dancing in their high school talent show two years before.

As he grabbed the ringing phone from its spot beneath an old dirty napkin, Theo shoved the remnants of last night's dinner onto the floor. He didn't love the food his work served, but he wasn't too proud to take home the leftovers instead of throwing them out at the end of his shift. Most nights, that was his one meal of the day.

He lived in L.A. for almost a year now. All he had accomplished of his big dreams was talking his way into a single open mic night at his work, Proper Bar.

"Teddy?" the sweet voice on the other end asked.

"Hey, Mats." Theo scratched his grumbling stomach. He should have saved the sandwich the night before. He didn't work until five.

"I've been trying to call you for days. Where have you been?"

Theo imagined Mattie sitting on her clean white and blue bedspread, her sturdy legs crossed beneath her. The great expanse of her pristine room on its second story, overlooking the water in her beautiful seaside home back in Cape Rose. He had to imagine her exactly the way she was when he left her. The long dark hair, the bright green eyes, the way she had a small scar on her lower lip that grew white when she would angrily purse her lips at him. What he wouldn't give to kiss that scar one more time.

"Around. It's been busy with work, pulling extra shifts at the bar. I have almost enough saved up for some studio time."

She hesitated on the other end. "Do you need money? I can send you money."

Annoyance flickered inside him. Not at her, never at her, but at himself. He was twenty years old; he came to LA to make something of himself. And now his eighteen-year-old girlfriend was offering him money. She was still in high school and didn't work. It would be her parent's money. Her parent's who hated him. "No, I don't need your money."

"I'll come down to see you. Maybe next week?"

Theo opened a pizza box that was sitting on the kitchen counter, picked up the hardened crust, and knocked it against the counter where it made a dull *thunk* noise. It would probably chip a tooth and he certainly couldn't afford a dentist. He dropped the crust back into the box. "What are you talking about? Don't you have school?"

She let out an irritated huff. "Fuck school, Teddy. I'm practically failing classes as it is. You told me once you get settled, you'd send for me. I miss you so much it's palpable. What's the point?"

Leave it to her to use SAT words while waxing poetic. Theo let the pizza box close as he sat back in the single plastic lawn chair they had for seating. "What do you mean, you're failing? You can't flunk out of high school."

She scoffed. "You're one to talk. You did."

Theo swallowed the shame of that statement. It was true he had left high school in his junior year, but the circumstances were different. His uncle needed help in the diner and whatever he was going to do with himself wasn't going to involve an institution of higher learning. "But you're not me, you're supposed to do more..."

"It doesn't matter. Teddy, I'll come down and we can live together and you'll be a famous rock star and no one will care if we graduated from high school."

"I care! You can't fail high school. Promise me. No matter what, you'll finish high school and you'll go to college and you'll be more."

On the other end, Mattie snorted. "College? Why would I go to college? That's not our plan."

Theo sighed. He wouldn't let Mattie throw everything away for him. When he left, he told her as soon as he got a place, she would join him. But that was the talk of a teenage idiot who had never lived outside Cape Rose. That drive over the California border was his first time being outside of Oregon. Before he left, her mother warned him not to ruin her daughter's life.

Yasmin Lewis told him all the things he didn't want to admit were true. He was a high school dropout with nothing but a car that leaked oil and a beat-up guitar. That if Mattie followed him, it would ruin her life. At the time, he thought Yasmin didn't understand how deeply in love they were. But now he faced the truth. It didn't matter how much he cared for her. It wasn't love to ask her to give up all her potential so he could chase his dreams.

"Plans change, Mattie. You're not coming down here. You're not doing anything." He glanced around the studio apartment he shared with two other guys. Single twin mattresses on the floor. The dead cockroach carcasses that lined the floor of their kitchen, the shots that rang out at night, and the drug deals that went on outside his doorway. What kind of life was this for Mattie? It was all he could afford and was enough for him, but he would never have Mattie there. She had no idea how hard life was outside Cape Rose.

"What do you mean? I thought you wanted to see me?" Her voice was softer now, an edge of panic creeping in.

Every minuscule piece of him was begging for him to tell her the truth, to beg her to come down. To abandon all her dreams so he could have her beside him. But if there was one other thing Theo Blake knew, it was that he would always love Matilda Lewis more than anything in the world. Even if that meant letting her go. He fingered the small bag in his pocket. The item inside too precious to let go. She had given it to him with the promise that he'd use it to start a new life. He couldn't give her back the time she wasted on him, but he was going to give her back the life she deserved.

"No, I don't want to see you. Things aren't going to work out for us..."

Chapter One

Mattie

I F THERE IS AN art to avoid your ex, Matilda Lewis had it down to a science. Granted, her methods were different from your average person's. Most people avoid the diner their ex frequented. Would drive out of their way to a different coffee shop or make tea at home. Even in a small town, there are ways. But when the man who broke your heart at eighteen is the lead singer of the world's biggest rock band, it gets tricky.

It was easier in the beginning. Sure, she cried herself to sleep for months after Theodore Blake unceremoniously dumped her over the phone. But once she left for college far away from Cape Rose, she could start new. There were the little things that might remind her of Theo—a shaggy-haired man bent over a guitar, the scent of Irish Spring soap, when someone would snort-laugh. But these were brief pangs of hurt.

She knew Theo wasn't on her campus. In many ways, she could move on—never forgetting or stopping the nurturing of that little space deep in her chest that loved him above everything—first loves will do that. But she got older, wiser, and could tuck that part of herself away. She could date boys and eventually, when they kissed her, it would only be a fleeting thought to compare their lips to her Teddy's.

She was fine until she heard his voice again. By junior year, she and her roommate Emily lived off campus. Emily hung her bras to dry on the kitchen chairs, but she also knew the best clubs and parties. Emily had the best taste in music and was constantly playing new artists for everyone. At parties she would hijack the speaker, putting on whatever new playlist she had curated for the event, to groans and lighthearted admonishments. Mattie bopped her head to the first few chords of the rock song as soon as she heard it, but the second his voice rang out, her body grew cold. It didn't matter that at that point it had been four years since she had heard Theo sing. She recognized him immediately. Bile rose in her throat as she excused herself from the party. Her new boyfriend, Jay, found her standing outside. Her hands on her knees, painful gasps scraping her throat as she tried to get enough oxygen to make the ringing in her ears go away.

She told Jay she was suddenly sick and asked him to take her home. He didn't ask why. He was a sweet guy, through and through. Jay West was nothing like Theodore Blake, who left her behind.

When she got home, she typed his name into the search engine, wondering if she was wrong, that maybe it wouldn't be him. But it was. Theo Blake; lead singer and guitarist of Prevalent Notion. The band had recently been signed with the prestigious Repercussion Records. Beside him in the press release were two other men she didn't recognize. They even had a Wikipedia page, though the members didn't have enough fame to warrant their own. Alone in her room, she played video after video of them, mostly grainy footage from bars around Los Angeles, and one amateur music video. In the years since they had been apart, he had grown a beard, a few shades darker than his golden hair. Her fingers tingled as if they could remember the bristle at the nape of his neck as she would pull his face down for a kiss. He was tan and bulked up. She always loved the sturdiness of his arms as he wrapped himself around her, but now his biceps were huge. He was never a tall man, but when it was the two of them, it didn't matter. No matter what heels she wore, Theo was taller than her. Bigger, stronger.

There were comments about Theo calling him a golden boy. Talented musician, the hair, the tawny skin, the voice. She understood the comparisons, but to her, he wasn't golden. Gold was soft, it was shiny, and malleable.

Until the moment he broke her heart, she would have said he was sturdy, unpretentious, and would never waver in his convictions.

Seeing his picture, she wondered how she could have read him all wrong.

He would hate the label of golden. But he had that face, he had that voice. And golden he would be to everyone else.

She spent hours researching every detail about Theo and Prevalent Notion until there was no inch of the Internet she hadn't combed. Then she set blocks on her browser and phone to never give her information about them again. For the next few years, as they climbed into the music collective, she carefully avoided mention of Theo and the band. She would change the channel when they were on talk shows. She'd switch off the radio if she heard the familiar sound of his voice. Avoiding your ex-boyfriend was hard in most situations, but when he was shirtless on the cover of every magazine in the checkout aisle, it was damn near impossible. She never told a soul about Theo. At first because it felt self-aggrandizing then later, because who would believe her? A handful of people over the years put it together that they were from the same small town on the Oregon Coast. By then he had his own Wikipedia page, multiple fansites, and paparazzi swarming him, but if they asked if she'd met Theo, she'd say, *sure, of course I did*. Before changing the subject.

Because Theo Blake belonged to the world, but Teddy was hers, and even after all those years, she couldn't let him go.

She and Jay graduated from law school and they both found jobs in the Seattle area. They settled into a small northwest craftsman in his hometown, the exclusive island of Manzanita, a short ferry ride from Seattle. Six months after they graduated, Kamari Yasmin West was born. Mattie took a leave of absence at the law firm where she was working and threw herself into being the best mother she could be. Despite their beautiful home, in the middle of a Pacific Northwest oasis, the cracks in their marriage began. Jay was always kind and the divorce was the textbook example of amicable. He let her keep the house since his long hours at the firm in Seattle had him gone for long stretches at a time. By the time of the divorce, she had gone back to part-time work at a small firm. Not nearly as prestigious as Jay's, but it paid the mortgage and allowed her to be down the road from Kamari's school, the newly named Agate Elementary.

Their island was an odd mix of new money transplants from elsewhere and Manzanita locals who kept the homes of their forefathers from the days when the island was little more than strawberry farms and logging. Mattie's home was nestled between two sprawling mansions on the bay. While different from Cape Rose, it was nice to once again live close to the water the way she did in her early years. Watching the tides as they came in and out, the seabirds making a glorious racket as they fished for their breakfast, and the occasional boater venturing out. In the summer months, the small bay would have families paddle boarding in the chilly water, their water shoes on to protect their feet from the sharp oyster shells and barnacles that lined the rocky beach.

Every morning, she would pull on her boots and warm fleece to take her cup of tea onto her back porch. For ten minutes, she would have uninterrupted time to gaze at the water. This was her private time before the roar of being a single mother would take over. Before the pressure of whatever case was being worked on, or the newest fundraising event at the elementary school was being held. There were always shoes that had been outgrown, laundry that needed to be treated, a property line dispute, or complaints about how many Christmas decorations it took to be called light pollution. But for those minutes, before she woke up Kamari, it was an easy silence.

Leaning against the back of her wooden chair, Mattie listened as the branches moved against each other and waves lapped on the rocky shore. She closed her eyes, savoring the bite of the early morning on her skin. Bundled up tight in her warm clothes, the cool air nipped wonderfully on her cheeks. While the tides in Manzanita weren't nearly as drastic as in Cape Rose, she could still smell the familiar scent of sand and salt. She never felt far from home when she was near the water.

She should invite her parents up for a trip. It had been over six months since they had gotten together. Both her parents refused to retire, though they were both eligible. She had been what her mother called "a lucky accident" born fifteen years after her sister, Ida. Mattie was closer in age to her niece, Noor, than Ida. The rest of the family was still in Cape Rose. Her parents tended to host most family events, but it might be nice to invite everyone up to her place for a change. No one in her family had been to her home since before she and Jay divorced almost two years before.

"Hey, neighbor."

The tea in Mattie's mug sloshed over the side, scalding her hands, she jolted from the intrusion. A familiar man stood in front of her, with longer, dark hair and warm brown eyes. He was very handsome, tall and lanky, with a slightly olive complexion. His hands were shoved into the front pockets of his jeans and his blue graphic tee said Fresno. He read her shocked expression and took a big step back from her.

He pulled his hands out of the pockets of his jeans, putting them up, palms facing her. "Sorry, didn't mean to startle you. I moved into the house next door and wanted to come over to say hi."

Mattie set her half gone tea on the chipped mosaic table and shook out her wet hand. "Sorry, hi."

The man came one step closer, still far enough to show her he was safe but close enough to talk. He motioned to the imposing mansion beside them. "We bought the house a few weeks ago and I figured there aren't many people on this street. I saw you out here and thought I'd introduce myself before it got weird. I'm Keller."

Mattie walked down the three wooden steps into her backyard and put out her hand.

"Matilda. Mattie." He had a firm handshake and she liked his warm demeanor. He reminded her of something, but she still couldn't place him. "Have we met before?"

He blinked at her a few times as if the question was unexpected before he shook his head. "I doubt it. Maybe. If you're from around here, you might remember my wife. She grew up in Ridgewood, Eloise Dunning?"

Again, a niggle of something familiar, but she couldn't place it. "No, I don't think so. I moved here about five years ago with my husband...well, it's ex-husband now, but he was my husband then and, oh, I'm going to stop talking. Sorry." She gave him a sheepish look.

He laughed warmly. "Don't apologize, I like a good overshare session."

Mattie wrapped her arms around herself, the early morning air seeping through her thin fleece jacket. "Where'd you move from?"

He rocked back on his heels, grimacing. "Los Angeles. Truthfully, this is our second home. We live in L.A. for work, but like I said, my wife is from the area and her family is here."

A lot of the locals complained about the influx of California transplants, particularly the ones who were buying second homes. It drove up housing costs for the locals and people said it took away from the charm and personality of the town. As a transplant herself, she didn't have much room to criticize.

"Manzanita is great. One of the best school systems in the state, good restaurants, low crime. Almost all the stores close at six, but I think that's a small price to pay. Plus, we're a quick ferry ride from Seattle."

"That's what my Eloise said."

"She sounds like a smart woman."

"She is. Smarter than me, but of course, I used up any brain cells I have in convincing her to stay married to me."

Mattie laughed. He was obviously besotted with his wife. What a shame, too. He was incredibly attractive. She wasn't sure if she wanted to get back into the dating world yet. Six months before, she downloaded Tinder on the suggestion of her friend, Shea. The only match was a twenty-one-year-old who was looking for "a fit lady who doesn't take herself too seriously" and called her "sexy momma" three times in their brief exchange. While not opposed to a quick hook-up, in theory, she had higher standards than that. She was a thirty-year-old single mother. Focusing on Kamari was more important. As for her baser needs, she had an assortment of tools to get the job done.

Keller slapped his hands together, rubbing them for warmth. "I won't keep you. I wanted to introduce myself. We're having a few people over tonight. Nothing big or fancy. Mostly a few friends and my wife's family. You should come by."

"Oh, I'd hate to impose."

Keller gestured for her to stop. "Please, it will give us something new to talk about, then the same five stories we always tell. Come over, around six?"

Before she tried to refuse him again, he was walking away, taking the small path through the woods that connected their two homes.

J AY HAD TAKEN KAMARI for the weekend, and for the first time in a while, she had nothing to do. There were shows she could watch—the kind with bad words and naked bodies she had to save for when Mari was sleeping. But she wasn't in the mood for sitting on her couch alone, the way she had been for the past year.

After snagging an unopened bottle of local wine off the kitchen counter, she took the small wooded path between her home and the mansion beside her. The couple who lived there before were older, in their mid-seventies, when they put the house up for sale. They had custom-built it ten years before. When she and Jay had moved in, they came over with a bouquet and request that they never use pesticides on their shared hedge. Through the years, Mattie had limited contact with the neighbors. It was a very Northwest thing to do. Everyone is nice, but hardly ever welcoming.

The front door was propped open, and sounds of people talking and music filtered through the doorway. The clock on her oven said 5:58 when she left, so she knew she was exactly on time.

Timeliness had never been her strong suit, and she was working on getting better at that. Her family called her "the world's slowest human." When her brother-in-law was afflicted with the same issue of showing up on time, she was more than happy to hand the title over. They had spent the last five years trading the honor back and forth at different family events.

In the five years she lived beside the home, she had never seen the inside firsthand. The inside was vastly different from the Internet pictures she looked up when the house came up for sale. In the day and age of technology, she knew of few people who didn't snoop on real estate websites. As she approached the door, she reminded herself not to act like she knew where everything was inside the house. She could do some online sleuthing, but to admit it? No way.

Following the bright hallway down to where the noise and music was coming from, Mattie kept her eyes off the pictures lining the hallway. She didn't want to be a gawker before even meeting her new neighbors. The view of Manzanita Bay was much better from their floor-to-ceiling window than it was from her house. Rounding the corner, she found a group of people standing around a large marble island. The guy, Keller, saw her and his face brightened.

"Hey, you made it!" He walked to Mattie, taking a bottle of wine from her hands. He inspected the label. "Looks expensive."

She shook her head. "Nah, it's a local bottle I had. I figured since you're new to the area, you'd want to try some. A small housewarming gift." It was silly to bring a twenty-dollar bottle into this mansion when they obviously had some serious money, but it was already done.

"I love it. It's the first of our new place." He set the bottle down on the counter and turned to a pretty woman with blond hair that faded into a bright teal color at the tips. "Lou, come meet our neighbor."

The woman stuck out her hand; her nails were cut short and brightly painted. "Mattie, right? Keller mentioned he invited you over. I'm glad you could make it. I'm Eloise."

She motioned to a redheaded woman and man with dirty blond curls beside her. "This is Ana and Xander."

She pointed at a few people mingling around the room. "And we have George, Nathan, Ilsa, Trihn, and Alexis. We'll have a few more people coming in the next few days."

Mattie gave a halfhearted wave. Everyone was incredibly attractive. Is this what it was like being in Los Angeles? Mattie considered herself to be presentable, but beside these people, all polished to perfection, her hair seemed too unruly, her teeth crooked.

Eloise gestured for her to come into the kitchen. "What can I get you to drink? We have wine, beer, sparkling water." She held her own glass of water with a lime wedge inside.

"A beer would be great."

Eloise handed her a Freedom Bay Ale from the fridge. Mattie popped the top off and took a sip to settle her nerves.

"Good choice."

Eloise motioned to the redhead. "Ana brought it. They live down the road from the brewery in Ridgewood."

"Keller said you grew up around here."

Eloise nodded. "Around here, but certainly not here. Manzanita is worlds away from the neighborhood I grew up in, in Ridgewood. I don't think they have a single low-income house here on this island. But that was a long time ago. I moved away to LA at eighteen to be a songwriter. I met Keller and the guys, and the rest is history."

Mattie had been to Ridgewood plenty since moving to the area. The closest twenty-four-hour grocery store was in Ridgewood. A cute town that was fashioned as an old Nordic fishing village.

"You're probably right," Mattie agreed. Keller came to stand behind Eloise, a possessive hand over her lower belly. Eloise absentmindedly tangled her fingers with his.

"Tell us all about you, job, kids? Is there a guy in your life?"

"The only man I've got is six inches long, rubber, and requires batteries." There was a long moment of silence where Mattie wondered if she had said the wrong thing. These people were strangers, and just because they were musicians from Los Angeles didn't mean they wouldn't be offended by a comment about vibrators.

Keller broke the silence by letting out a loud laugh. "Oh my God, you two are going to get along wonderfully." He motioned between Mattie and Eloise. "Lou, I think I met your new best friend."

Mattie gave them a relieved smile.

Down the cavernous hall, a door slammed and the sound of a suitcase hitting the floor echoed into the kitchen. Beside her, Eloise set down her drink, calling out, "We're in here, Theo."

Mattie's fingers chilled around the beer in her hand as all the blood rushed to her head. Her heartbeat picked up as she glanced around the kitchen, the truth dawning on her.

I'm a singer

Moved her from Los Angeles

Keller

Eloise

They were familiar because they were in Prevalent Notion. All her avoidance, all her denials, had been for naught. What cruel twist of fate had led to her standing in the kitchen, about to confront the only man who broke her heart?

Theo rounded the corner, and though she tried to say there was no way it was him, his face was there. Her grip tightened on her beer as she shuttered out his name, "Teddy."

Chapter Two

Theo

NEVER IN ALL HIS years of searching for coins below the bleachers did he imagine he would join his friends at their waterfront mansion for the summer. Keller and Eloise had invited everyone up for a housewarming trip. With Keller and Eloise in marital bliss and Nathan and Ilsa equally bad, he was the odd man out. His friends were getting lame.

Everyone was changing, settling down and he was, what? Newly dumped by his fake girlfriend. He wasn't mad at Aria for telling him they were over. She was right to want a man who actually liked her. Sleeping with her earlier that week had been a mistake, but tequila and loneliness are a wicked combination. The next day, Aria told him they were warm bodies to each other. She was twenty-four. Far too young and successful to be wasting her talents on a guy like him.

Guilt washed over him at the expression on her face when she said, "I should get good dick *and* a healthy relationship. It's obvious you don't want me. I don't know who you want, but it's not me."

He wouldn't argue with that. Once again, Aria proved to be far too good for him. He wasn't going to convince her to stay in this sham. She deserved to find someone who would appreciate all her good qualities. Years before, when they started "dating," he had tried to build up feelings for her. Kissing her was warm, it was wet, and it was nothing like being in love.

He knew what it was to love someone. The heartache of when they are away, the way your face warms when they walk toward you, the electricity of their touch, and the way your hands fit together.

What he had with Aria wasn't love. A few years before, he thought he had found someone he could fall for, someone to help him forget about the life he left behind in Cape Rose. But even having the world's hottest supermodel on his arm didn't help the ache go away. He fucked up his relationship with Safiya Khan the same way he did everything else, by only thinking of himself. Safiya deserved better. He knew that, so did Aria. But he didn't have it in him to give it. He never would. The one and only person he was truly happy with had moved on long ago. He had no right to think about her, and yet he did. Constantly. He could still taste the bitterness on his tongue as he broke up with Mattie all those years before. He couldn't help comparing how much easier this conversation was to have. He had spent years in this fake relationship with Aria, and letting her go was as easy as talking about the weather. Still rumpled from his flight, Theo slumped in his seat as they drove toward the mansion Keller bought for Eloise; once again, proving his bandmate was a better man than him. He only wanted to give a woman a screaming orgasm and a ride home.

Almost any woman.

No, he wasn't going to think about her. He worked hard to put that piece of his life behind him. If he didn't, the regret would consume him. Over the years, he had made many personal mistakes in his pursuit of his career. Years before, he had nearly broken up the band when he drunkenly tried to kiss his bandmate's wife, Eloise. Yeah, Eloise was his friend first and he was the one who brought Eloise in as an assistant for the band before they got big, but still. The next day, he realized how badly he screwed up. How Keller didn't want to kill him for that stunt was mind-boggling for him.

Since then, he had been trying to be better at being a friend to his bandmates. As much as people commented on his appearance as the reason for their success, without Nathan and Keller, he'd still be singing at open mic nights at dive bars, scraping sticky singles from his guitar case. Theo knew he had a part to play in their success. He was the heartthrob, the soulful lead singer all the women wanted to sleep with and the men wanted to be around. It was fun for years, sleeping with a new groupie at each spot, the light of the stage and roar of the crowd as he sang. But after his disaster of a relationship with supermodel Safiya Khan, once again his fault, it was clean it up or get the boot. Executives at Repercussion Records sat him down alone and told him they would replace him with some other golden-haired pretty boy in a flash. His relationships in shambles, and his career on the brink of collapse, he did the only thing he had left. He complied. He sang the songs they told him to sing. Dated Aria Kingston, the star of a teenage paranormal show. He wore the outfits and took the pictures.

All the while, he was floundering.

Outwardly, it worked. The label loosened its chokehold on him; the band got new management who helped them record better material. He contributed more to their most critically acclaimed album, *Vermilion*. Keller forgave him, though he didn't love it when Theo hugged Eloise. Nathan was supportive, running with him a few times a week, even though he hated running.

Theo should be on top of his game, but he couldn't shrug off the persistent weight on his shoulders. Nathan and Keller were married now. They had homes set up for their respective families.

The last time he saw Eloise, she had shown him a commercial of a puppy running home to its owner, and was crying so hard over the video that she couldn't get the words out. His knowledge of women's hormones was slim, but in the almost ten years they were friends, he never saw her crying over a dog video before.

Yeah, sure, he would have more freedom to party now, but hangovers were lasting longer now. The three Bloody Marys he had on the two-and-a-half hour flight weren't helping the pounding in his head.

At least Keller and Eloise would have more booze. He didn't want to risk going up to the galley on the ferryboat, opting instead to stand on the car deck against the bright orange plastic barrier and watch as Seattle grew smaller. The soggy air was welcome on his skin. He had forgotten the sting of the sea. How long had it been since he was near water and enjoyed it? Years, probably. Going to events, his best clothes on, a beautiful woman on his arm. It wasn't the same as the riotous water beneath you and taking in the smell of brine and cedar.

The ten-minute drive through the forest-lined Manzanita streets was quiet. His driver, thankfully, was a quiet man. Didn't ask for an autograph, maybe didn't even realize who he was. His assistant, Beatriz, deserved a raise for getting him this driver.

They pulled down a long-wooded drive. Ancient thick cedars hung over the gravel road. Theo was surprised to see there was no gate in front of the home. In L.A., everything worth having was behind a gate. Entry only allowed for a select few.

He handed a hefty tip to the driver and pulled his suitcase out of the back before the driver had a chance to get out.

He craned his neck up to take in the house. All Pacific Northwest design, it boasted white trim over dark cedar shake siding. Along the entryway were smooth rock pillars and a deep green front door that stood half-opened. Briefly, he wondered what the crime statistics were in Manzanita. Nonexistent he'd wager.

Walking through the door, he heard the chatter of people inside. He was late for the party, but that wasn't a new thing.

Setting his suitcase down on the stamped concrete flooring, he marveled at the bare wood walls. The aesthetic lent itself to a much homier vibe despite its grand size. It was understated. In Los Angeles, the buildings were modern, sleek, and minimalistic.

Along Eloise and Keller's walls were framed black-and-white photos of the couple through the years: At the beach in front of their home in California; them wearing horned helmets at some parade; them singing together at Eloise's debut album release. Early pictures of when they were living out of a beat-up van for shows. Eloise sitting on an amp beside Keller, looking annoyed as he tried unsuccessfully to flirt with her. Their original wedding photo, taken in a sleazy Vegas wedding chapel. The black-and-white format hid the terrible purple velour of Keller's jacket, but not the size of the poofy veil that was plopped on Eloise's head. He was in a few; a background player in their love story. He was the lead singer in the world's largest rock band, and yet he had the sense he was a ridiculous sidekick in others' epic tales.

When he first met Eloise, he was still nursing a guilty conscience for the way he left Mattie. They couldn't have been less alike on the surface, but something about Eloise was right to him. Sure, he thought about kissing her a few times; she was beautiful and he was still a twenty-one-year-old single guy. But from the moment he brought her to the first rehearsal with Nathan and Keller, it was obvious that would be a mistake.

It was no secret, Eloise had a crush on him then, but she was too good for him. Eloise was more than a one-night stand. She was his best friend for years. That, and Keller was insanely in love with her, pining for years before she noticed. Despite his one or two screw-ups with them, he supported their being together.

This house was a home. His own condo was cold, with all dark shiny surfaces and little decoration, with its white leather couch he never sat on. A fridge that housed only alcohol and the pre-made meals his dietitian insisted he eat. He couldn't remember the last time he had a home.

Yes, you can. You know exactly when that was.

He had been thinking about her far too much these days. From the moment Eloise told him they were buying a house in Manzanita, he knew there was a chance he would see her. Where Matilda Lewis lived was only one of many things he had memorized over the years. The thought of running casually by her house one day flittered in his mind since hearing the news. Still, how likely was it he would see her even in a city of five thousand?

Shaking his head, he moved farther inside. The sound of voices led him into an open-concept kitchen with a large granite island in the middle covered in plates of small snacks and half-drunk glasses. The floor-to-ceiling window overlooked a cove where sailboats were moored. It looked like something out of a postcard.

Eloise and Keller were standing in a group of people he didn't recognize. This home wasn't far from where Eloise grew up; she might've invited some friends over. He couldn't remember Eloise talking about many friends aside from Ana and Xander, and he didn't see them. Just as well. They didn't like him. How was he supposed to know he shouldn't ask Ana if her pubes were red? Seems like a common question to ask a hot redhead.

He heard Eloise laugh, and then a low voice said something back. The sound was muffled enough that he didn't make out the words, but he stopped in his tracks, his eyes on the group.

Stepping out behind Eloise, the small woman brushed her long, dark hair off her shoulder. Watching her, Theo remembered exactly how that hair slipped between his fingers. How those green eyes warmed as they gazed upon you. Fumbling on his feet, he knocked into a wrought iron coat rack, sending it toppling. He reached out his hand to catch it before it hit the floor, but it slipped out of his fingers. The clang sent everyone staring at him.

Some entrance.

Both the women looked at him, Eloise slightly annoyed, the other woman shocked.

"Teddy?" her voice was so soft, he could barely hear it. But he didn't need to hear her voice to remember how his name sounded on her lips. It was the expression he wallowed in as he drifted to sleep each night. It was his biggest regret and his greatest triumph.

He opened his mouth, then closed it, feeling like a wide-mouth carp. Clearing his throat, he realized the group in the kitchen was watching him with concern. With a hard swallow, he attempted a small smile.

"Hey, Mattie."

The woman blinked a few times before turning to Eloise. "I should get going. Great talking with you, Eloise. Thanks for the beer."

Setting her half-full bottle down on the marble countertop, she rushed past him. Frozen to his spot, he watched as she left, her long dark hair swinging behind her as she walked out the door.

For the second time in his life, Theo let Matilda Lewis go, only this time it was her running away.

CHAPTER THREE

MATTIE

H ER SENSIBLE SHOES SLIPPED on the polished wood floor as she hustled past Theo. She couldn't look at him, because it couldn't be him. It wasn't possible. How could it be?

Once outside the clear air burned her throat as she made her way to the small dirt path between the houses. She had to make it out; to get away. She had to wake up.

Goddamn it, wake up Matilda. This is a dream and you'll wake up and it will be done and...

"Mattie." His voice sounded behind her.

She stuttered to a stop. That same voice. Sometimes she had caught snippets in interviews before changing the channel. It was slightly deeper now, a man's voice, but it was his nonetheless.

"Matilda."

Swallowing down the lump in her throat, she begged for the ground beneath her to fall away. Over the twelve years they had been apart, she had envisioned seeing him a thousand times. That he'd show up at her dorm in the middle of the night with a bouquet of pink peonies and tell her he hadn't slept a wink since they last parted. That he could never touch another after her.

Even the day she married Jay, she wondered what she would do if Theo showed up at the church. She was ashamed of her own thoughts that day.

Even so, they were there.

In her visions of their reunion, she would have glossy hair and a formfitting dress that flattered her curves. Not shorts that were too snug around her middle and a plain green tee with a small stain above her right boob. She'd be wearing heels, not clunky hiking sandals. Over the years, she had pictured it in so many ways, but she never envisioned what she would do after seeing him.

What could she say? What could be done?

She heard him stop behind her. Though they were outside, she knew he would still smell of his favorite soap. All the money in the world, and he still used the same two-dollar soap. An ache formed inside her chest she had long ago thought was healed.

One steading breath, then another. She slowly turned to face him. The sun was setting over the bay, casting pink and gold light over his face. He was tan now. Whether that was from living in California or a cosmetic thing, she couldn't tell. He smiled at her and she noticed his chipped front tooth had been fixed. Something about that made her sad. He had always been handsome, there was no arguing that, but now he was stunning. It wasn't fair. In the years since they parted, she had grown into herself. Learned how to tame her unruly curls, had a better skin care routine than three-dollar face scrub and tap water. But she was older now, a mother. Her body had carried and delivered an eight-pound baby. Her hips would never be the same slim set they once were. Not to mention the stretch marks that never faded from her ass and stomach. In the real world, she knew she looked good, but Theo didn't live in the real world.

"It's really you." He took a step forward and she mirrored him, taking a step back.

"I didn't know. I…" Her words died out. How dumb must she sound not to realize before going over there? The entire world knew who they were. For her, to go into the party blindly was foolish.

"I can tell. I saw how shocked you were."

She motioned to her home. "I live next door. Keller invited me over. I didn't realize."

"That I would be there?" He finished for her.

"No. Who they were. I didn't put it together. I..." She swallowed hard, unsure. Would admitting all the effort she had put into avoiding him make her seem more pathetic? "I wasn't thinking in a million years I'd see you again."

He stepped forward, and this time she didn't step back. She was right. He did smell of the same soap. His clear blue eyes held the same warmth he always had when he looked at her. His hair was longer now and in need of a haircut. She knew if she reached up, it would feel the same. Her fingers tingled a phantom want and she squeezed her hands into fists at her side. His beard, once scraggly as a teen, had grown a shade darker and redder than his hair. His biceps were stretching out the arms of his tee shirt. It was criminal how good he looked.

"I can't believe it's you. I mean, I always hoped I'd see you again, but I never thought it would be like this." He gave her that same crooked smile, the scar next to his left brow, creasing.

Offering a small smile, she fought back the panic rising in her chest. "You did?"

Stepping closer, his left foot wedged between hers. "Of course I did. As the rain."

The spring Theo and Mattie started dating, a country singer came out with the song "Rare as the Rain." A love song about his wife. While the artist was singing from his hometown in New Mexico, rain in Cape Rose was neither rare nor beautiful, but an ever-present part of life on the Oregon Coast. Theo would sing the song to Mattie, an inside joke between them that while the weather was not rare, how they cared for each other was. The song became a shorthand for how they felt for each other. All the other had to do was say, "As the rain," and the person would know they were loved.

Mattie's chest seized with the familiar phrase. One she had long since buried alongside his voice.

From inside the house, someone laughed loudly and there was the sound of cheers. Theo glanced back. "I think Eloise told everyone she's expecting. They're all great. I think you'll like them."

Like them? Why would he care if she liked them? She wasn't part of his life anymore. Celebrations with his famous friends, expensive champagne, and fancy parties. That was his life. Not standing on a dirt path with his ex-girlfriend. Their lives were worlds apart. She didn't have to cyberstalk him to learn that. It was all over his tanned and smooth face. He dripped wealth and extravagance she would never touch. And she was happy for him, but trying to picture what they could have in common now was a fool's errand. She had seen him. He was okay and now she could be, too. Motioning behind her, she stepped back from him. If she wasn't touching him, she could almost think straight. "I should get going. You need to go see your friends. I won't keep you."

"Do you want me to walk you back?" he asked.

Glancing at the twenty steps it would take to get to her back porch, she shook her head. "No, it's really fine. I'm practically home already."

"If you're sure." His fingers came up, brushing a curl away from her face and behind her ear. Her face heated as his fingertip skimmed above her forehead. His hand stayed there, holding her hair but not quite touching her. The nearness of him was all too familiar, the sweet gesture flooding her body with warmth. "I'm going to be here for a few weeks. Can I see you tomorrow to catch up?"

"Uh, I don't think that's a good idea. I have a lot going on and..."

"Perfect, I'll stop by." He bent down and pressed a kiss to her cheek before whispering in her ear, "We were meant to see each other again."

Nodding at him with a shaky smile, she turned away, walking on trembling legs to her back door. Once inside, she locked the deadbolt, something she hardly ever did. With her eyes closed, she counted to one hundred by twos, a calming trick she had always used. Finished, she peeked out the small side window to see if he was still standing in the path. Bathed in the gold and pink light of the sunset, he stared up at her small house, his hands stuffed in his pockets.

THE LAST TIME SHE had such a terrible night of sleep was when Kamari had a double ear infection a year prior. She couldn't remember the last time her anxieties caused insomnia. All night, she was punching her pillow and grumbling as she tried to drift off, replaying her brief exchange with Theo. It wasn't fair that he would show up out of nowhere and disrupt her perfectly simple life with a crooked smile. She considered what she would do if he showed up while she was in college; deep down, despite how badly he hurt her, if he asked her in those early days to run away with him, she would have. But she wasn't running away now. She was a mother. A professional. She had a career, and that part that loved Theo, as deep-rooted as it was, couldn't sway her from the person she was today. It had been hard work to forget him. She would do it again. She couldn't allow herself to wallow in the thoughts of what could be with Theodore Blake.

At six a.m., she considered sleep a fruitless endeavor and climbed out of bed, pulling on her grubby gardening clothes. She could take out her emotions in the garden.

One cup of strong tea and a bucket full of weeds later, she pushed a wayward curl off her sweaty face using the back of her glove. A smear of dirt lined on her forehead, but she didn't care. She had little time for spa treatments, so here was her mud bath. Once the strawberry section was completed, she moved on to her sweet pea trellis, where she had been battling unsuccessfully to get the vine to climb up.

The crunch of footsteps made her pause and she glanced over her shoulder to find Theo coming through the trees. Catching sight of her, he paused. The black rain jacket he wore was slightly too small for him, tight around his arms.

"Nice coat." Wiping a clod of dirt on her already dusty leggings, she stood up. "I'm assuming it's not yours."

He glanced down at the neoprene coat. "I don't know, I grabbed it of the coat rack. I didn't think it would be this cold here."

"It's early June. It doesn't feel like summer until after the Fourth of July." Mattie pulled her gardening gloves off, shoving them in the front pocket of her old Manzanita Hay and Feed hoodie. Frowning, she looked him up and down. "It's not that much colder than it would be in Cape Rose. Has L.A. thinned your blood or something?"

His hands in his coat pockets, he rocked back on his heels. "Might have."

Jutting her chin at the house, she asked, "You want a cup of tea or something?"

"You got coffee?"

He followed her into the house, kicking his shoes off beside her dusty gardening clogs at the back door. As she came in, the speaker connected to her phone, the playlist streaming through the small house.

Theo took a seat at the counter of her breakfast nook as she made him a coffee. She grabbed the small carton of half-and-half from the fridge, then turned to him and paused. "I don't know how you take your coffee."

As kids, he always took it with lots of cream and sugar, same as her. But her preferences had changed since then.

"I'll take it however you want to make it."

She set her favorite hand-thrown mug down on the counter in front of him, now filled with cream and lots of sugar. Theo picked it up, taking a tentative sip. His face grimaced as he set the mug back down.

"Too sweet."

Sheepishly, he smiled. "A little. I haven't made my coffee like that in years. My dietitian would murder me."

She took the mug from him, dumping half in her own empty mug before mixing more black coffee in both mugs. As she handed it back to him, his finger brushed against hers. The spark that flew between their touch was enough to almost make her drop the cup. She took a step back, resting her hip on the other side of the small kitchen, holding the mug between her hands, as if it was the only thing keeping her from drifting away.

"I was coming back from a run earlier and I'm hungry. Any good breakfast places around here?"

Warming her hands on the mug, she tilted her head to the side. "A few little spots. No one makes hash browns like your uncle's place, though."

The warm memories of going to his family's diner in Cape Rose flooded through her. The ripped pleather chairs and sticky jam jars on each table. Sugar and bacon scent filled the air. Every day after school, she would stop by and sit at a small table in the back corner while Theo did his closing duties from the lunch rush. Back in those days, she thought the nearness of him was the epitome of love.

"How's your mom?" Mattie asked. "I haven't seen her in years."

Theo scratched his head. "She's good, moved to Santa Fe a few years ago. She met some guy and they got married. He's nice. Treats her well. I try to visit a few times a year."

The long, tense silence stretched out between them. She couldn't figure out why he was here. Did he feel bad for her? What were you supposed to talk about with your ex-boyfriend after twelve years apart?

"I like your place," he commented. As he glanced around the room, she saw it through his eyes. The drawings on the fridge of penguins, Kamari's new obsession, the mismatched candles on the side table, the thick blanket strewn over the back of the couch.

"It's small. I didn't think anyone would come over, or I would have picked up."

Smiling over the rim of his coffee mug, less sweet. "It's a great house. You remember the house I grew up in?"

She scratched at a small scab on her wrist from a gardening mishap a few days before. The edge of the scab came up, and she pressed down on it with her fingertip, centering herself. She didn't want him over here doing this. Making her remember all the wonderful things about him and not how much it hurt when he was no longer around.

She wouldn't think about the small apartment he shared with his mother behind the diner. The old couch in the living room barely big enough for three people, the faded orange color of the carpet that should have been replaced decades before. The way he sheepishly had guided her into his room the first time, apologizing from the space. How much she didn't care in those moments because she only wanted to be near him.

"I bet your place in L.A. is amazing."

Shrugging, he took another sip of the coffee. "It's okay. It's not a home, though. I don't cook in my kitchen, it's just a place. In the early years we were traveling so much, it didn't matter where I lay my head at night."

Or with who, I'd imagine.

Internally, Mattie shook that thought from her head. It was none of her business who Theo found himself with. He was in the past.

"That's a shame," she remarked.

He was staring down at his coffee mug, swirling the half-empty contents around. "I suppose it is, but that's the tradeoff. You want to be a musician, travel the world, and play sold-out stadiums, let go of the idea of a home base. That's the sacrifice."

On the surface, those words sounded boastful, but there was a heartache behind them. That word, *sacrifice.* Is that what she was, another sacrifice on his journey?

The song on the speaker changed, and Theo's shoulders stiffened. It was an older song from the midnineties. As a dancer, she performed a lyrical dance to this song at several competitions. She was never good enough to win a big prize, but she loved dancing.

"You danced to this song the night I met you."

It wasn't the night she met him, but it was the night he first noticed her. He had been dragged along to the high school talent show. Mattie performed her dance. She got second place that night behind an air guitar act. When she came backstage, she found her friends talking to Theo and she almost ran away. She had a crush on him for over a year, a tender innocent thing most girls in their small town held for the musician.

"You're an amazing dancer," he told her and it took all she had not to melt into the floor at his words.

Mumbling her thanks, she said something slightly self-deprecating, and he laughed. Then he asked her out. Right there, in front of all her friends, in front of the town. For months, they were inseparable. Until he left and his promises to love her were proven false.

He set his coffee mug down on the counter, putting a handout. "Dance with me."

A glance around the room and she frowned. "It's the kitchen."

"Come on, dance with me. For old time's sake."

This was a mistake. To dance with him would be a mistake, but she took his hand anyway. He didn't fight the smile on his face. His arm wound around her waist, pulling her closer. His body was different under her hands, his arms muscular and firm. He was skinny when he left Cape Rose those twelve years before, but he wasn't any longer. She was different, too. Her hips had widened from the pregnancy and her stomach would never be as flat as it was when she was in high school. But she had never been a slender girl to begin with. Her body was powerful from working outside in the garden and yoga, but it was not the body of an eighteen-year-old. And yet their bodies fit together the same as they did when they were teenagers. She closed her eyes, letting the ethereal song wash over her as they moved to the song.

For someone who was a talented musician, he never had a good sense of timing for dance. It wasn't so much dancing as it was two bodies swaying to the hypnotic music. He ducked his face down, breathing into her neck, and she was transported to that place where his lips had kissed the spot below her jaw. The way his hands would burn warm as they traced up her back. The slide of his mouth on hers. A chasm inside her chest was splitting open. With his arms around her waist, the smell of the clean soap on his skin, and the press of his hand firm on her hip, she could allow herself that moment where she wasn't someone's mother. Where she didn't have relentless research to fact-check, and disputes to handle. A place where she indulged that small flicker inside her that told her it was okay to still care for Theo.

"How could I forget how beautiful you are?" he whispered in her ear. A thrill ran through her at the words. And then the harsh reality of it. He had forgotten her. He had left her. Why was she giving him attention when he was the one who threw all they had away? How did this man have the power to make her feel like she was a raw seventeen-year-old?

A clearing of a throat separated them, then sprang apart. Jay stood in the living room holding a small pink backpack in his hand.

"Hey Mats, I knocked but you didn't answer, um." His eyes darted from Mattie's face to Theo's hand on her waist.

Stepping back from his embrace, she wrapped her arms around her body, as if to hold herself together. "Uh, hey, Jay. This is...um." She glanced at Theo.

"You're Theo Blake," Jay finished, confusion lacing his features. Mattie had told Jay about him, of course. Her parents would casually mention it, but she downplayed their relationship. What was the point in rehashing a sad story?

Theo put out a hand, his features smoothed over. "Yeah, how's it going?"

Jay took his hand, shaking it slowly as if Theo wasn't real. "Uh, good. I'm Jay. Mattie's, um...I'm Kamari's father." He looked at Mattie as if to say, WTF, Mattie?

She shook her head at her ex-husband. How would she explain this? She was acting like a fool.

"Right. I've got to get going. Her homework is done for tomorrow. I'll come to get her after gymnastics?"

Mattie nodded. She wanted to walk him out, to explain, but leaving Theo and Mari in the house together seemed ill-advised if she was trying to appear as a stable person to her ex. At the door, Jay turned back to her. "Call me later, okay?"

"I will," Mattie assured him.

The whole time Kamari was glancing from Jay to Theo and back to Mattie, an expression of suspicion on her face. This was not the way her daughter should meet Theo, but of course, she never pictured a day when her daughter would.

The door closed behind Jay and Mattie took a calming breath, blood pumping in her ears as she bent down to Mari's level. She motioned to Theo. "Darling, this is an old friend of Mommy's from when I lived with Nani and Pop-pop." Mattie hoped seeing her daughter might scare Theo away enough. Here was evidence that Mattie was an entirely different person from her eighteen-year-old self.

Instead, Theo bent down until he was at eye level with Kamari. "Hi Kamari, I'm Theo. As your mom said, we knew each other when we were younger," Theo told her. "I like your name."

Kamari blinked up at him, trying to gauge how much she wanted to talk to this strange man. "It means 'moon.'" She turned away from Theo to her mother. "Can I watch my show now?"

Mattie nodded at her daughter, making a shooing motion. Kamari left clutching a tablet. Her fingers tight on her upper arms, Mattie held herself, waiting for a reaction from Theo. Kamari thundered up the stairs to her room. How a five-year-old made so much noise, she had no idea, but Kamari had always been that way.

"Is she...how old is she?" Theo asked.

Mattie blinked a few times, processing his question. Theo's serious face broke into a grin. "I'm fucking with you. I have my talents, but swimmers that can last seven years isn't one of them."

"Glad to hear it. I didn't want to think being some big shot had burned all your brain cells away."

"Oh, there are plenty of brain cells that got ruined, but I can still do basic subtraction, and twelve years, three months and five days does not make a five-year-old."

"That's a very specific number."

"Is it?" Theo asked, glancing around the room. He picked up a small figurine off the shelf, a chipped clay snowman Kamari made in her preschool class, painted a bright teal color.

"Theo, why did you stop by?" Mattie asked.

He set the snowman down carefully and turned back to face her. "I wanted to see you."

"But why?"

It was impossible to imagine that he would want to see her. It had been twelve years since he dumped her over the phone. While the pain was no longer jarring, it was still there, buried deep. A slow ache that never really went away. To miss your first love isn't always about the person you loved, but the loss of who you were at that time.

Once you have your heart broken, you will never be as innocent. A part of you is irrevocably changed. Mourning your first love isn't unique. It wasn't strange, and it certainly didn't make her special just because the man who broke her was a celebrity now. Her pain was the same as billions of other people in the world who had been through the same thing.

"Because you're my home."

Mattie plopped down in her wooden dining room chair, her knees knocking against the table and shaking the vase of irises she picked from her garden. Bringing her hand up to her forehead, she rubbed her temple, urging the sudden pounding to abate. With a bracing sigh, she glanced up at him. "You can't be serious. I haven't seen you in twelve years, Theodore. You can't show up here and ask me to dance with you and look the way you do and say something like that."

He had always been good with words. The first night he noticed her, he was the same way. Sweet, confident, telling her exactly what she wanted to hear. But she wasn't going to fall for this act again. She wasn't eighteen and impressionable.

"The truth? I can't tell you the truth?"

"I'm not your home. Theo, I haven't been your home for over a decade. I have a life, a child, and it doesn't involve me being your *home*."

With his hands stuffed in his pockets, he surveyed her as if she was a petulant child and he was a patient parent. "I freaked you out."

Blinking at him, she tried in vain to come up with a response. Theo had always been sure of himself. It was one of the things she loved about him when they first started dating. Now he was looking at her as if he had answers to questions she never asked.

"Theo, what do you want me to say here? I haven't seen you in twelve years and you come in here and tell me I'm your home at nine in the morning." She shook her head at him. "I think you should head out. I have to make Mari breakfast and I have stuff to do today."

He didn't argue with her, leaving out the back door with a promise he'd see her again soon. She didn't think it was possible. His life was far from Manzanita. No matter how tempting his hand felt on the small of her back, she could never be a part of his life again.

Chapter Four

Theo

Once again, Theo was forced to face his absolute truths. In the early years of trying to get big, he would repeat his mantra in his head. Every failed audition, every poor turnout at a show, he would tell himself that he was destined for more. He was talented, driven, and had what it took to make it big. And in the back of his mind, he thought he would love Matilda Lewis for the rest of his life. Over the years, he allowed that part to grow quieter. What was the point in thinking of how much he still loved Mattie when he was the one to leave? When she had obviously moved on with her life? He watched from afar. She graduated, she got married; she had a baby. At first it was through his mom and uncle, who still lived in Cape Rose, then the Internet. She had a life that had nothing to do with him. He wasn't meant for her; she was meant for more. But fate had other plans.

Fate was never something Theo gave a lot of credence to. He worked his ass off for the career he had. Sure, his looks had played a part in getting them noticed initially. But he toiled for years to prove he was worth it. His bandmates gave him a hard time about how many takes they'd record before he could deem a song ready, but inside he knew he had more to prove. Especially now. Nathan and Keller had their families and homes, and what did Theo have? Talent, golden hair, and an empty condo.

No, until he saw Mattie the night before, he would have said fate was for other people.

There she was, back into his life, and it was as if there was a cord wrapped around his chest, pulling him to her. When he awoke that morning, his first thought was to make sure she was real. The house was quiet and empty. From his glance out the side window, he couldn't see into Mattie's yard, but he somehow knew she would be there. She had always been an early riser like him. What was the harm in going over and saying hi?

Standing in her kitchen, his hand outstretched as the song played on the small speaker. He willed Mattie to accept his hand. Her eyes darted from his hand to his face, hesitation clouding her features.

She had told him once he was impossible to say no to. He hoped for that moment that was still the case. The guitar solo before the second verse played, and his chest clenched at the thought that she might turn him down. This song, this moment, might be the only chance he'd get to hold her again after so long apart. But she took his hand, and for a moment he could hold her the way he used to. He could pretend he didn't fuck up his one chance at happiness years before. His face buried into her soft curls, the smell of her shampoo and the earth on her. Pulling her even closer, he could feel the curve of her stomach against him. He always loved the lushness of her body. She was never slender, even as a teenager, but now she was soft in a way that only led to dirty thoughts of exploring her body. He knew by the way they swayed together to the haunting melody that her body was reacting to him. He knew how they would fit together once more.

Her ex-husband coming in the door was bad timing, for sure, but what could he do? After briefly meeting her daughter and saying his piece, he left again.

It would take some time to show Mattie he was serious. Until he walked into the kitchen and saw her again, he didn't know where his life was taking him. But now he did. Everything was leading back to this place with Mattie. He had a chance to get her back, and he wasn't going to waste it.

Returning to the house, he found Keller standing in front of the coffee machine, frowning at it. He pushed a button on the top and watched as nothing happened. Cursing low, he glanced at Theo as he settled onto a high stool at the island. Theo ran a hand down his face, the scruff bristling against his palms.

"So…" Keller drawled, a devilish glint in his eyes. "You know our neighbor."

Theo grabbed an orange out of a small fruit bowl in the middle of the island. "From Cape Rose."

Keller slapped his hand on the top of the coffeemaker, grumbling, before turning to face Theo. "Cape Rose?"

His nail in the peel, Theo stopped what he was doing. "Yeah, where I grew up. You knew that."

"There is no way I knew that. You never talked about where you grew up." Keller flipped the top open to the coffeemaker, peering inside before closing again and pressing more buttons on the side.

Theo studied Keller, trying to see if he was telling the truth; thinking back, it might be true.

"She was my girlfriend, back home."

"Your girlfriend. From back home," Keller recited the words back as if Theo were speaking in a new language.

"I've told you about back home before," Theo exclaimed. Why was Keller so weird about it?

"No, you definitely have not. Which is fine, you didn't enjoy talking about your life before, neither did I. I mean, I could tell you had as rough of a go of it as I did."

Theo knew a little about Keller's upbringing. He had been opening up more since he married Eloise. The absentee father, being raised by his grandparents, the snotty half-siblings.

"It wasn't that bad. We were poor—electricity cut off in the winter, food banks and couch surfing at friends' houses sometimes poor—but my mom and my uncle were good to me. Lots of kids have that life."

"Not Nathan, though," Keller reminded him. He unplugged the coffeemaker, then plugged it back in with no success.

"No, not him." Their bassist, Nathan, had grown up with a picturesque set of parents. The first time he met Nathan's parents, his mother, Jean, had fussed over the state of his shirt, offering to mend the small hole in the collar. His own mother tried her best, but Lori Blake was fifteen when she had Theo. They were always more akin to roommates than mother and son.

"But Matilda was your girlfriend before you left."

"What! Are you kidding me?" Eloise came into the kitchen, her blonde and blue hair a mess from sleep. She pressed a quick kiss to Keller's shoulder before turning to Theo. "Is that true?"

Theo regretted letting this little piece of information loose. If there was one thing Eloise enjoyed doing, it was fixing things. For years, it meant she was great as an assistant to the band. But once she went her own way and married Keller, it meant she meddled in everyone else's business.

"It was years ago."

"Tell me everything," Eloise demanded as she turned to the coffeemaker, pressing a few buttons, and the machine began to bubble and hum. Keller narrowed his eyes at the machine but said nothing.

"It was a long time ago..." Theo trailed off.

"Not by that silly expression on your face. Anyone could see something was going on when you ran after her last night and then we didn't see you for the rest of the night."

"I was tired from the flight up and went to bed early."

"You? Went to bed early?" Eloise repeated back at him.

"Yeah."

Eloise and Keller exchanged glances. Why do smug married couple always have their own language? So annoying. Theo scrubbed a hand over his face. He shouldn't have to explain himself to his friends. He knew Eloise would try to force him and Mattie together in contrived ways, and Keller would be smug and pick fights with him. And Nathan, Nathan would probably charm Mattie to make him mad. He loved these people like family, but they were the worst.

"I'm going for a run."

He pushed off from the counter, the spinning stool catching him in the hip as he got down from it.

"Leave my coat in the hallway closet when you're done," Eloise called out to his back. He kept walking from his friend, leaving them snickering together in the kitchen.

T HE BACK ROADS ON Manzanita were winding, tree-lined, and best of all, devoid of people aside from the rare car passing him. His legs pumping beneath him, Theo pushed himself further and further down the tree-lined streets, away from Eloise and Keller's home. The music blasting in his ear pods was at a level he was sure doctors would be aghast at, but his life was pounding bass lines and drums. Losing his hearing at a certain point was an inevitability.

He ran until his legs burned and then he ran until they felt like jelly beneath him. Down the street, he went until he reached a wooden boardwalk out into the water. Grasping the railing, he stopped, the salt air burning his lungs. He had pushed himself too hard. Already his calves were aching from not warming up properly. In the distance to his left was the ferry boat about to dock. He could see the Seattle skyline across the Salish Sea. It seemed close enough to touch from where he stood. The last time he was in this area was for the band's Hellions Tour. He was nursing a bruised ego over being dumped by Safiya Khan back in New York. That was a terrible night. He got too drunk and tried to kiss Eloise. One of the bigger mistakes he made during that trip. By the time he got to the West Coast, he was drinking all day, had to be dragged to performances by his assistant, and made a mess of his life.

That was his low point. When they returned to L.A., the label brought him for a meeting alone and informed him his behavior would not continue. They were about to sign a new contract with the label for three more albums, but the label let him know with his erratic behavior, he was more of a liability at that point unless he straightened up. Faced with losing his career, his first thought should have been to his bandmates. Nathan and Keller didn't deserve to lose their recording contract because of Theo, but it wasn't. No, his only thought was of Mattie.

He gave up days of food to save up to get to gigs, he sweated and toiled for years at his craft. He was willing to sacrifice everything he cared for to get his fame, including the only girl he loved. If he lost his career, it would all be for nothing. The press, the groupies, the music, the celebrity status - it was almost enough to keep the regret from ravaging him on the inside. But to not have Mattie or his career?

What if he could have both? When he went to see Mattie that morning it wasn't with forethought or a motive. It was a need, inexplicable and unrelenting. Alone in his thoughts, he could reflect. There had to be a reason they were thrust back together. Was this his second chance at happiness?

He wasn't sure he deserved a second chance with Mattie. He knew when he left her behind that there was a possibility she could never forgive him. Hell, he knew he wasn't worth her forgiveness.

But Theo was a selfish man, he knew that to his core, as much as he knew he was a born performer.

Leaning against the railing, his breath evened out. Small dots of commuters walking in the sky bridge to the waiting ferry were a rainbow of colors. The sun peeking out behind the white clouds. A low murmur of the announcer sounded the last call for walk-on passengers. From where he stood, he watched as a lone man jogged down the bridge waving his arms, then a minute later walked back to the building dejected.

Turning back around on the boardwalk, Theo made his way into the downtown area where small cafés and art studios lined the street. An honor system farmstand sold glass jars of honey and bouquets of flowers. He stopped to touch the petal of a flower. A peony. They were Mattie's favorite. He remembered she told him once how they were special because they only bloom once a year. The time you can hold one in your hand, fleeting and precious. Only a few blocks long, the front of each store was pristine. While Cape Rose got a share of tourists in the summer months, it always had a sea-ravaged look; paint peeling and everything out of date by ten years. Manzanita was obviously built up to be a cozy destination. If someone was building a set for a Pacific Northwest town, this is what it would look like. He opened the door to Goldfinch Café and made his way to the counter.

The young woman behind the register widened her eyes, then smoothed her face. This was a welcome change from other places he had been hounded by fans. Some might say the area wasn't friendly, but he'd take the anonymity.

Settling into a small table by the window he fished out his phone as he waited for his drink.

Aria says, "No MORE!!" An AllCeleb exclusive!!
By Trinity Flay

Theo Blake has been dumped. A close friend of actress Aria Kingston said that the teen soap star has kicked the aging rock star to the curb.

"She wants someone she can count on, and everyone knows Theo Blake is nice to look at, but you can't count on a guy like that," the anonymous source reports.

Kingston and Blake had been dating for over two years, and there were even reports of wedding bells in their future. Here at AllCeleb, we have been following the romantic intrigues of Prevalent Notion's lead singer for years now. His previous relationship with supermodel Safiya Khan ended in equally drastic measures. It begs the question, what is wrong with this man that sends these women running?

If you have information regarding this story or have any other celebrity news,

please email us at our tipline at gotcha@allceleb.com.

Theo scrolled through his messages, sending a *WTF* to Aria, who quickly replied that she was having her people handle it.

Aging rock star.

He was thirty-one. In his prime. Or something. And yeah, he didn't want to marry Aria. But did the tabloids have to make him sound undesirable? The barista called out his name and he grabbed his raspberry mocha from the counter. The barista's cheeks were pink as she smiled at him, but he turned away. A cute girl, but she couldn't be older than twenty.

Shoving his phone into his pocket, he moved down the street, glancing in shop windows and watching the people around him. He couldn't remember the last time he had felt like he blended in. Stopping in front of a bookstore, he studied the display of different books on wildflowers. In the window's reflection, he saw a dark-haired woman getting out of her car. Turning he watched as Mattie balanced a stack of files in her own hand and coffee mug in the other as she walked into the law office. Fate was helping him out once again.

CHAPTER FIVE

MATTIE

AN ERRANT CURL STUCK to Mattie's forehead as she walked into the Goldfinch Café behind her friend Shea. A fellow lawyer at the firm, Shea had talked her into using their lunch hour for the new hot yoga class in town. Mattie didn't realize it was taught by Jay's new girlfriend, Suze until the class started. Mattie had thought about leaving but she liked Suze well enough and there was only one studio in town, so she ended up at the twice-weekly classes.

Shea approached the counter, ordering her usual drink before glancing over at Mattie, her long box braids pushed over her shoulder. "Raspberry mocha?"

"I can get it, you don't have to..."

Shea ignored Mattie, giving the order to the barista. Grumbling, she followed her friend to the counter.

"Mats, don't look now, but I think I see Nathan Ayers. Behind you." Shea glanced over Mattie's shoulder, then back at Mattie. "Damn, that man is fine. Sure, he's a white boy, but I'll admit I wouldn't mind those bulky arms holding me tight."

"You're married, to an amazing man." Mattie reminded her, hoping to change the subject. They grabbed their drinks off the counter, the paper cup hot in Mattie's hand.

Shea flapped her hand at the comment. "Lee can't say a thing about this.

The number of times I've had to listen to that man wax poetic about Devlin Teague is a lesson in wifely patience."

If Nathan Ayers was around, there was a possibility Theo was too. It wasn't that she didn't want to see Theo. It was that she wanted it too much.

For days after they danced in her kitchen, she could still sense the weight of his palm against the small of her back. Could smell the soap of his skin and regret of not getting closer. No, her life needed to go back to how it was. The sooner Theo Blake left town, the sooner she could do that. Instead, she was forced to watch from her bedroom window like some creeper as he returned to the mansion every morning, sweaty and strong, his cheeks flushed from the crisp air. One time he saw her watching and waved from the road. She ducked down and hit her knee on the edge of her bed frame. She was still sporting a nasty bruise.

Mattie turned to the exit and almost ran into Eloise who was standing beside an especially tall and bulky Nathan Ayers.

"Mattie!" Eloise chimed, her face breaking into a huge smile. "I was hoping I'd see you around again." She motioned to Nathan. "You remember Nathan from the other night, right?"

Mattie nodded; she could sense Shea shooting her a laser glare beside her. "Right." Her voice came out shakier than she meant. She coughed before turning to Shea. "This is Shea Montgomery. She's a senior associate at the firm I work at. Shea, this is my new neighbor, Eloise, and, um, Nathan."

Nathan stuck his hand out to Shea, who shook it carefully, his large pale palm engulfing her small hand. "Ladies, it's wonderful to see you." His voice had a slight southern drawl she hadn't noticed the last time they met, but she had been distracted that night.

Eloise was talking about their errands of the day, buzzing on about the long line in the Manzanita Market, the only grocery store on the island. "...and then Nathan suggested we grab a coffee for everyone else. I mean Ilsa, that's Nathan's wife," she explained quickly. "Ilsa's going to still be in bed, but Keller and Theo will be up."

Mattie should say something, but she wasn't sure what. Shea was going to grill her within an inch of her life the moment the duo left their sights. Finally, Shea cleared her throat. "That's sweet of you. If I may, I'm a big fan of

Vermilion, Mr. Ayers. I know some critics didn't like the departure the band took from your previous work, but I enjoyed it. Especially your collaboration with Sakina Green on *The Stars Are You.*"

"That's very kind of you, ma'am. We always appreciate hearing that." Nathan brightened up. "Sakina is going to be doing a show here tomorrow. We were gonna go support her and sing a song or two. You should come. Both of you, bring your husbands or something."

"Oh, I'm not sure, it's short notice, and I..."

"Yes. We would be honored. I am a huge Sakina Green fan," Shea interrupted. "Mattie, I bet Jay would take Kamari, even if it's not his night."

Eloise grinned, a glint of something behind her eyes. "Wonderful! Why don't us gals all go together? The boys have to go early, sound check stuff." She leaned in and winked. "It's a secret, don't tell anyone, though."

The barista called out their orders, and Nathan and Eloise grabbed the multiple drinks, calling over her shoulder as they left, "I'll stop by later, and we'll work out the deets."

Gripping her coffee in her hand, Mattie turned slowly to Shea, who had narrowed her eyes. "Matilda Lewis. I about want to kill you for not telling me your new neighbor is Nathan from Prevalent Notion."

"Well," Mattie drawled carefully. "Technically, it's Keller and Eloise's house. The band is visiting them right now."

Shea glared at Mattie. "What aren't you telling me? You love sharing gossip with me. You called me at five a.m. about that blogger."

"Because Everslee Tracy was caught using peat moss! That is an enormous story in the sustainable gardening world. It was news."

"At five a.m. When all good people should be resting. But you can't tell me you live next door to a rock star?"

"It slipped my mind?" she offered weakly. "It's complicated, I knew Theo when I was younger and I never thought I'd see him again..."

Shea grabbed the coffee out of Mattie's hand and motioned to an empty table in the corner. "You sit down. I can already tell this conversation requires a muffin."

WHEN THEY ARRIVED AT the venue, there was a line around the block to the front entrance. Riding in the town car the short drive from the ferry terminal to the venue, Mattie fought the urge to check her phone for the seventh time. Jay had agreed to take Kamari even though it wasn't his usual day. She rarely had a night out, and even when she did it was more happy hour wine tastings with a friend downtown. While she could tell he was curious, Jay wasn't the type to pry, telling her, "I'll mind my business, but be careful, Mats."

Nothing about this trip felt careful. She had long prided herself on being somewhat responsible. Sure, she had her moments of being perpetually late and yeah, she could do better at keeping her house organized—but she wasn't reckless.

But seeing Theo, this night out, it was as if she was careening toward the edge of something. Despite the voice telling her she was in no danger from Theo, there was no way a man like that could want her, she was tormented by thoughts of him. To see him again, the way he looked at her, made her feel the way she did as a teenager. And that teenager was a fool.

"I hope we can find parking," Mattie remarked as she eyed the long line to get in. "Or we'll be waiting forever outside."

Eloise laughed beside her, giving her a confused expression. "Line? There is no line for us."

"What? But I thought..."

Eloise called out to the driver to go around back. Her turquoise hair was curled and pinned to the side showing off a small tattoo of the lower-case initials *mc* behind her ear. She wore a short rainbow sequin dress and tall platform sandals. Beside her, Mattie tugged on the hem of her jean skirt and purple shirt. It had felt cute in her bedroom before she left, but not anymore. If she had put more thought into it, she might have worn heels, but almost every trip to downtown Seattle involved walking and the streets were notoriously unpleasant on feet.

Huddled beside Shea, Eloise banged four times on the back door with her fist.

A tall dark-haired woman with a shaved head opened the door, a scowl clouding her face. Upon seeing Eloise, she snarled, "No groupies allowed."

With eyes narrowed Eloise, crossed her arms over her chest. "Is that so?"

The women looked Eloise up and down. "You seem like the worst kind of groupie if I've ever seen one." Then her face broke out into a grin, exposing braces. The two hugged, the security guard lifting Eloise off the floor.

Turning to the rest of the group Eloise smiled. "Dawn was our head of security for the boy's last tour."

"The same one where this gal up and married that man-whore," Dawn teased as she held open the door for the group to walk through. Mattie looked to Eloise to see how the comment landed, but Eloise was chatting with Dawn about some acquaintances.

Following the group down the hall, Dawn knocked on a door before opening it slowly. "Put your pants back on, Nathan, we got guests."

On different chairs were the members of Prevalent Notion. Keller sat in one chair, his long legs stretched out in front of him, crossed at the ankle. Nathan was on the couch his arm over the shoulders of a beautiful blonde woman wearing high-waisted leather shorts, a sheer top, and over-the-knee boots. Strewn across the room were various clothing items and empty beer bottles. In a chair in the corner, Theo sat tuning his guitar. Her chest tightened at the sight of him, his hair flopping over his forehead as he bent over the instrument. He could have been eighteen again, sitting on her bed in Cape Rose. When he glanced up, his eyes went straight to Mattie, a lightness flooding his features. A pang echoed through her. How many times had she envisioned him looking up at her like that? And now he was here and she didn't know what to do. As she glanced away from his face, her eyes caught on something on his guitar strap, a glint of green and gold pinned to the fabric. She sucked in a breath at the sight.

When Theo left for L.A., she didn't have any money to give him to help with the move, but she had her grandmother's old brooch. The idea being he could pawn it if money got too tight. She never thought she would see it again, but there it was pinned to the strap of his guitar, twelve years later.

It doesn't mean anything. He still left you.

To the side, she heard Eloise introduce the blonde woman as Nathan's wife, Ilsa, who she vaguely remembered from the party. Shea sat down and accepted a beer from Keller. Mattie hugged her small cream-colored clutch to her chest. It was the wrong color for her outfit, but it was the only small purse she had. Normally she had a plethora of snacks, bandages, lotions, and gum alongside her wallet and keys. She was practically naked without her big purse.

The indistinct sound of another band on the stage filtered down the hall. Theo was going to play on that stage to these fans. He had everything he could ever want on that stage. By leaving her, he had given himself that. Steeling herself, she walked to the other side of the room, leaning against a wall and watching as Shea and Lee made themselves comfortable on the couch, chatting with the band. When Eloise handed her a beer, she drank it, not caring how it tasted. The heavy weight of Theo's eyes on her. She couldn't look at him. If she looked then he would see how conflicted she was about being near him. She had to maintain her composure. She had argued cases in a court of law, and had finished law school while pregnant. Surely, she could ignore one sexy rock star for a night.

The door opened again and this time it was a statuesque black woman coming in. The sheer ethereal dress swirled around her legs as she moved and her long black hair cascaded down her back like a waterfall. Her makeup was immaculate, with gold and green stripes on her lids and a dark purple lip that contrasted with her rich dark skin. Her cheekbones were highlighted to a shine that could have reflected the lights above.

"Hey boys, you got a beer for me?" Sakina Green asked.

With a quick flick of his wrist, Theo popped the top off a beer and handed it to the singer. Sakina came into the room, sitting across from Shea, who was practically vibrating with excitement at seeing her. Mattie was happy for her friend. This was why she wanted to come. Soon they were chatting, and Mattie watched her friend's face, seeing the happiness there.

Draining her beer, Mattie set it down on the counter behind her. Eloise came to stand beside her, another beer in hand. She glanced at Theo, then back at Mattie.

"Man, he's got it bad." Eloise cocked her head to the side to motion toward

Theo who was now sitting apart from the group, drinking whiskey straight out of the bottle.

"What?" Mattie took the offered beer from Eloise.

"Theo. I've never seen him so twisted up before. I've seen him with women he considered friends, and I've seen him with women he wanted to sleep with. The way he watches you. It's different. I've known him a decade and I've never seen him stare at a woman the way he does you."

Mattie snorted into her beer. "It doesn't mean anything. All that was a long time ago."

With a shrug, Eloise allowed her comment to stand.

A young man poked his head into the door and told the band it was showtime. Nathan kissed Ilsa before getting up. Keller followed suit, pulling Eloise in for a deep kiss and whispering something in her ear that made her blush.

"Get out of here," she admonished with a grin.

As Nathan walked out the door he turned around, shooting Ilsa some finger guns. "Hey Petal, thanks for coming to my show, you should try my face sometime."

Ilsa's cheeks turned pink but she laughed at him.

Guitar in hand, Theo followed his bandmates out, his exit subdued. In the doorway, he turned and looked at Mattie; his ocean eyes deep as he opened his mouth, then closed it. She recognized the look. It was one he had many times over their relationship. A fissure was forming in her chest at the familiar vulnerability.

In the green room, Shea and Ilsa were discussing some show they both loved watching and Ilsa was sharing how she had a run-in with one of the actors on the show once, and how it ruined her experience. "...tiny dick, and had no clue how to work it. Not everyone can be well endowed, but you have to find other talents if you want a girl to stay." Ilsa laughed.

"Illy, stop ruining these gal's experiences for that show," Eloise scolded Ilsa.

With an eye roll, Ilsa glanced at Eloise. "Oh, come on, you've heard that story a million times, too. Everyone knows he's a dud."

"You are a married woman now," Eloise quipped.

"I'm married but I wasn't a nun before Nate and I got together. If he doesn't care, why should you?"

Ignoring her friend, Eloise stood up, motioning to Mattie. "You want to watch from the side? It's pretty fun getting that viewpoint. Ilsa says the side of the stage is too loud for her." Eloise looped her arms through Mattie's, pulling her out the door.

"They're only playing three songs before Sakina comes out," Ilsa called out.

In the wings of the stage, Mattie stood back, watching as Keller walked out first, his drumsticks in hand. He waved at the crowd, who emitted ear-piercing screams at the sight of him.

Eloise glanced at her. "They have a lot of female fans." Her words weren't quite an apology.

Nathan jogged out and did a dance with his bass while walking to his spot. He blew kisses into the crowd, and the chorus of "Oh, my God!" sounded over the racket.

"Show-offs." Eloise laughed. Theo took one step toward the stage, then turned back to face Mattie.

"Thanks for coming to watch me play." Theo pulled his guitar over his head. She couldn't look at the strap, couldn't see the evidence in front of her. Her thoughts jumbled in her head. In the audience, a chant started, first a few voices, then a cacophony.

Theo

Theo

Theo

The voices didn't seem to register for him. Was this his experience every time he played?

"I didn't come to see you. I came for Shea. Because she wanted to see Sakina."

The strap smooth on his shoulder, he smirked at her. "We both know that's not true, Matilda." He bent down, pressing a quick kiss to her cheek. His mouth found her ear. "Pay attention during the show, I think you'll like it."

He jogged out on stage, a showman's mask over his features. His head bowed over the microphone he waited the crowd out. When the hush fell on the crowd, he leaned forward his clear voice ringing out. She recognized the song; it was featured in a big movie a few years before. From her spot on the stage, she watched as they played, the way Theo controlled the crowd with the rise and fall of the song. The pace quickened and Keller came in with the drums.

She had never seen Theo this way. As children it was him on an acoustic guitar, singing his songs to whoever would listen. This music was full and lush. The three of them in unison as they played and sang together.

"I wrote this one," Eloise said, leaning into Mattie. "It's Keller's favorite." With a glance at the drummer, Mattie saw him shoot a quick wink to his wife beside her.

The song ended with a long echo drumbeat.

The crowd cheered, and Theo and Nathan exchanged big grins. This was obviously his best self, performing out there under those lights with these men. For years, she'd cursed the band for its popularity, for keeping him away. She told herself if he failed as a musician, he'd come back to her. To watch his talent onstage, she saw how wrong those ideas were.

With one hand wrapped around the microphone stand, Theo shook his hair off his forehead, sweat glistening at his hairline under the bright lights.

"How many of you remember your first love?" Theo asked the crowd.

Screams and whoops echoed up to the stage.

Theo glanced over at the wings, his eyes on Mattie as he spoke. "I've never admitted this publicly before, no matter how many times I've been asked, but Stone Castles is about someone. It's about the first girl I ever loved."

The crowd quieted down, listening as Theo talked. Beside her, Eloise grasped her arm, murmuring, "Oh, God."

From the corner of her eye, Mattie could see the concerned expression on Eloise's face, but she couldn't look away from Theo as he spoke.

"I'm sure you all know what that feels like, to have something perfect and to lose it."

With one more side glance, he began to sing. She tried to pay attention to the words, but they were drowned out by the pounding of blood in her head. Breaths came out sharp, stinging her throat. Her chest was too tight for her thudding heart against her ribs. Life was fine before he came back with his confusing words and beautiful songs and stupid, perfect smile.

The song ended, and they began a third one, with Nathan taking the lead on the vocals as Theo stood back. Beside her, she could sense Eloise tense up.

"He does this sometimes, runs his mouth on stage. I'm sure if you give him a chance to..."

Before Eloise could finish her sentence, Mattie had turned around, searching for an exit. She couldn't be there when Theo got off stage, she wouldn't know what to say to him.

I still care for you.

You broke my heart.

"I'm going to get a drink," Mattie murmured.

"Okay, the green room is fully stocked, whatever you..."

"No, at the bar. I'm going to the bar out there, and I'm getting a drink." Their song was ending, and they introduced Sakina. The Afro-punk singer glided by them, stepping on stage for her first song. Still glancing around the area, she spotted a side door that would lead out into the concert hall. She willed her feet to move, but she couldn't. Theo was exiting the stage heading toward her.

Joining her in the wings, Theo took a bottle of water offered by an assistant. Tilting the bottle back, Theo drank half the bottle in a long movement. Matilda watched as his Adam's apple bobbed as he swallowed. She could still feel the stubble of his throat on her fingertips from the last time she touched him.

No, stop, do not proceed, turn away.

"Did you like your song?" he asked, stepping closer to her. Somehow, she got turned around, and her back was facing the stage. If she took a step back, she'd be visible from on the stage. The scent of his soap clung in the air between them. How could he smell good after being on stage under those lights?

"It's not my song." She refused to accept that. They had to be meaningless words. He couldn't mean that, because that meant he was still thinking of her but didn't want her, or else he wouldn't have let her go the way he did.

His head cocked to the side, as if assessing her. "Who else's could it be?"

Matilda stepped back, getting away from the pull toward him that was reaching out from below her belly button. Her mind realized she needed to stay away. Her nether bits had a whole other idea. Damn horny clit, getting in her way.

"Theodore."

His bright blue eyes watched her as she moved, a lion about to pounce. No matter how many years it had been since she had those eyes on her, they held the same sway. She was right back to that little auditorium on that tepid May night, dancing on stage, the awareness of those feline eyes on her as she moved.

"Teddy, please. You called me that once, why can't you again?"

"You know perfectly well why." She narrowed her eyes at him, setting her jaw tight. That first day she saw him at Eloise and Keller's, it slipped out, but now that she had control over her tongue, she wasn't going to give him that endearment ever again.

He stepped closer, his foot between hers. The warmth of his leg between hers radiated up her thighs and straight to her center. Dammit. It was just a little leg brush, and her clit was pounding for release; what would happen when he actually touched her again?

If. If. Not when. Dammit.

"In case you were wondering, no one. Not the guys, not anyone, not even Eloise, is allowed to call me that. Only you."

His words were a warm wave crashing through her ribs. No matter how much she fought against the aching, it stayed buried deep in her chest.

His movements were so subtle, she didn't notice his hand until it was resting on her cheek, the rasp of his calloused fingers hot on the hollow above her ear. His thumb touched the edge of her mouth, a soft brush of sparks that made her face flame.

"Only you. Twelve years later. And it's only you. As the rain, I swear it."

She found her voice. "You can't say things like that to me. Not anymore."

"Why, because you like it?" A smile ticked up on those soft lips. Would they taste of whiskey and his favorite gum?

Closing her eyes, she willed herself to step away. To remember why she was angry. She couldn't allow him to sway her like this. She had spent years in turmoil, getting over this man, to have him saunter in and destroy everything?

No.

Bringing her hand up to her face, she grabbed his hand, pulling it off her face.

"Because your words don't mean anything to me. They didn't mean shit twelve years ago, and they don't mean a damn thing tonight." Dropping his hand, she stepped around him, too quick for him to react. Stalking away from the backstage area and down into the venue, to be swallowed up by the concertgoers. In there, she could escape him.

Coming was a mistake. She was a fool for that man, time and time again. The best course of action would be to stay as far away from Theodore Francis Blake as she possibly could.

Chapter Six

Theo

H E'D GIVE HER A few minutes to cool off, and then she'd be back. There was no way she'd up and leave him. At least he didn't think so.

Okay, yeah, maybe she would. He shouldn't have come on so strong, but between the drinks, before he went on and the adrenaline pumped through him while performing, it all came out. He wasn't ashamed of how he felt or what he said. Every word was true, whether she believed it or not. She was his, and now that he had her back, he was going to see to it that she understood that.

Eloise offered to go find Mattie for him, but her friend volunteered instead, knowing her better. Her friend gave him a nasty frown as she walked by, though. That might be a problem. Ten minutes later, she announced that Mattie was fine, she was having a drink with some guy at the bar, and she'd meet them at the car after the show.

Some guy? Fuck that.

The security guards at the side door moved to the side as he stomped past them, making a beeline to the bar in the corner. As he passed, there were shocked whispers and comments he ignored. It wasn't to say he hadn't interacted with fans after a show; it had been over five years since he was comfortable going into the general admission area. At that moment, he didn't care about his security. The only goal was getting to Mattie.

Hip up at the bar, she was gesticulating wildly to a man in a flannel shirt who was smiling down at her. A scruffy beard and tee shirt with a large capital "R" in front of a mountain range on it added to the man's aesthetic. He had a tall can of beer in his hand that matched the shirt.

"What are you doing out here?" Theo demanded, stepping in front of her. Around them, a crowd had formed at the sight of Theo, but his eyes were on Mattie alone.

Narrowing her eyes at him, she took a sip of her tall can of cheap beer.

"Oh, man. Theo Blake. I love you, man. Huge fan," the scruffy-bearded man gushed, putting his hand out for Theo to shake. With a single narrowed-eyed glare, the man put his hand down and stepped back.

"Come on, Matilda, let's go," he demanded.

Her beer can made a low thunk as she slammed it on the counter. "I told Shea where I was. Now please go. I'm having a conversation with Sage, here."

"It's Satchel," the man interrupted.

"I've heard all I need to hear from you tonight, Theodore. Go find yourself some groupie, and try your lines somewhere else." She turned her body until she faced the other man and avoided Theo's eyes. "Now, what were you saying about your crypto-currency?"

Every muscle in his body tensed at seeing her flirt with this douchebag. Pushing the other man to the side, Theo wrapped his arms around Mattie's middle, picking her up and throwing her over his shoulder. His grip was tight on her upper thighs as he made his way through the crowd.

Mattie wriggled against his shoulder, trying to free herself from his tight grip, but he wasn't putting her down yet. People had pulled out their phones, recording him. It would be fodder for the gossip sites in a matter of minutes, but he didn't care. Mattie needed to be on the other side of that door with him. Mattie needed to be with him. Period. Full stop.

"Put me down!" she hollered, raining light punches on his back as he walked.

Getting to the side door, he glared at the two security guards. "Let us through," Theo demanded.

The security guards glanced at each other. "Mr. Blake, sir. I don't think it's appropriate..."

"I don't give a damn what you think." The men crossed their arms over their chests and glared down at him. So, that wasn't going to work. Behind him, the comments were getting louder.

Who is that girl?

Rock stars, man, losing their minds.

I can't wait to tell my sister about this.

"I'll put her down on the other side of this door, just let us through first. Talk to Dawn if you don't believe me." The guards hesitated, giving each other looks of disbelief before one of them shrugged, moving aside to open the side door.

Once the side door closed and they were fully backstage, he walked into the first dressing room he found. Once inside, he slammed the door behind him and flipped her back to rights, setting her down on the ground. Her skirt rode up her legs, bunching around her waist. Angrily, she shoved her skirt down over her exposed legs.

"How dare you? You entitled asshole. You can't pick me up and carry me like I'm a sack of potatoes."

"I could have done that all night I have great stamina." Rubbing his hands together, he gave her an expression of pure glee at her reaction.

Matilda's lips curled at his comment. "Those little lines are ridiculous. *I have great stamina.* No self-respecting woman would fall for that."

"My legions of fans disagree."

"I am not one of your fans."

Theo's eyes flashed at his comment, and the corner of his mouth ticked up. "Of that, I have no doubt."

She walked to the door, grabbing the handle. "I was having a perfectly fine time talking to that guy before you ruined it."

He slammed his hand over the door, not letting her open it. "That's a lie, and you know it. You don't want that dickhead."

Both her hands wrapped around the door knob as she tried pulling it open, but it stayed shut under his hand. "You have no idea what I want."

He slid his body against the door. "I am exactly what you want. You think I don't remember how it looks when you're attracted to someone? The way your pupils dilate, the hitch in your breath, the way you suck on your lower lip."

He was pushing her limits, but he also knew if she wanted out, she would leave.

Brushing her hair off her face, his fingers wrapped around the nape of her neck, pulling her closer. Her lips parted, and she stepped closer, letting him lead her.

"If you think for a moment I've forgotten how these lips taste, or the little sounds you make when something feels good, you are mistaken. I remember everything, Matilda."

"That was years ago," she said, but the fight was leaving her voice, replaced by something lower.

"And I've only gotten better since then." His fingers moved from the nape of her neck to her chest, holding her against the door.

"You don't have that power over me any longer. I'm not that eighteen-year-old girl anymore."

"I know exactly what you are." As she watched his face, her tongue came out to lick her lips. His hand moved from the center of her chest to spread against her throat. "I've pictured this a million times over. You can't imagine how it hurts knowing you've had other men. I have no right, but I don't care. This skin—" His thumb traced against the side of her throat. "This body. It belonged to me once, and it will again.

His lips descended on hers, devouring her mouth, her hands fisted in his hair as his tongue battled hers. Grasping her thighs, he pulled her up, wrapping her legs around his waist and then turning to wedge her between his body and the door.

The kisses she returned were as frenzied. With her legs around his waist, she moved against him, rubbing herself over the front of his pants. He thanked God she was wearing a skirt, the thin fabric of her thong riding his ever-growing cock. Her skirt hitched up around her waist.

"How can you still kiss like that?" she murmured against his mouth. It wasn't a love declaration, but it was enough for him. Thrusting against her, his mouth moved from hers to her throat. She groaned at his motion, throwing her head back, where it hit the door with a low thunk.

"Are you okay?" he asked.

"Keep kissing me," she demanded, wriggling against him. By this time, his dick was hard and begging to be inside her, but he had to hold off.

His kisses rained down her neck, savoring the taste of sweat on her skin. With one hand firm on her ass to hold her up, his other hand reached between them to pull up her shirt. Her body slipped down, and she grabbed his hand, placing it under her ass to hold herself up. With both hands doing the work, she hitched her body up, tightening her leg's grip on his waist.

Her shirt came up over her head. The bra she was wearing wasn't fancy; a cream-colored one with a little bow between her breasts. They were bigger than he remembered them being, but the left one still had the small birthmark peeping out of the lace trim. He wanted to kiss that little spot, but the angle wouldn't allow it.

Her hands moved from his hair to between them, where she grasped at the front of his jeans.

The motion stopped him. "Wait, I don't want to push you to do anything you don't like. I can't believe I'm saying this. I've waited years to have you again, but we should stop."

"Don't you dare stop," she demanded.

He pushed her damp hair from her face; how did she become more beautiful in the past twelve years? And still she remained the same, her skin was as soft as it has always been, her hair the same wild tangles through his fingers.

"Why don't we get a hotel room, or at least..."

"Less talking, more kissing," she said before taking his mouth.

This wasn't how he pictured having Mattie again. But with his raging hard-on and her moving against him, he was only going to stop if she told him to.

With his hands on her ass, lifting her, it was easy to push the thin material to the side. His fingers found her wet and ready for him. As he pushed a single digit inside her, she groaned, her pelvis moving against his hand. He moved inside her, two fingers fucking her as his other finger circled her clit.

She was getting heavy in his arms; for all the workouts he did, this was using muscles he didn't know he had. Setting her on the floor, he kneeled in front of her. She stared down at him, her fingers tangled in his hair. Hooking his fingers on each side of her underwear, he pulled them down to the ground. When Mattie stepped out of them, he grabbed one of her ankles, bringing it over his shoulder. He should have been tender, taking his time teasing her, but all he wanted was the taste of her on his tongue. Burying his face in her pussy, his tongue circled her clit as his fingers moved in and out of her, hitting the spot that made her curse.

"You taste so good on my tongue." His thumb traced over her clit. A glance up showed her head tilted back, her eyes closed as she gasped.

"Stop talking," she groaned as her fingers dug into his scalp. He wondered if she was pulling out his hair, deciding he didn't care as long as she felt good.

As he worked over her, licking and teasing her closer, he heard the sweet sound of her humming with pleasure. He tightened his grip on her ass, feasting on her until she cried out. Around his fingers, she tensed. With half-lidded eyes, he peered up to see her cover her mouth with the back of her hand, biting the soft skin there to muffle her cry.

As she was coming down from her orgasm, he pressed a kiss to the spot where her pelvis met her hip. Rocking back on his heels, he watched as she slowly opened her eyes.

"I never want to forget that look on your face," he remarked. "We should get back, though. The security guards are probably worried about you."

She grabbed the shoulder of his shirt, pulling him up to his feet. With a hand firm on the nape of his neck, she pulled at the front of his pants, unbuttoning them. Pulling him out before he realized what she was doing, her hand wrapped around his shaft, warm and strong in her grip.

"You're not done. I need you to finish what you've started. You owe me that."

"I owe you a lot of things."

"I don't want to hear that right now. Just make me feel good. Show me."

His resolve was crumbling as her fist moved up and down his cock, pumping him. "Mattie, last chance to back out. We don't..."

"Fuck me, Theo. You want me, don't you? Prove it."

His kiss was crushing, his hands bringing her hips flush with his, and then he was picking her up again, slamming her back into the door as he sunk inside her in a single motion. Her stuttering cry was beautiful in his ear as she stretched around him.

"Oh, God," she cried as he moved.

He wasn't going to last long inside her. He tried slowing down; he wanted to make this good for her. For him, it had been too long since anyone felt this good, maybe never. He owed her more. If this was his last time to be inside her, he owed her a pleasure she'd never dreamed of.

Her hips rose up to meet him, and her tug of his hair was demanding. "You can fuck me harder than that, Theodore," she taunted him.

With those words, all semblance of control he had snapped. His grip on her hips was so tight, he was sure she'd bruise. He bounced her up and down on his cock, edging them closer to orgasm, each thrust a penance for all the years that had built up between them.

He knew talking might break the moment, but he couldn't stop himself, the words flowing over his tongue as he thrust inside her. "You ruined me for other women, am I supposed to try and be with someone else? Years I tried and it's never enough. Who else has this birthmark on the inside of their thigh, just begging to be kissed? The slick of your cunt against my cock as you move. The silk of your skin on my lips, the way your breasts are heavy in my hands. The scar on your back that I run my fingers over again and again. No other women whimpers softly as I kiss their neck. There is no one else for me, Matilda. There's only this, all I want is you, your tight pussy around me, your throat exposed as you throw your head back. All I need is you whispering those words in my ear as I fill you up. No one is going to compare to you. You've destroyed me for every other woman."

Her fingers raked down his back, deep enough to sting, but he didn't care. He was sure to have red knuckles from the way they hit the door with each thrust he gave her.

"What do you have to say for yourself?"

"Come closer," Mattie gasped in his ear. "And ruin me too.'"

With every thrust, she took more and more of him. He wanted to claim her, to make her his the way he was irrevocably hers now.

She cried out, tensing around him, finding his shoulder and biting his skin to muffle the scream that came from deep within her.

He followed, coming inside her with an anguished noise. Slick with sweat, he pulled away. Her head still on his shoulder, her eyes were closed. Dropping her feet to the ground, he cradled her face in his hand. This kiss was soft, reverent even.

"I'm so glad I have you back," he whispered against her lips.

Mattie jerked her head back, her eyes dazed. "What?"

Rubbing his thumb over her cheek, he smiled down at her. "Us, together again. I'm so glad."

Blinking several times, as if to clear her vision, she stepped away, glancing around the small room. When she found her discarded underwear, she pulled them on, her eyes downcast from him.

"I have to go."

"What?" he asked, confused, using the wall to steady himself. He had barely put himself back in his pants, while she was pulling her shirt over her head and straightening her skirt.

"Yeah, this was...something. But I should go."

He watched as she opened the door, speedwalking to the green room, where everyone else was still sitting. Mattie's hair was a mess, half-pulled out of the sleek style she showed up in, and her shirt was backward, the tag sticking up. He didn't need to look into the mirrors to know he was equally messed up, but chasing after Mattie seemed more important than finding a mirror. From the surprised looks on everyone's faces, he must have looked worse than he thought.

But Mattie didn't notice their stares as she approached her friend.

"I'm ready to go. You ready?"

"Mattie," Theo called out. "Come on, stay."

She refused to look at him, grabbing her purse from the counter and slinging it over her shoulder. Her friend must have read Mattie's face, because she shot Theo a dangerous look and shook her head. The room was quiet as his bandmates glanced from Mattie to Theo, then back to Mattie. He was going to be in for a mess of questions later.

Shea got up, pulling on her own bag. "Of course. Thanks for the VIP treatment, guys. I'll see you around."

Eloise's brow furrowed as they walked away. "What did you do, Theo?" she hissed before she chased after them.

When Eloise returned a few minutes later, it was with a disappointed expression on her face. "I asked the driver to take them back to the ferry and then return for us later."

For what must have been the first time in his life, Nathan was quiet, watching Theo with a concerned expression.

"I did nothing wrong. Why are you all looking at me like I did?"

Eloise huffed, her hands on her hips as she glared up at Theo. "Because whatever asshole-ish remark you said or piggish thing you did scared her and her delightful friend away."

"It wasn't like that. I didn't say or do anything bad. I know I'm no saint, but this wasn't like that at all." With a glance at Keller, Theo grimaced. "Keller, come on, you know me."

Keller put up his hands up. "Hey, don't look at me. Whatever Eloise says we're doing, I'm doing. If she says you're an asshole. You're an asshole."

"We all know I'm an asshole. You don't need your wife for that." Theo went to the fridge, grabbed a beer, and popped the top off. "But this time around, it wasn't something I did."

"Care to explain yourself, then?" Eloise asked, an authoritarian look over her face.

Theo chugged the beer in his hand, trying to find the words. How could he explain this to his friends? As he set the empty beer bottle down on the floor at his feet, he shrugged his shoulders. "I honestly don't know."

"Did you fuck her?" Nathan asked.

"Nate!" Ilsa chided.

The bassist threw his hands in the air in an innocent gesture. "What? It's a legitimate question. He comes stumbling in here after her, his pants still unbuttoned, and her hair all messed up. What's a guy to think?"

"It's none of your business," Theo grumbled, grabbing the whiskey bottle off the table.

Around him, his bandmates and their wives made varying sounds of annoyance and glee at his words. They were such a pain in his ass.

CHAPTER SEVEN

MATTIE

THE ENTIRE FERRY RIDE back, Mattie was silent. At one point, Shea asked her if she was okay, to which Mattie told her, *No, not really, but it's fine.*

Luckily, Shea was a good enough friend to see Mattie would talk in her own time. Leaning her head on her friend's shoulder, they sat in a cold leather booth at the back of the ferry. The lights of Seattle grew darker and smaller in the white wake of the boat.

She wished she could blame the few beers she had, or that she hadn't had physical intimacy with another person for almost two years. But even as she tried to rationalize her choice to have sex with Theo again, she knew the argument fell flat.

His touch held the same magic it always had for her. She wanted him in that moment, she wanted that control and power over the man who had hurt her all those years before. To see him on his knees before her, taking her over the edge of pleasure, and then to have him give her more. It was intoxicating. In that small room off the side of the stage, she could pretend she was the type of woman who slept with a rock star. But with those brief words, she was cut off.

I'm so glad I have you back.

He couldn't have her back. She wasn't his anymore; he had seen to that years before. Did he think two orgasms and a backstage experience at a concert were enough to upend her entire life and years of pain? She had always been a fool for Theo, and she couldn't regret having him one more time. But it wouldn't happen again. Couldn't.

For twenty minutes, she could pretend to be wanton and desired by that man, but at the end of the day, she was still herself. And there was no world in which she and Theo were going to make sense again.

T HE NEXT DAY, SHE wasn't home for more than an hour before Eloise showed up at her door, carrying a bouquet. Unsure of how to act around her new neighbor, Mattie let her in, inviting her to the breakfast counter.

"Have a seat. I'm making some muffins for Kamari's class Flag Day party tomorrow."

Eloise rubbed her lower stomach as she sat on the stool opposite Mattie. She was already showing, her small belly stretching her dress.

"How far along are you?" Mattie asked. "Those might be ligament pains."

Eloise rubbed a circle with her thumb. "I'm fifteen weeks, and I'm pretty sure they are. My sister, Ana, said it's common, but every pain worries me."

"It's extremely common. The baby has to grow, and your body might not like it. I had terrible ligament pains with Kamari." Mattie smiled at her comfortingly.

Eloise glanced at a small school picture on the wall nearby. In the picture, Mari had refused to let Mattie do her hair and insisted on wearing her glitter barrettes that always slipped down. They were perched near her ears by the time the photo was taken. "She's a beautiful child, she looks like you."

"Except her ears, thank God." Mattie touched her left lobe, as if to remind herself that her ears were still there, large and sticking out from her head. "As a kid, I got teased horribly for these things. Luckily, she's like Jay in that regard. Maybe she'll have a little more height, too."

"You and your ex, you're good?" Eloise asked carefully.

Mattie nodded as she dumped the coconut oil into the mixing bowl. Setting the mixer to low, she kept her eyes on the mixture as she talked. The consistency looked off, but with the rabid allergies at the school, vegan substitutions were her best option. "He's a good guy. He just wasn't the right guy for me. We had been dating for two years, he proposed when I got pregnant, and it made sense to get married. We tried for a few years, but after Kamari was born, it was obvious we weren't meant to stay together. I couldn't imagine co-parenting with anyone else, but he was a better father than he is a husband, at least for me. He got engaged a month ago. She's nice. She has a daughter a few years older than Kamari who is an absolute doll."

Mattie liked Suze. She felt leagues different from herself, but maybe that was what Jay needed. A yoga instructor, she owned a studio in the old part of town. She was lean and blonde, and if she wasn't nice, Mattie would be tempted to hate her. She was apprehensive the first time she met Suze, but hours later they were chatting like old friends. Best of all, Suze and Kamari adored each other. Jay was going to move on eventually and Mattie was pleased with his choice. Now that he was seeing Suze, Kamari could spend more time at their house. It began to feel like a better co-parenting situation.

Eloise took a sip of her mug of decaf coffee, then made a face. "Ugh, decaf. People say it tastes the same, but it's not the same."

"Do you want real coffee?" Eloise reached for the canister of beans on the counter.

Eloise flapped her wrist at the comment. "No, I already had more than my caffeine limit at the coffee shop earlier this morning. I'm being grumpy."

"I remember the feeling." Her eyes glued to the mixture in the bowl, she asked the question that had been nagging at her. "That brooch Theo has on his guitar strap, um—" She took a steadying breath. She could sound nonchalant, she didn't care, truly, not at all. "Is that normal, or something he always has on there?"

With a furrowed brow, Eloise set her chin in her hands, pondering. "It's always been there since I've met him. I'm sure I asked at some point, but he said it was his good luck charm and left it at that. I don't think I've given it much thought for years."

Swallowing down the bile rising inside her, she choked out the words. "It was my grandmother's."

Eloise set her mug on the counter, blinking at her in surprise. "Your grandmother's. For the past decade, Theo had your grandmother's jewelry on his guitar strap?"

Mattie nodded, the words falling flat on her tongue. The implication of what that meant hovered the air between them.

"I don't know you well, and I'm sure I'm overstepping, but..." Eloise raised herself up taller. "Listen, I don't know what happened with you and Theo. He doesn't really talk about his life before L.A. and the band. But all I know is, he has never looked at anyone the way he looks at you."

Mattie's breath caught in her throat, choking her words. Swallowing painfully, she trained her voice to even out. "How does he look at me?"

"Like you're the only one he knows. I think a lot of people hear his songs, his voice, and they think they know him. But they don't. He doesn't want anyone to know him. He puts up this sensitive facade, but it's not real. To be honest, I thought I knew him better than anyone. But I don't. Then one day with you, and it's like he's been peeled away. I've never seen it before."

"He's not like that with you guys?

"Vulnerable?" Eloise laughed. "No, definitely not. He's a bit of an asshole, to be honest. Says all the right things to get into a girl's pants and then leaves them. I've consoled many a groupie."

Mattie focused on the way the sugar fell into the bowl, the cascade of white crystals mixing with the dough. She knew he must have slept with other women; it had been years between seeing each other. The opportunity to sleep with women was probably given to him at every stop he made.

"I'm not a groupie," Mattie said. She didn't disparage women who slept around. But it wasn't her style. She had a single one-night stand in college before she started dating Jay. It was fumbling, awkward, and sloppy.

The mixer off, she scraped the sides with a rubber spoon.

"Yeah, that's pretty obvious, based on the way you hightailed it out of there after fooling around with him in a closet."

Mattie whipped her body around to face Eloise, the spoon still in her hand. "Did he tell you we slept together?"

Eloise raised a brow at Mattie, letting out a single chuckle. "No. He didn't have to. Your shirt was on backward, your hair was a mess, and his fly was down. We could all put two and two together on that one."

Eloise got up from her seat to grab the spoon out of Mattie's hand before the mixture dripped on the floor. "Don't worry about shocking me. You wouldn't believe the crazy stuff I've seen. The Seattle show was positively children's theater compared to what a night on tour looks like. Twenty-four hours before I married my husband, I had to kick a groupie out of his hotel room."

Pacified slightly, Mattie wiped her hands on her apron. "It wasn't a closet, by the way."

With her hands up in a mock defeat expression, Eloise shrugged. "Hey, no judgment here. When the need arises to get some, who am I to stop you?"

Growing up, her mother had drilled into her the importance of sex being between a loving couple, that a woman should only give herself to a man in a committed relationship, ideally marriage. When Mattie needed to get on the pill, she had a friend take her to the clinic two towns over, so she wouldn't be seen. While her sex life with Jay had been fine, it was nothing compared to the few instances with Theo at eighteen. She always chocked that up to her romanticizing her first boyfriend. But being with him again, even for those brief moments, had shown her they were what was good together. Him and her, it was about the way they moved together, how he could read her and know exactly what she needed from him.

It was the opposite of a casual encounter for her, but she had to lock it away under that label. To do otherwise would be opening herself up to hope, and she had too much at stake in her life to hope for a rock star.

Her focus shifted back to the recipe she mixed in beetroot for the red coloring and blueberries. The kids deserved a little color.

"I don't know how much Theo told you about us, but we dated when I was in high school. He was my first boyfriend." Mattie cleared her throat, trying to dislodge the lump forming. "When he moved to L.A., I was supposed to join him, but that didn't work out."

"He ended it?" Eloise leaned against the counter, her arms crossed over her chest. "Of course he did. Damn, he is such an idiot."

Biting her lip, Mattie stared down at her bare feet; she needed to touch up her toe polish. "I never thought I'd see him again. Honestly, I don't think I wanted to. But I can't pretend it's not bringing back all sorts of memories and emotions I didn't know I had."

"If it's any consolation, he was wrecked when you left last night. Sulked like a baby for hours. Refused to go out with Sakina and the band for a late dinner. I've never seen him react that way; normally when he has his ego bruised, he'll drink too much, kiss the wrong girl, pick fights. But last night, he was so quiet, I forgot he was there. That man lives for the spotlight, and it was as if he wanted to fade away."

She wanted to be relieved about hearing that, but a hollowness formed inside her chest.

She was supposed to hate him, to despise the way he hurt her as a naive girl, but still, after all this time, she couldn't. But he didn't need to know that, and despite how nice Eloise was being to her, she couldn't trust that everything she said wouldn't be reported back to Theo.

"Good. He deserves it." Mattie steeled her voice with more conviction than she felt.

Her finger tracing the edge of the coffee mug, Eloise looked at Mattie with something akin to an inspection. Mattie must have passed some test, because Eloise set her empty mug down on the counter beside her. "I'm sure he did. If I can be totally honest with you, I had my bouts of thinking I was in love with Theo. Now I know, it was a silly crush and nothing more. He never saw me that way, so it didn't matter. But over the years, I've seen the way he acts with women, even the women he claims to be in love with, and you? You're different."

"I'm not a supermodel, for sure," Mattie griped.

Eloise flapped a hand at the comment. "Trust me, I've been around enough of those people to tell you, they're equally flawed. So what if they have a perfect little slope nose, when they can't cut their own steak or drive a car or know which 'there' to use in an email?"

Mattie wrinkled her nose at the statement.

"Anyway, I should get going, Keller wanted to try that little Mexican restaurant downtown. Ilsa is from Arizona and is the snobbiest when it comes to Mexican food. I can't wait to see her face when they bring out the food."

Though they didn't know each other well, Mattie didn't protest when Eloise wrapped her arms around her for a hug. As she pulled away, Eloise's gaze met her eyes. Pausing, she furrowed her brow. "You have green eyes."

"Uh, yeah?" Still in Eloise's embrace, Mattie pulled back slightly. "They're not that unusual, more of a mossy green, not like a pretty emerald or anything—"

Letting Mattie's arms go, Eloise blinked a few times. "Theo mentioned a girl with green eyes once. He was really drunk and all broken up about his girlfriend, Safiya dumping him at an industry party. He said, *I loved her from the moment I saw her. All dark hair and green eyes and...the first time I saw her dance, I was done for. But she didn't love me, or else she wouldn't have left me.*"

Mattie blinked at this revelation, the words sinking in. "I didn't leave." Mattie's voice was small, a pain woven in the words. "He did."

Eloise nodded at the statement. "I'm sure that's true. I love Theo, I do. But he has a way of rewriting history when he feels hurt. He's been working on it, therapy and all that, but it's still there. I'm not telling you to give him another chance or anything, you obviously have a life here. All I know is, Theo cares for you. Whether that is enough, I can't say."

When Eloise left, Mattie sat at the counter, her chin in her hand. What Eloise shared was echoing around in her head. It could have been any girl he was talking about; he had years between them. But deep down, she knew it was her. That when Theo was at his lowest point, he thought of her. It could be a yearning for a time he lost or an idealized version of her he had built up in his head, but it was still there for him. Just as it was for her. She had no idea what Theo wanted from her. If it was a one time sex thing, she could get over it eventually. Yeah, it meant something to her, because she had no idea how to be casual about Theo. But she wasn't going to hope for more.

With the timer beeping, Kamari emerged from her room, the little girl's eyes on the muffins cooling on the counter. "I want this one tonight." She pointed at the biggest muffin.

Even though she knew this would ruin Kamari's appetite for dinner, she handed the muffin to her daughter. Mattie's life was full of poor choices these days, what was one more?

T HE DAY AFTER THE concert, he wanted to visit Mattie, to talk some sense into her, but his schedule called for him to fly down to L.A. for reshoots on a commercial he was doing for a high fashion brand. It was clothes he looked ridiculous in, but they were paying him an astronomical amount of money to sit on a bed with a smirk on his face while scantily clad models were draped around him. A month before, he was thrilled with the idea of doing the campaign. Now, his skin felt too tight beside these women, and he couldn't wait to leave, to return to Manzanita and Mattie.

Upon returning, he had a mind to go over to her place but stopped himself. What could he say to her? He knew his own feelings, and the moment he saw her face, it clicked with him. But getting her on board was proving to be more challenging. In the morning, he swung by her house to try to catch her before she left for work, to find the place dark and her sensible sedan gone. At night, he saw her return home with her daughter, a stack of papers in one hand and her daughter's backpack in the other.

Theo had never given much thought to children. He liked the idea of having them, of being a father. But seeing Eloise pregnant, the way Keller was excited for his wife was changing him. Keller confided in him that he was scared when Eloise first told him. Raised by his grandparents, Keller never had a father around.

Theo knew what that felt like. His mother never told him who his father was, only that he was a drunken mistake made while on a trip to Florida with some friends. Telling him that even if she wanted to let the man know, there wasn't a way to track him down. How many men named Dennis were out there?

He didn't need to mourn the loss of his biological father too much. His Uncle Rich, who was ten years older than his mom, more than made up for his lack of a father. Rich took him to Portland Blazers games and helped him with homework when his mom had to work late. He even bought him his first guitar. A perpetual bachelor, his uncle used to take him to the park, where he would pick up single mothers. Looking back, he didn't think a single relationship lasted longer than two months. Rich was hard-partying, drinking a beer every morning as he got ready to open the diner. Theo learned to drive early, so he could pick his uncle up from the bar when he called. The police looked the other way the few times he got pulled over. A sober fourteen-year-old was better than a drunk thirty-five-year-old. Was it what therapists would call a life of co-dependency? Sure. But Theo knew no different. He always had food, somewhat clean clothes, and a warm home. Rich was the best father figure he could be for his nephew.

But seeing how much better Keller wanted to be for his child made him wonder if he could be more, too. It was obvious Mattie was a great mom, caring and patient. Kamari was a package deal with Mattie, and if he wanted to be a part of Mattie's life, he would need to figure out what to do with her daughter.

Almost done with the first leg of his jog, he made a mental note to look up an article about kids when he got back to the house. He pulled one ear bud out as he slowed his pace. As he passed the law office where Mattie's name was listed at the bottom, he peeked in the window.

Only a young receptionist was behind the desk, a phone pressed to her ear. Continuing, he stopped at Goldfinch Café to get a smoothie.

Smoothie in hand, he walked out the side door of the small business, to hear the mention of his name.

"...and Theo Blake. You had to have heard that Prevalent Notion is here? Someone told me they did a surprise concert in Seattle the other day." He glanced around the corner to see a short blonde woman at a table talking to someone he couldn't see.

"I don't know if that kind of gossip is really my thing," a vaguely familiar voice chimed in.

The woman seemed to disregard the comment. "I heard from Remi at the market that the whole band is here, that Keller Grant bought a house on the island, can you believe…"

"If so, they wouldn't be the first celebrities to live here."

Theo had his share of overhearing things about himself; it came with the territory. He knew it was rude to eavesdrop, but he couldn't help himself sometimes.

"Who cares. It's not as if they're curing cancer," another voice sniped, and his breath caught. It was Mattie. He'd recognize her voice anywhere. Sitting at a small table to the side was Mattie, alongside her friend Shea and another woman. Fate was dealing him a lucky hand indeed.

"Mattie, come on. It's cool. I'd love to bump into one of them. Do you think they make it into town often?" the woman said. "I wouldn't mind getting thrown around by Theo Blake. He looks like he knows what to do with those fingers, if you know what I mean."

There was a coughing and sputtering noise, and then the assurance that she was okay, that the coffee went down the wrong tube. He knew the polite thing to do would be to leave her and her friends alone, but he had never been a polite person.

Approaching them, he noticed Mattie wasn't dressed in her normal business clothes, but in tight pants and a strappy tank top. Her hair was up in a ponytail on the top of her head, with little curly wisps falling out at her nape. He wanted to brush those tendrils away and taste that spot.

"Theo!" Shea said loudly, her eyes darting from Mattie to the other woman back to Theo. "Hi."

He nodded at Shea, but his eyes could only see Mattie. Her face paled as she took him in. "Matilda."

Her knuckles around her coffee cup went white with how tight she was squeezing the cup. The lid popped off, and coffee sloshed over her hand. Cursing, she set the cup down, grabbing a wax paper bag that still had blueberry crumbs on it, trying to mop it up. The liquid pebbled on the wax, aiding only to move it but not soak it up.

Theo kneeled at her feet, pulling his shirt away from his stomach to wipe the spilled coffee off her hands. Beside him, he saw her friend look from his exposed stomach and then lower before her eyes snapped away. Mattie allowed him to dry her hands off for a moment before jerking herself back. "I'm fine. It was lukewarm."

Shea handed Mattie a napkin, helping her friend clean up. The entire exchange, Mattie was staring away from him.

"You sure?" Theo asked, grabbing her hands again to inspect them for burns.

Her hands were pulled from his grip and she tossed the napkin down on the table with a *splat*. "I said I was fine, Theodore."

"Do you two know each other?" the woman asked, a gleeful twinkle in her eyes.

Mattie opened her mouth, then closed it, her eyes darting from Shea to Theo. "Uh, yeah, a little."

"Theo Blake. I'm an old friend of Matilda's." He extended his hand to the woman. "Matilda and I go way back. Don't we, Mats?"

"Patrice Woods. Fletcher Bay Real Estate and Equity." The small woman shook his hand with a firm grip. "It's wonderful to meet you, Mr. Blake."

She held his hand for a few moments longer than was appropriate. When he got his hand back, he had to take a step back. He recognized the gleam in her eyes. She was hungry for something; whether that was physical or financial, he wasn't sure. She seemed to be deciding if she either wanted to jump his bones or sell him a house, neither of which was going to happen.

Mattie's cheeks were flushed, and he wondered if she was either going to scream or pass out.

Theo smiled at Shea. "Nice to see you again, Shea. I hope you had fun the other night at the concert."

"I did. Lee had a great time. It's a shame we had to leave early." She shot a warning look to Mattie, who was inspecting her nails, as if it might tell her the secrets of the universe.

"I'm glad. Sakina said she enjoyed talking with you."

While they were chatting, Patrice seemed like she was mentally recording every word, to replay later for her group of friends. Mattie was silent, avoiding his eyes.

Clapping his hands together, Theo stepped back from their table. "Well, ladies, I'll let you get back to your coffees." He bent down, taking Mattie's hand and kissing her knuckle. "Matilda, I hope to see you soon."

As if those words knocked her out of her trance, she blinked at him several times.

"Can I talk to you for a second?"

He motioned with his hand for her to show him the way. Stomping past him, she walked across the courtyard to a small fountain. He watched as her hips moved. Damn, her ass looked amazing in those pants.

So focused on her ass, he almost ran into her when she suddenly whipped around to face him. "What the *fuck* do you think you're doing, embarrassing me like that?"

"What—I—"

"And stop staring at my ass, you think I couldn't tell?"

He put his hands up in surrender. "Sorry, it's such a great ass, I couldn't help myself. I was thinking about how it felt in my hands the other night."

With a long huff of air through her teeth, she grimaced. "Please, don't remind me of that mistake."

"Mistake? That night was many things, but we both know it wasn't a mistake."

Perching her butt on the edge of the concrete side of the fountain, she looked down at her shoes. "It should go without saying, I don't do that kind of stuff."

He sat beside her. "I know that. You're obviously not skilled at the whole one-night stand thing, based on your reaction."

"Not skilled, what are you..." Her face flooded with heat, and anger flickered in her eyes.

He chuckled. "Hold on, I didn't mean it like that. The sex was incredible. We both know that. But the after? Most women don't run off as if they're on fire, especially after I confess my adoration."

"You didn't confess anything. You were being a drunk idiot and getting sentimental. It's not the same thing." With a sideways scowl, she said, "Look,

I don't need to follow your exploits to know what kind of life you lead. I know you're super famous and probably have a million groupies out there, and yeah, maybe ten years ago I would have followed you anywhere, but I'm not some groupie you take home with a single nice word anymore."

Pain lanced his face as her words hit. "I would never put you in that category."

"So I'm right, there's been millions of groupies."

"Millions is an exaggeration."

"How many?"

He studied her, a small smile ticking up on the corner of his mouth. "Are you asking me how many women I've slept with since I last saw you?" He leaned forward. "Are you jealous?"

She crossed her arms across her chest. "What? No. That's ridiculous. I have no claim on you. All I'm saying is, you obviously live a certain kind of life, and I don't."

"You're jealous."

"I promise, I am not." Each word was enunciated carefully.

"It's okay, I'm jealous of any man who has been with you."

"I'm sure all three of them will be glad to hear that."

"Aren't you a busy girl," he joked, knocking into her shoulder with his.

Grimacing, she glanced across the way, where Patrice and Shea were sipping their coffees and trying to make it appear as if they weren't watching them. "Thanks a lot for embarrassing me, by the way. Patrice is the chair of the gardening committee I was trying to get into, and the school board. The last thing I need is for her to be judging me. At this rate, it'll be halfway across the island by five tonight."

"What? She doesn't know a thing, she's a busybody. L.A. is full of them; doesn't matter where you go, you'll encounter them. Ignore her." He was no stranger to people talking about him. When he got his first brush with fame, he made the mistake of going out to drink with a guy he met at a show. The guy liquored him up, and they talked all night. The next day, there was an article in the tabloids about his exploits. He had been sold out by dates, by stagehands, and by his dietitian even. Everyone was loyal until there were a couple bucks in it for them. Being talked about was part of his life; he had long accepted this.

"I can't ignore her; her son is in Kamari's class. You have no idea how these small town politics work, do you? Or even the stigma about being a single mother. It's bad enough I didn't stay with Kamari's dad - who, by the way, everyone loves. But to hook up with some musician? It's tacky. I'll be labeled a bad mother and whore."

"It's the twenty-first century. That's a pretty archaic view, don't you think? I thought this area is progressive?"

Mattie snorted. "Sure, a Black Lives Matter sign in their yard but refuse to pay their housekeeper more than minimum wage. No, Timmy can have two daddies around here, but they better be the picture of flawless, or else it won't work. I have to work twice as hard as Jay to get the same amount of respect as Kamari's mother."

She wiped a hand over her face, and Theo realized she had started crying. "Oh, God. Why am I doing that? It's fine. I'm fine."

Screwing her eyes shut, she took several calming gulps of air before opening them again, her dark lashes still wet and the green glistening under the line of tears. "My point is, you shouldn't have done all that in front of Patrice, or anyone, really."

"Why? Because you're embarrassed of me?"

She snorted, wiping away a single tear. "Yeah, you're the embarrassing one, not me, who threw herself at you, even though I know you're not sticking around."

"Who said I'm not sticking around?"

Mattie cocked her head to the side, the tears drying up. "Teddy, be serious, that's not funny."

"I'm not laughing, am I?" he asked.

The point of her tongue clicked against the roof of her mouth as she surveyed him. "I don't have time for this right now. I have to get back." She stood, brushing off little specks of gravel from her hands.

"Can I see you soon?" he asked.

Standing above him, Mattie hesitated. "I don't think that's a good idea. The other night was fun and maybe that can be closure or something, but it's not happening again. It can't."

He reached out to take her hand, to try to draw her closer. "I don't want closure with you."

A hollow, sad laugh came from her as her eyes grew dark. Stepping back, she crossed her arms over her chest, as if to protect herself. Her words were cold. "Maybe that's because you already got it twelve years ago."

She left him, her spine straight, joining her friends. He waited on the edge of the fountain, watching as Mattie gathered her things up and they walked away.

Maybe fate needed him to work a little harder.

CHAPTER NINE

Mattie

T IME SPEEDS UP WHEN you are a working mother trying to get your child out the door. When she checked the clock, she had over twenty minutes to get herself and Kamari dressed and out the door. Once she wrestled Mari into pants her daughter insisted were the wrong kind of green, Mattie had only two minutes before they needed to be in the car. Snagging earrings out of her jewelry box, she shoved them in the small pocket of her blazer - really, why make pockets on those things if they are only an inch deep? - and was pushing Mari out the door with one hand. Her travel cup of coffee, keys, and purse in the other hand, she pulled the door closed with her elbow. Halfway to the car, Mari stopped in her tracks, watching between the two houses. Theo emerged from the path, wearing a tight athletic shirt that hugged his biceps and low-slung shorts. A baseball cap was pulled over his blond hair, and his cheeks were pink.

"Mommy, it's your friend." Mari smiled up at her.

Mattie patted her on the back, motioning to the car. "Go get buckled, please. Mommy will be a minute."

Theo walked over to her, his steps crunching the gravel of her driveway. "Hey. I was hoping to catch you. I've stepped by a few times, but you never seem to be home." He gave her a wide smile. Her stomach dipped at the sight, the same as it did a decade before. Traitor reactions. "Or it's dinner, and I didn't want to intrude."

Mattie glanced at Mari in the car. She was climbing between the front seats to the storage compartment, trying to find the gum Mattie hid there. "Yeah, I've been busy. Work. Kamari. You know."

He nodded as if he could possibly understand. She wondered when was the last time he worked a job he clocked in and out for.

"I was hoping to catch up some more. You've been avoiding me since Sakina's concert."

"I'm not avoiding you. I have a life and obligations that you have no impact on." This wasn't entirely true; she had been making excuses to leave the house early and come home late, even at night, since she saw him at the coffee shop.

Mattie opened the front passenger side of her car, dropping her purse into the seat and making Kamari scamper into the back seat, a handful of gum in her hand. Mattie pulled out her phone and cursed. She could make it to the school before the doors closed if she didn't hit any red lights between the school and her house. "Theo, I got to..."

He stepped forward, something in his hand. "I wanted to drop this off. I found it on my run earlier, and it made me think of you. I was going to leave it on your porch with a note and my number, but here you are. " He held up a green rock. Mattie held out her hand, and he slid the small, opaque green stone into the center. His long fingers brushed against her palm, a tingle running down her arm at the contact. She should pull her hand away. She should step back.

His fingers stayed over her palm, his calluses firm against her skin. The first time he played guitar for her, he explained how the calluses form on your fingers to protect your skin from the strings. How it was a badge of honor and you should never trust a musician who didn't have calluses. His middle finger moved over her wrist, tracing a slow line. They both stared at her hand, holding the small rock. "It's pretty." Her voice came out lower than she intended.

"It's the same color as your eyes, and it's a heart, see." He traced the outline of the stone with his fingertip, the contact burning her. "I saw it, and I thought of you. Do you remember how we used to search for beach glass?"

She nodded at him. The memories of being on the beaches of Cape Rose with him. She could almost feel the weight of his hand in hers, the coarse sand under their bare feet. The way the corners of his eyes would crinkle as he smiled at her, holding up a piece he could take home. How he made her feel like she was the only person in the world.

"That was a long time ago, Teddy." Her voice soft.

Wrapping his fingers around hers, he closed her hand over the stone. "Not to me."

With the stone gripped tight in her palm, she took a steadying breath. "Look, I have to get going, I'm already late getting Mari to school, and the lady at the front desk has it out for me."

Walking around the car, she reached for the driver's door to find Theo had already opened it for her. "Could I see you soon? Maybe we could get dinner or something?"

As Mattie climbed into the car, she got close enough to him to smell the soap on his skin. How could a man who just ran still smell good? A single look in the rear-view mirror told her Kamari was holding gum in her cheek like a chipmunk. Thrusting her hand back between the seats, she motioned to her with an open palm. "Spit it out, baby. You know Mrs. Truett won't let you have gum in class."

Turning back to Theo, she wrapped the wad of chewed-up gum in a napkin. Other women might be embarrassed by the display, but she was too rushed and tired to feign anything but resignation. "Theo. It really is nice seeing you again, but I've got a lot going on."

"Lunch, then. You have to take a lunch break, right?"

"Theo."

"Coffee. We can get coffee. I'll bring it to you; you don't even need to leave."

"Why does that sound like a threat?" she joked.

"It's a promise."

A promise. He gave her all sorts of promises. She couldn't be silly enough to believe them again. Gripping the door, she started pulling it shut. "I really need to go."

"I'll see you soon," he assured her. Theo stepped back, allowing the door to close. He watched her as she started the car and backed out of her driveway, fifteen minutes late once again.

RRIVING AT WORK, SHE found a bouquet of peonies on her desk, the gem-colored petals velvet soft as she brushed a finger over them. Only one person would get her these. Jay used to buy her roses for all the romantic days; beautiful, extravagant bouquets that cost hundreds of dollars, their cloying scent filling up every room they were in. She liked getting roses, but these were something else.

On their first date, Theo picked her up after dance practice in his old, beat-up truck, a bundle of peonies wrapped in newspaper and tied with a thick blue rubber band on the seat. He told her he snuck into Mrs. Crawford's garden to cut those for her. While she didn't approve of the thievery, it was the first time anyone got her flowers. There was a small snail still clinging to one of the green stalks.

She had come a long way from that girl sitting in the front seat of his truck, hoping for a goodnight kiss.

A small card was between the stalks. She couldn't bear to open it yet. Whatever was inside was only going to twist her stomach into more of a knot than it already was.

Still fingering the delicate petals, she missed the first knock on the door frame as Shea poked in her head. "Oh, did you get flowers?"

Mattie dropped her hand, tucking it behind her back, as if she was caught sneaking candy in class. One hand on the back of her chair, she sat quickly, trying to train her face to appear nonchalant.

"Are they from..." Shea raised a brow.

"They might be. I haven't read the card yet."

Shea walked in, plucking the card from the bouquet and turning it over in her hands. "Do you want me to read it to you? Is it really that scary?"

Lips pursed; Mattie glared at her friend. "Give it to me."

Shea handed the envelope over with a well-manicured hand. With shaky hands, Mattie pulled the small card out of the envelope.

There will never be closure for me. I won't let you go. As the rain.

There was no name, but it didn't need one. His handwriting was the same as it always had been, little block letters, squished together too close and tilting to the left. A small smudge as the ink bled from him writing left-handed. She could recall the pages of songs in his notebooks, filled with that writing. Closing her hand around the card, she felt the sharp edges of the stationary dig into her palm. With her other hand, she cradled her forehead, squishing her eyes shut.

"That bad, huh?" Shea asked.

Mattie slid the card between two fingers and held it up for Shea. Through closed eyes, she heard the sharp intake of breath and a low whistle.

"Woo. That is something. What does he even mean? Closure?"

Cupping her cheek, Mattie opened her eyes, her head cocked to one side. "The other day, at the coffee shop, I told him what happened at the concert was a one-time thing and it was a good opportunity for closure. He apparently didn't agree."

Shea set the card down, blank side up. "Sure looks that way. He's coming on awful strong for a guy you haven't seen in a decade."

Mattie opened her mouth, sighed, and closed it. How could Theo's single-minded determination be explained? It was insane that he swooped into town and expected Mattie to, what? Get back together? Preposterous.

But maybe hook up a few times, sure.

It would be insane for anyone else, but to her, knowing him, it was the way he did things.

Grabbing the card, she shoved it into her drawer on top of her extra staples. "He can try."

"Looks like he succeeded the other night, too." Shea raised her brow at Mattie, with a knowing gaze.

"Had to bring that up, didn't you?"

Shea sat down in the seat opposite hers, folding her hands in her lap. "I wasn't going to say anything that night, because you were all torn up about something, but now, when he's sending flowers and showing up at coffee shops looking for you, that is a whole new story, and you know it."

Avoiding her friend's eyes, she wiggled her mouse around, focusing on her overflowing inbox. "Have you heard from Driscoll about the Santos case?"

With a cock of the head, Shea narrowed her eyes. "Don't you change the subject. I know what you're doing."

"I'm working, or trying to work. This isn't the time or place to be discussing my love life or lack thereof. I'm already in hot water with Mr. Mackie about missing all that work a few weeks ago."

Shea waved a hand at the comment. "Don't worry about Mackie. He doesn't understand how it is to be a working mom. He's barely a partner. Plus, he doesn't wear socks. Can you imagine how gross his feet are?"

"I'd rather not," Mattie snorted. A barely partner was more her position as a junior associate.

"What are you going to do about this boyfriend of yours?"

Opening an email, Mattie scanned the first few lines, the words blurring together. "He's not my boyfriend, he hasn't been for a decade."

"Does he know that?" Shea asked.

Her eyes leaving the screen, Mattie glared at Shea. "Don't you have work to do?"

"Always. But here I am, helping you out."

Mattie softened to her friend's words. Growing up, she had a hard time making friends. She was so focused on dance and academia that she had little time to spend with girlfriends. Even in college, she'd join her roommates at parties, but she was never the first call they made to confide in, never the first invitation. Theo was the first person she met who picked her first, her before all else. Until he didn't.

"He made some comment about maybe sticking around," Mattie admitted.

"Do you think he meant it?" Shea asked.

Using her thumb, Mattie pressed on the center of her palm, the spot her mother always said was where the tension lived. Holding it for five seconds, she waited for the anxiety to abate, but it lingered.

"I doubt it. Theo does what he wants, he always has. He might be interested in rekindling things for a few weeks, but I doubt he's serious."

"And how do you feel about a brief fling?" Shea leaned forward, her voice dropping at the word, *fling*.

Mattie wiggled her fingers. Focusing on the movement instead of her words. "I wouldn't know how to have a fling. I've never done it before, and having one with the first boy I said I love you to seems like a terrible idea."

"So don't. Tell him you're not interested."

Mattie wanted to do this. She wanted to resist him. But when he was near her, she forgot how to be truly mad at him. Her sense of self-preservation flew out the window. "And if I am?"

Shea whistled under her breath. "Well, shit. You got it bad."

Burying her head in her hands, she shook her head. "You have no idea."

It had been days since he came back, and already he was making her want things she had long let go of. She knew she would never be the girlfriend of a rock star, living out of suitcases and following him around the country as he performed. Those were the dreams of a silly girl. But she still felt the same sweep of warmth in her chest at his words, the same dizziness in her head at seeing his face. All his sly talk of sticking around was exactly that. She had learned her lesson long before.

He wasn't her home, he wasn't her Theo. No matter how much she wanted him to be.

Chapter Ten

Theo

A CUSTOMER AT PROPER Bar once told him he could charm the skin off a snake if he wanted to. At the time, he had been working sixty hours a week to cover the cost of his apartment in L.A. and slept on a bare mattress. Whatever charm he had was feigned, until the band got their first big hit. That being said, he was not above using his wiles to get what he wanted, and that day he was going to make Mattie have lunch with him. Walking into the law office, he spotted the young receptionist at her desk, a phone wedged between her shoulder and ear as she took a message. When she saw Theo, the phone slipped from her shoulder, and she had to scramble to pick it up.

The young woman's eyes were large as she stared at him while the person on the other line kept talking. "I'll have Mrs. Prescott get back to you regarding your case." The person on the other line started talking again, but the receptionist hung up the phone, missing the cradle and then fumbling to right it.

"Hi, can I help you?" she asked, her voice shaky.

"Is Matilda Lewis in?" He leaned forward on the desk, shooting the woman a smile. "I'm an old friend and wanted to say hello."

"You know Ms. Lewis?" she asked, blinking several times at the information. He could see the woman swallowing hard before picking up her phone. "I can, um, call her office and see if she's available."

Theo flapped a hand at the comment. "Don't do that, just point me in the right direction and I'm sure I'll find it." He wasn't entirely sure Mattie wouldn't flee out a window if she got advance notice. She had been jumpy that morning.

"I don't know. They don't want me to let anyone back unless..."

"I'm sure you can make an exception for this old, dear friend." He leaned closer to her, motioning to the outline of a castle on her wrist. "Nice tattoo, by the way."

Her cheeks got pink. "It's from your song. It's one of my favorites. I love you guys. I saw you when you were last in town. You were amazing."

The song was one of the few he wrote the label allowed them to put on the album. They had pushed for other songs that were better for the arenas they wanted to sell out. They called his music too morose for general audiences. Sure, he could get a song or two of his own on the record, but in the beginning, they were so excited about getting a deal, they would have played anything.

"'Stone Castles' is one of my favorites, too." He told her. He wondered if Mattie recognized herself in the lyrics. "I'm glad you like it."

There was the sound of a throat clearing. He glanced over to find Mattie standing in a doorway behind the desk, her hair pulled up in a bun since he last saw her that morning. He noticed the earrings she wore didn't match. Her green eyes watched him with hesitation. Her lipstick was fading, giving her mouth a lined look. How he wanted to kiss those lips.

"Theodore, stop distracting Cheyenne. She has work to do." Mattie shot the receptionist a raised brow, and Cheyenne pursed her lips together.

"I wasn't distracting her. She was being especially helpful and profession-al."

Mattie clutched a binder to her chest and scowled at him. "You are not a client here, she does not need to be professional with you. What do you want?"

"I came for our lunch date. Remember?" Still leaning on the front desk, he shot Cheyenne a look of *can you believe this gal?*

"I didn't agree to anything, Theo. I have a ton of work to catch up on and will be eating lunch at my desk."

"Excellent. I'll get takeout and join you." He could see she was fighting an internal battle.

"You can't stay here for lunch. It's unprofessional. I could get in trouble."

"So go out with me."

"You're not taking me seriously." She set the binder down and crossed her arms over her chest.

"It's lunch, Matilda. You have to eat."

Narrowing her eyes at him for a moment, she let out a huge puff of air. "My place, tonight, six-thirty."

He took the win. "Sounds great, I'll bring some wine. Red or white?"

"Neither." Mattie picked up the binder, once again bringing it to her chest. "And Theo, you can't bother me at work again."

She left him in the front with the receptionist. As she walked away, he admired the swing of her hips in her tight pencil skirt. Dinner would be fun.

Joining Eloise as she came out of Manzanita Market, he helped her put the groceries in the car. Her hands free, she crossed her arms across her chest and studied him. "Did you finish your 'errand?'" She used air quotes.

"I did."

She let out a noise of incredulity. "And what was your errand?"

With his thumbnail, he scratched the side of his nose. "Um, you know, odds and ends. Did you get any wine? I need a bottle for tonight." His assistant was going to get him a rental car, but he told her not to bother. Now he was rethinking that request.

"Since when do you drink wine?" The keys in her hands jangled as she peered at him. "Do you have a date or something?" She let out a laugh. When he didn't laugh, too, her voice cut out. "Wait, do you? How do you have a date? You've been here for, like, a week. Who did you meet that—"

She stopped, cocking her head to the side. "No, no way. Are you going out with Mattie? Theo. Don't do that! I like her."

"So do I." Theo set the bags in the back of Eloise's SUV and hit the button for the door to close. "A lot. We have a history."

"That's exactly what I'm worried about, I have to live next door to this woman. It's bad enough you two do whatever it was that happened at the concert. But for you to go over there tonight? You'll get all charming and sleep with her, and then when you break her heart, I'll have an angry neighbor for the rest of our lives."

"Who says I'm going to break her heart?" Theo asked.

Raising one brow, Eloise stared him down. "Do I really need to list off the trail of brokenhearted girls I've had to console over you? I was your assistant for years, Theo. I know all your dirty details."

"Mattie isn't those girls."

Eloise opened the car door, climbing in, and Theo followed suit. She turned the car on and paused, staring at him expectantly.

"What?"

"Buckle up, Theo."

Petulant, Theo pulled the belt over his lap. "And you don't know all my dirty secrets."

Maneuvering out of the tightly packed parking lot, Eloise checked her mirrors. "I know enough. Mattie is a really great person, and I would like to have a friend up here. And you know your track record with women is bad. I saw that article in AllCeleb about your breakup with Aria."

"That article was bullshit, and you know it."

Stopped at a red light, Eloise leaned against her seat and glanced over at Theo. "Obviously. But Safiya wasn't bullshit. The groupies I had to kick out of your hotel rooms the next morning weren't bullshit. Honestly, you're lucky Aria has a good head on her shoulders, or she could have easily been another one of your victims, too."

"You make me out to be this villain. I'm not."

"Really? Are you sure about that?" Pulling into a confusing roundabout, Eloise's eyes darted around the road. "You know I love you. But when is the last time you did right by a girlfriend? Or even a one-night stand?"

"Hey, all the girls who leave my bed, leave satisfied."

"I'm not talking about sexual prowess. I'm talking about emotionally. When is the last time you took care of someone's emotional needs before your own? The last time you were vulnerable?"

The car was silent as the question hung in the air.

"Exactly. I'm the closest thing to a healthy female relationship you've had in years, and we both know you fucked things up with me more times than we can count."

The night he tried to kiss Eloise and ensuing drama he created from that still burned bitter in his chest. How Eloise forgave him, he still didn't know.

"You know I'm sorry about that."

Eloise nodded at him, sparing him a quick glance. "I do. The mighty Theodore Blake humbling himself to me was quite a sight, I'll admit. My point is all those girls, even Safiya. They know the score. Do I like the way you treated them? No, of course not. But they know who you are. But someone like Mattie? She's normal. She's nice. Please don't fuck things up with her."

They pulled into the long gravel drive of their home. He glanced at the small bungalow next door, the lights off and house quiet.

"I never want to hurt Mattie. At least not again. But Lou, seeing her again. Having another chance? I'd be the biggest idiot in the world if I didn't take this chance, don't you think?"

Eloise killed the engine, turning in her seat to face him. "You really care about her, didn't you?"

Theo nodded.

Eloise's face grew soft. "Okay, I'll help you."

Their phones buzzed, and Theo glanced at his screen and cursed. He saw the headline, quickly followed by a text from their manager, Tamara, who succinctly said, "What the ever-loving fuck are you doing up there? I thought this trip was for you to lie low."

He ignored his manager for the moment, pulling up the article, with its grainy flash photo.

Mattie's legs gripped tightly as he made his way through the crowd. He didn't remember how many people took pictures and at the time he hadn't cared, but now, seeing Mattie in this position, and only having himself to blame, he felt like shit. Luckily, you couldn't tell it was her, but it was obviously him carrying her.

The Pickup Artist
Trinity Flay for AllCeleb

Playboy and lead singer of Prevalent Notion, Theo Blake wasted no time licking his wounds from his recent breakup with Aria Kingston. The singer was seen by a large crowd at the Sakina Green's Seattle show, getting quite cozy with a mystery woman. According to eyewitness accounts recorded on varying angles of video footage, he talked with a mysterious dark-haired woman before picking her up and carrying her backstage.

Witness Satchel Berkwood had this to say: "They obviously knew each other. He was kind of rude, actually. I was talking to her first and we were really hitting it off, but he interrupted our conversation. The girl, I think her name is Addie, didn't seem like she wanted to talk to him first, but then he picked her up, and off they went. Dating is hard here, you know? I'm a good enough guy to buy her a beer, and then this man swoops in and she goes off with him? Women don't like nice guys like me, they want {expletive} like Theo Blake. It figures." The witness then went on to attempt to sell this reporter crypto-currency.

Theo is no stranger to the ladies, being linked to several high-profile women since rocketing to fame with his band's first record, *Glazed Eyes* eight years ago.

An inside source close to his ex-girlfriend, Aria Kingston, shared this statement:

"Theo is welcome to do what he wants. He always has. Are his actions hurting Aria? Of course they are. Most people don't spend years with a person, then move on after a few weeks. Hopefully, whoever this girl is, she's worth it."

AllCeleb reached out to a representative from Blake's camp, but as of this publication, there has been no comment.

If you have information regarding this story or have any other celebrity news, please email us at our tip line at gotcha@al lceleb.com

Theo let out a low curse. It was a matter of time before this news spread to more gossip sites. How long it would take until Mattie saw it, he didn't know. Warning her would be a smart move, but judging by the way she was on edge with him, he wasn't sure she wouldn't go off on him for it.

Getting Mattie back would involve some creativity and persuasion. Maybe he came on a little strong with her, but once he made up his mind, that was it. He was confident with time, he could get her back. Now, he had to figure out what that looked like.

CHAPTER ELEVEN

Mattie

T HE NERVE OF THIS man. She knew she had to get him out of his office before one of the senior partners saw him. That was all she needed, to seem even more unprofessional after being late that morning. What game was he playing with her? He didn't live there. He couldn't come to her work and disrupt her whole life, then blow away whenever the mood struck him.

All morning, she had been distracted. When she arrived at work, she pulled out her earrings to find the small green rock in the same pocket. She hadn't remembered putting it there. Setting it beside her pencil cup, she tried to work, but her eyes kept straying to the small green stone. Smooth to the touch, it was cool under her fingers. His words echoed around in her head so much, when she heard his voice hours later, she at first thought she was imagining him some more. But no, it really was him, standing up front, flirting with Cheyenne. The sight of him leaning over the desk, his golden hair flopping over his forehead as he grinned at the twenty-year-old. A hollow pit formed in her stomach at the sight. Her throat thick as she steadied her breath. And then she invited him over for dinner.

Mattie surveyed the grocery bags on the counter, cursing herself for spending too much at the more expensive Manzanita Market instead of driving into Ridgewood to their Safeway. Considering the chicken parmigiana, she paused. Did he even eat meat? He used to eat everything, but she didn't know him now. He could be vegan or gluten-free or something else she hadn't heard

of. The population of Manzanita had its share of dietary restrictions. The first time she brought cupcakes for Mari's preschool, the teacher handed them back to her with a note
that all foods must be dairy, nut, and sugar-free.

Her hands were slick as she sat on a stool with a thud. This was a mistake; she shouldn't have invited him over for dinner. At the time, it seemed like the best way to get him out of her office and away from her for the rest of the day. But now, faced with making him dinner and having him *in her home*...she couldn't do it.

All day long, she thought about calling him and telling him not to come. That she was busy. But she didn't have his number, even if she wanted to. Taking a steadying breath, she got up, grabbed the milk out of her bag, and set it in the fridge. It was a simple meal. She could get through an hour with Theo Blake and come out okay. She could guard herself against his charms, and when he left, she could go back to how things were. Maybe even get some resolution. He likely had picked up some horrible rockstar habits, a big ego, disgusting manners, a penchant for throwing guitars around the room, something.

Walking up the stairs, she heard the skittering of Kamari playing with her LEGO blocks. Her daughter built them together like little tops and then had them battle each other in death matches. The baseboard molding was full of tiny dings from ricocheting plastic blocks.

"Not against the door, please!" Mattie called down the hall. Her daughter was quiet, but the sound of the blocks changed to a softer sound.

The clock said six-fifteen. She glanced down at her clothes, still in her skirt and blouse from the office. She should change into something more comfortable, but her comfortable clothes weren't sexy.

Clad in her bra and underwear, she flipped through her closet. Most nights after work, she changed into leggings and an oversized tee shirt. She hadn't tried to dress sexy for someone in years. Would her sexier clothes even fit her anymore? She kept them, of course, in an ill-advised ploy to lose the baby weight from Kamari. Giving them away felt like admitting she'd never look the way she did at twenty-three.

Holding a black dress against herself, she shook her head. Too formal. The last time she wore that dress was for a holiday party of Jay's, back when they were still married. A fuzzy sweater, too hot for the June weather. Clothes piled on her bed as she assessed her options. A knock sounded on the door below, and Mattie went to her window to see the golden top of Theo's head as he stood on her front porch.

She mumbled a low curse and grabbed a cotton sun dress out of the closet, pulling it over her head as she descended the stairs.

As the dress came down over her butt, she was yanking the door open. On the other side, Theo was clutching a bouquet of peonies and had two bottles of wine wedged in the crook of his arms. His dark blue button-up made his tan skin look ever more golden. His cool blue eyes brightened as he took her in.

"You're here," he said, with a hint of surprise. "I wasn't sure if you'd answer."

"Well, yeah. I guess." Her words came out oddly petulant. "You didn't give me much choice."

"These are for you. " He handed her the bouquet. Stepping closer, he pressed a quick kiss to her cheek, his nose brushing against the shell of her ear. "You look amazing."

He pulled back, looking over the front of the dress. "Though, I think your dress is backward?"

She glanced down to see the tag sticking up on her chest. "Damnit," she cursed, beckoning him into the house and closing the door behind him. Hustling around a corner, she stuck her arms back into the dress, twisting it until it was on correctly.

"Sorry, the house is a mess," she called out as she returned, glancing at all the discarded items she forgot to pick up before he came over. Nudging Kamari's backpack into a corner, she pointed at the kitchen, where half the groceries were still sitting on the counter. "I didn't have time to plan anything fancy or tidy up."

"The house looks lived in, it's great." He set the wine down on the counter alongside a small paper bag. "And you know I'll eat anything."

"Still? I would have thought you'd want to get some organic wheat grass smoothie or something."

He walked into her kitchen, grabbed the box of cereal and opened cabinets until he found the right one to place it in. "That can be our second date."

"This isn't a date, Theodore."

"We'll see." He took out the fruit, brought it to the sink, and began washing it.

Coming behind him, she took the grapes from his hand and set them on the counter. "Stop, you're not putting my groceries away for me."

"I'm trying to help."

She pointed at a stool. "Well, stop. Sit down, and I'll start dinner."

"Can I at least pour you a glass of wine?" he asked, motioning toward the bottles on the counter. She recognized the labels as an expensive bottle from a local winery. "Red or white?"

Pinching her lips together, she glanced from the wine to him. "I shouldn't. It's a school night."

"One glass?" He gave her that smile, with now such perfectly white and straight teeth. She wished she didn't miss that chipped incisor. She liked the man with that chipped tooth; he was real and dependable and loved her. But he was also the man who dumped her over the phone. She had to remember that. This gregarious man in front of her was a stranger. She wasn't in danger from this stranger because he wasn't the same man she fell prey to years before.

"One. White, please."

Kamari came downstairs, stopping when she saw Theo. Handing the glass of wine off to Mattie, he turned in his seat to face Kamari.

"Hello, Mari."

She stared at him with suspicion. The number of strange men who had been inside their home could be counted on one hand.

"I'm Theo, your mom's friend. I brought you something." He grabbed the small paper bag off the counter. "Since your mom loves these, I thought you might, too."

From out of the bag, he extracted a small cardboard container of raspberries.

Mari stepped closer, taking the container from his hands. Her voice solemn. "They're my mom's favorite, not mine, but I'll eat them."

He nodded at her, seeming to understand that was the biggest vote of confidence he'd receive from the five-year-old. "I had a feeling. I knew they used to be her favorite when we were kids."

He glanced up at her, a deep look that told her, *I remember.*

Mattie brought her hand up to her mouth, running her short nails over her lips as his words sunk in. He couldn't sway her. A lot of people like raspberries. It meant nothing.

"Mommy, can I watch TV in your room?" Kamari interrupted her thoughts.

Blinking a few times at her daughter, she fought to put a mask of normalcy on her face. "Only until dinner time. And don't get raspberries all over my bed, like you did with the crackers last week." Kamari fled the kitchen, with the berries in hand.

"She seems great, Mat."

"She is," Mattie agreed. Squeezing her hands into fists, she wrung them together. Her whole body buzzed with something she couldn't place.

Theo motioned to the stove. "Do you need any help with dinner? I'm still pretty good with the griddle. Just like Uncle Rich taught me."

Matilda felt a softening in her chest at the mention of the uncle who'd raised Theo. But she wasn't going to let *him* know that.

"No. You stay there. It's a quick dinner. Mari will only eat three things right now, so options are limited."

Once the water was boiling, she started on the roux for the alfredo sauce. The chicken was cooking in the oven. Mari would likely eat two bites of the meat and then insist on more of the pasta the same as almost every night. The only protein that girl liked was either in dino or string form.

She hadn't meant to, but she finished her glass of wine before the chicken was done. Before she could set the glass down, Theo was there with the bottle, refilling it. Their eyes caught as he stared down at her. He was closer now; she could see the little flecks of green in his eyes. The glass felt as if it would shatter in her hand, she was gripping it so hard. The heat from him was leeching into her. If she set down her glass...if he took another step toward her...she had to get control.

Taking a steadying breath, Mattie shut her eyes. "Look, I don't know what your game is here. But earlier at my office? You can't show up at my work like that. I've worked my ass off to get to where I am today. The last thing I need is you coming in and being charming and making me seem unprofessional. You have no idea what I have done this past decade to get here. What I've gone through, what..."

Mattie's teeth slammed together before she could say another word. She wasn't ready to talk about how much his leaving had hurt her. She couldn't give him that power.

"Of course I know how hard you worked."

Mattie glared at him. "You don't know the first thing about me anymore." Theo cocked his head to the side in a come on, now gesture. "Matilda Iman Lewis. You graduated salutatorian from Cape Rose High. You majored in law, with a minor in dance from Northwestern University, graduating Magna Cum Laude seven years ago. From there, you got your JD from Seattle University. You married Jay West seven years ago, and six months after that you had your daughter, Kamari Yasmin West. The two of you settled in Manzanita together until last year, when you filed for divorce, citing irreconcilable differences."

Mattie's whole body went cold as his words washed over her. "How do you know so much about me?"

"It's all public record, if you know where to look," Theo said.

"And you looked," Mattie added. "When? The day you saw me at Eloise and Keller's? After?"

Theo set his wine down and stared out the window, his words slow. "I have an alert. Whenever there is mention of you on the Internet, I get a notification."

Matilda stepped back, assessing Theo's face for traces of dishonesty. Would he lie about this? She wasn't sure; she didn't know him now. She wanted to think this was exactly the kind of thing a nineteen-year-old Theo would have done, but this man? This thirty-one-year-old man in front of her? She didn't know.

"Is this some line?"

Theo blinked a few times, surprised. "No. I would never give you a line."

Mattie frowned, cupping her hands around her glass, as if to anchor her to the spot. Heat flooded her face at his admission. She didn't blush easily, but her face felt like it was on fire. He had no rights to her anymore.

She had to get through this dinner, and then maybe she could have her life back. He'd see how boring she was. How settled and domestic. A single mother, gardener, and baker. What would a rock star want with someone like that?

MATTIE WAS A LIAR. For all the good her pep talks about guarding herself had done, twenty minutes into the dinner, she found herself hanging on his every word. In the years since they last saw each other, she had told herself there was no way he was that charming, but here he was, asking Kamari all about her last ballet recital. He didn't seem bored when she described the music cutting out halfway through the snow pea soliloquy and how it was a pandemonium of five-year-old girls twirling on stage until the instructor came out to escort them to the wings.

He asked questions about both of them. Things that felt so trivial to her, but he soaked up each word, asking follow-up questions.

The hour grew later, and Mattie excused herself to tuck Kamari into bed. Theo assured her he would be fine waiting on the couch while she tended to her daughter.

After teeth brushing, two stories, one silly song, and a long routine of goodnight kisses, goodnight hugs, and eyelash kisses, Kamari was tucked in with Pennyworth, her favorite stuffed penguin.

When she descended the stairs, she found Theo in the kitchen, the water running and him elbow deep into the sudsy water.

"What are you doing? Leave those, Teddy."

He shut off the water, turning back to face her.

"It was the least I could do for the fantastic dinner. I can't remember the last time I had a home-cooked meal." His eyes got far away for a moment.

"You don't cook at home?" Mattie asked as she grabbed the wooden salad bowl off the table. He took the bowl from her hands. She opened her mouth to protest, and he shot her a warning glance.

He talked as the water rinsed the dishes. "I'd need a home to have a home-cooked meal. No, honestly, I eat out mostly or have pre-made salads and stuff my assistant sticks in my fridge. Nothing like this. I doubt my handlers would approve of this on my diet plan."

"Diet plan?" Mattie turned in her seat to look at him. His waist was as trim as the day he left Cape Rose, but his muscular shoulder and arms filled out his shirt. He had rolled his sleeves up to rinse the dishes, and his forearms were flexing as he moved. They looked solid, and she wondered what they would feel like under her fingers. A flash of his arms, bracing themselves above her as he pushed inside her struck her.

Nope, don't go there, danger, danger. Exit, stage left.

"You are in the best shape of your life."

Shutting off the water, he turned to face her, drying his hands on a towel. "Yeah, and you don't get this by eating chicken parmigiana, I can assure you. Honestly, it isn't even a big deal. I've never been a big food guy, not like Nathan; you should hear him bitching about some of the food we eat. And working out is good for my pent-up anxiety. It's part of the job. I have to maintain a certain..." He paused, staring over her head as he searched for the word. "Mystique? Persona? Something. It's not enough to be talented in L.A.; you have to be handsome and talented. Or handsome and young and talented and good at public speaking, and so on. Every day, there is someone else who is younger, hotter, willing to do more to get where you are."

Something about the way he said it let her know this wasn't a boast. It was a simple fact. "That's a lot of pressure," Mattie murmured. She got up from the table, bringing the two empty wine glasses to the kitchen. Setting them on the counter beside him, she reached down and took his hand. It was warm against hers.

He watched their intertwined hands, the way her fingers wrapped around his. Standing in front of him, she was drawn closer. Bringing her hand up to his face, he pressed a quick kiss to the inside of her wrist. His full lips brushed against the tender skin there. "My life is not simple. It hasn't been in a real long time, Mattie. I don't think it's felt simple since..."

She watched as he swallowed hard. He wiped his free hand over his face, grimacing. His eyes got hard as he stared out the kitchen window at her backyard facing the bay. She held his hand for a long moment as he tried to find the words.

When he finally looked back at her, the softness was back. "Well, nothing worth having is easy, right?"

She wasn't sure how to respond to that. Where could she fit into this life he led?

"You want to sit outside for a bit? It's a little chilly, but still a nice day," she said. This whole idea was a recipe for heartache. But she asked it anyway.

The evening sky was a wash of white. Never letting go of his hand, she led him down the steps past her small backyard garden, to a stone bench that came with the property. In the bay beyond her trees, several paddle boaters glided through the water. A wind whipped over the water, making the little flags on the anchored boats snap in the air.

A small distance away, several seals were sunning themselves on a floating dock.

Theo gazed at the seals. "I don't know if I've ever been so close to a seal before." He looked over the water.

"Really? They have a bunch at the zoo," Mattie said. As a child, she went frequently with her family.

"I never went to the zoo as a kid. Never been as an adult either. Well, except for one time, we played a concert at one, but I wasn't walking around then."

"I bet that was fun, though."

He shook his head. "Honestly, I don't remember much from it. It was some charity thing, our old manager, Arnie, signed us up for it. We were only starting out back then, so we were one of the opening acts. After we performed, we all ended up at some dive bar together." He laughed at the memory. "Can't show up at dive bars anymore."

"Are you really that famous?" Mattie teased.

He smiled at her. "We're not getting mobbed at airports or anything, but yeah. If someone recognizes me, it's hard to have a private moment. The last few girlfriends I had, wherever we went, there were paparazzi hounding us. I'm not trying to complain, but Keller and Nathan don't have the same pressure to be on all the time. You know, before Keller married Eloise, he was way worse than I was with the drinking and the girls. But no one cared. But when I screwed up, the label flipped out. I'm sure you heard about me and Safiya."

Mattie shook her head. "No, I didn't."

Theo studied her, as if to see if she was telling the truth. This wasn't an absolute lie, but she also wasn't entirely truthful. She knew he dated the supermodel at some point; it was hard to avoid the magazine rack at the store. But she didn't know the story.

"Tell me about her."

He sighed, rubbing a hand over his face. The sun peeked out from behind a cloud, casting beams across his face. His unshaven whiskers were reddish in the light. "She was smart. We met at some industry party; I couldn't even tell you what it was for. One of those see and be seen type of events. You know?"

She didn't know.

"We had a lot of fun together for a while. She was separated from her husband at the time. I didn't really care, which should have been a clue that it wasn't going to work out. I thought that maybe she and I could have been something, but it didn't work out."

"Because of her ex?" Mattie asked.

Theo shook his head. "Me. I screwed it up. Safiya was never going to be it for me. I don't think I wanted to admit it, but she was too much like someone else I know."

His eyes caught hers, awareness coursing through her. Was it possible he had been holding on to this flame as long as she was?

"I can't believe you didn't hear about all this. It was all over the news for a week."

"I try to avoid all mention of you." Mattie shook her head. "And I don't listen to your music at all."

"No? Not even once?"

She knew the smart thing to do would be to play it off, to make him think he had no effect on her, but she couldn't do that. Somehow, he was able to see right through her. "I listened to everything you made years ago, back when you got signed. But never since then. I can't listen, it hurts too much."

"My music hurts you?" he asked, frowning.

"Of course it does, Teddy. Do you honestly think it wouldn't?" It was giving him too much, but that vulnerable part of herself that was reserved for him alone wouldn't allow her to be guarded. "The music was a reminder of you, and I couldn't face that."

His eyes grew far away as her words sunk in. "It's funny. You never wanted to think about me, and I never want to forget."

She sucked in a breath, hoping her voice didn't betray her. "The brooch on your guitar strap, it's—"

He nodded, folding his hands together, inspecting his watch with focus. "I couldn't get rid of it. No matter how hungry I was or close to living on the streets. "

"Could have bought a lot of instant Ramen," Mattie joked, giving him a halfhearted smile.

The wind whipped over the water, freeing her hair from its ponytail and getting stuck in her lip balm. Reaching between them, he curled his finger around the wayward strand, tucking it behind her ear. "It was practically all I had of you. I wasn't going to let that go." His finger lingered on the little spot behind her ear, trailing down the side of her neck.

"What are you doing here, Teddy?" Mattie asked, her voice throaty. "Why, after so long, are you back in my life?"

Resting his forehead against hers, she didn't pull away, their breath mingling in the air between them. "I don't know, Mattie. I didn't plan this. For years, I told myself I'd let you live your life. I'd let you go because I never deserved a second chance. And then I saw you, and it was like fate. Maybe all those nights I've thought of these lips. Years I've spent wishing for them. Something brought us back together, and I'm not going to leave you alone."

"Teddy, you can't say things like that to me." She knew it was a bad idea. When he took off back to L.A., she would be hurt again. She was allowing herself to wish for things that could never be with Theo. Her resolve was crumbling as his fingers traced the line of her jaw. His hand delved into her hair, pulling her mouth to his.

The first brush of lips was soft, a whisper or kiss. He pulled back to stare at her face, as if to gauge her response.

Her whole body felt light, as if a balloon was expanding in her chest. The sounds of the water, sea birds, and shouting teenagers in the bay all fell away. Wrapping her hand around the nape of his neck, she pulled him closer to kiss him.

Chapter Twelve

Theo

HE HAD FORGOTTEN HER. The feel of her skin under his fingers, the way she sighed when his lips moved down her throat. No memory conjured up in these late-night bouts of insomnia could have preserved how good she felt in his arms again. Holding her was like returning to a home he never knew he wanted.

He didn't have a plan to seduce her when he came over for dinner, but he wouldn't let this opportunity pass him by. Holding her face in his hands, he deepened the kiss. His tongue traced the seam of her lips, and she opened for him. Her hands slid down from his neck to his back.

"Take me to bed," she whispered against his mouth.

The bed was covered in piles of discarded clothes she pushed onto the floor. With her arms wrapped around his neck, she pulled him down on the bed with her. Her floral sun dress hiked up her thighs as he fit his body between them. The moment she opened the door and he saw the thin cotton sundress on her, all he could think about was how to get it off her. All night, he had watched as the lace hem fluttered around her knees as she moved. The way it rode up on her thigh when she crossed her legs at the table. The peak of cleavage he caught as she bent over the table to serve the salad.

Now, lying on top of her, his cock grew hard against the heat of her. His mouth left hers, trailing down her throat to pull her dress down over her shoulders. Freckles covered her bare shoulder, little brown dots scattered over her skin like a constellation. His mouth moved over each one, worshiping the softness of her. Beneath him, she wiggled, her legs wrapping around his hips to pull his cock closer to her. Kissing the exposed skin, he savored the taste of her on his tongue.

"Take this off," he commanded, fingering the edge of her dress. "I want to see you again."

Pulling the dress over her head, she wrapped her arms around her middle, covering her stomach.

"I have...I don't look the way I used to," Mattie said, her voice thick with an apology. When they were at the concert, their actions had been so frenzied, he hardly had a chance to see her; it was ruled by touch and want. This was different. In the golden light of the sunset, a rosy hue fell across them, bathing her in warmth. She was different under his hands, but his touch knew her. Wrapping a hand around her wrist, he pulled her hands off her stomach and pulled them over her head. She wore no bra, and her brown nipples pebbled in the sudden chill of the air. Tracing a finger around the pert tip, he watched her face as her lips parted. Teasing her, he flicked a thumb over the surface. His head bent low, he took one nipple into his mouth, swirling his tongue over the surface. Her fingers wrapped in his hair, her short nails hard against his scalp as he licked and teased her. Moving to the other side, he gave the other breast equal attention. Her legs wrapped around his hips, pulling him closer to her center. She writhed beneath him.

"More," she cooed. Letting go of her nipple with a pop, he moved down her body, his fingers trailing lightly.

Her stomach was soft, her hips wider, little white lines on her skin.

"You're beautiful." He leaned in, running his tongue over the marks on her skin. "It's a part of you. You are exactly what I want."

She let out a gasp as his lips dipped beneath her belly button. Her underwear was cotton, blue and white stripes, nothing like the fashionable lingerie he was used to L.A. women wearing. Hooking a finger into the edge of the elastic, he pulled it down, his mouth following the exposed skin. She lifted her ass in the air, and he tossed them on the floor.

When they had sex before, as teenagers, it was a fumbling, awkward thing done on his twin bed while his uncle and mother were away working. Back then, he didn't know how to touch a woman, how to make her feel good. He could show her now.

Gripping her hips, he pulled her mound to his face. He licked her seam, parting it with his fingers. He slid one digit inside her warmth, then two. His fingers moved inside her his tongue swirled around her clit. As she writhed beneath him, he held tight to her hip. A moan of pleasure hummed out of her, and he peered up to see her cover her mouth with the back of her hand. As he sucked on the tender bud, her grip on his hair tightened. Keeping pace to the rhythm of the fingers he pumped inside her, he took her closer to the brink.

"Harder," she urged, her hips bucking up to meet his face. "I need more."

Relishing in the taste of her on his tongue, he worked over her. A shudder ran over her body, and her legs tensed. He pushed further, moving his fingers in pace with her motions.

"That's it, come on my hand. Show me how good my hand can fuck you."

Her cry was soft, a wave descending her body more than a sound. A flush over her chest as she came. Sliding his fingers out of her, he brought his hand to his mouth, licking them clean.

She tasted better each time. Pressing a kiss to her inner thigh, he looked up at her. Her head was thrown back, and her hair was in a mess on the pillow behind her. Her eyes were closed, her face smooth from her orgasm.

He wanted to stare at her forever, to see her pleasure drunk on his touch and bask in the knowledge that he brought her there.

Opening one eye, she crooked a finger up at him. "Come here."

Sliding up her body, he braced himself over her. Her hands delved under his shirt, pulling it away from his back. Her fingers reached beneath his pants, grabbing his ass and squeezing it hard. "That has to be the most muscled ass I've ever felt."

"How many asses are you feeling up?" he asked, grinning down at her.

"Not nearly enough, I can tell you that."

"And mine is the best?"

She pursed her lips, gazing up at the ceiling, as if searching for an answer. All the while, her hands were squeezing his butt.

"It's up there. I'd have to assess a larger sample size to know for sure, and obviously, I'll need to visually inspect it first, before I can scientifically say it's the best."

His pants still on, he thrust between her thighs, rubbing his hard cock against her bare center. "You inspect me any way you need to, but there will be no other man. I'm it for you."

"Aren't you cocky?" She smirked. Her hands moved from his ass to the front of his shirt. She pulled the buttons through their holes, opening his shirt. "You're saying a lot of words, but I need to see you live up to them."

With those words, he made quick work of his shirt, tossing it to the floor. Her fingers traced over his chest, her small palm covering his left pec. "This is all muscly, too. How much working out do you do?"

"More than I'd like to admit. We're not supposed to let on, but it takes dedication to look like this. I haven't lifted in a week, and I already feel like I'm losing definition."

Mattie's hand stilled on his chest, over his heart. "You're a musician, not a male model."

"Maybe they can, but I can't afford that. I don't have enough talent to make up for a flabby waist."

Mattie's face softened. "Who told you that? That's ridiculous."

The conversation was going off the rails; he should be seducing her, not crying about his insecurities. "It doesn't matter. That's the business."

Mattie opened her mouth with narrowed eyes, then closed it.

"Don't feel sorry for me, I'm not complaining."

"I don't feel sorry for you. I'm angry. Teddy, you are insanely talented."

"I thought you didn't listen to my music?"

"I saw you perform. That was enough for me. You're a gifted musician."

Wiping a hand over his face, he shook his head. "Tell that to my label. Every conversation I have with them is about my image. It's never about the music. What am I wearing? Who am I dating? What club was I last seen at or premiere did I attend? Keller and Nathan, don't understand this pressure. I'm the leader of the band. If I mess up, the band will fail. So yeah, I have to keep my six-pack and have the fake girlfriend and..."

"Wait, fake girlfriend?" Mattie bolted up on the bed, pulling a blanket over her chest.

With a thumbnail, Theo scratched the side of his nose. "Aria Kingston. Our management team set it up a few years ago."

"You and Aria weren't..." She screwed up her face at his comment. "I don't get it. Why would you date someone if you didn't want to be with her?"

"It was 'mutually beneficial.'" He used air quotes as he spoke. "The label was worried about my image after I got trashed in the tabloid when Safiya dumped me. Aria needed more exposure."

"And you guys never—" She motioned in the air.

Theo grimaced. "A few times, but neither of us was feeling it. Aria's great, but it was never going to be real." He stopped, cupping Mattie's face in his hand. His thumb brushed lightly over the soft cushion of her lower lip, still swollen from his kisses. "There's only one person out there for me. As hard as I've tried, I've never gotten over you."

Mattie's breath hitched at his words. "Teddy. Why do you keep saying those things?"

Pain lanced his chest as she asked her, "You don't feel the same?"

Mattie shook her head, her eyes shut. "I don't know how to feel. You hurt me. Ruined me for every other man out there. Ruined my marriage. My trust in relationships."

He knew a stronger man, a better man, would be sad to hear this. But he couldn't be. Not when it came to Mattie. He was willing to lower himself to despicable depths to have her back.

"Good. I'm glad. I don't care if I've ruined the world around us, if I could get another chance with you. You have always been mine. You understand that?"

Mattie shook away the words. "I can't be yours. I don't know how to be."

"Like this." He pulled her face to his, taking her mouth. Her kisses matched his. He lowered her to the bed, covering her body with his. As their kisses became frenzied, she tugged on his pants, pulling them down.

Down the hall, a small creak sounded. Mattie's eyes flashed open as she pushed him off her and sat up. Flopping to his back on the bed, he watched as she scrambled for her underwear, pulling it on while staring at the dark doorway nervously.

Her breathing shaky, she was still as a statue. Theo hoisted himself up to a standing position, placing a hand on Mattie's shoulder. "Hey."

Mattie whirled on him, eyes bright with apprehension. "You should go. I have to go, um, you should, too."

"I can stay, if you need to check on Kamari."

Mattie shook her head, her eyes wild. "No, that's a bad idea. Let yourself out, don't worry about locking the door."

Without a backward glance, she climbed the stairs, pulling down the bottom of her dress, as if to hide the evidence. Down the hall, he could hear the creaks of her footsteps as she went into her daughter's room, and then the low singing of a lullaby.

As he buttoned his shirt back up, he tried to ignore the painful case of blue balls he had. Something had scared Mattie off, and he knew her well enough to know she wasn't coming back into her room until he left. He was going to have to take care of himself in the guest shower at Eloise and Keller's.

Heading down the stairs, he studied each 8x10 picture of Kamari on the wall. Baby pictures, pictures of her in a dance outfit, and in a small gold robe with a tiny blue mortarboard on her head. Mattie pregnant, lovingly holding her belly. Stopping at his picture, he touched the frame. The way the light pink dress flowed over her swollen middle, the pink of her cheeks, and the glow of happiness she had. Motherhood suited Mattie.

If he had made a different choice all those years before, that would have been his baby she carried.

It could be someday.

The thought came unbidden but strong. He ran a finger over the glass, where her hair was braided away from her face. It was a crazy thought; he was only starting to gain her trust again. Thinking about having a baby with her at this stage was madness. But he didn't stop himself from reveling in the brief sensation of its rightness. She belonged with him. He knew this as much as he knew he was a Sagittarius and hated the smell of patchouli.

S TEPPING THROUGH THE DOOR, he was greeted by Nathan and Ilsa, with their bags in hand.

"You out of here?" He vaguely remembered Nathan mentioning that Ilsa needed to get back for some event.

"Yeah, the plane is leaving in a few hours." He glanced at the doorway Theo walked through. "You coming back from Mattie's?"

Theo nodded, toeing off his shoes. "Yeah, we had dinner."

"Just dinner?" Nathan asked, with a devilish grin.

"None of your fucking business, man." Theo pushed past him into the kitchen, where he grabbed an orange out of the fruit bowl. He wasn't hungry anymore, but he needed his hands busy with something.

Nathan scratched the side of his nose with his thumb. "Look man, I know you don't want my advice."

"You're right, I don't."

Nathan kept talking, ignoring his friend. "I don't know what's going on with you and Mattie, and I'm not going to pry—"

"That's a first," Theo mumbled.

Nathan grinned at him. "Okay, maybe I'll pry a little. If you're trying to get Mattie to go out with you, or whatever it is you're doing, you can't treat her the same way you treated the other girls."

"I know how Mattie wants to be treated." Who was this guy, trying to assume he knew Mattie better than Theo?

"Do you?"

"I've known her for over a decade. I know her."

"No, you knew her. Big difference. You need to get to know who she is now. Teddy."

Nathan had a way of challenging a person, but saying it in such a nice way, you couldn't get mad at the big lug.

"Don't call me that," he grumbled. Slapping the orange rind down on the marble counter, he glared at Nathan. "Why is everyone trying to give me relationship advice lately?"

Nathan's normally jovial face got serious, and he raised a brow at his friend. "Come on, man. You know."

Theo stared his friend down, scanning his friendly face for a clue.

Nathan sighed. "She's different for you. We all see it. You know the biggest reason I was annoyed when you decided to bring Safiya on the Hellions tour wasn't because I didn't like her.

We all knew it wasn't real for you. You're different about Mattie. So yeah, I want to give you advice. Maybe for the first time in forever, you're ready to hear it."

Theo was dumbstruck by his friend. They had been through hell together, scraping and busting their asses to get to where they were, and Nathan had always been supportive of him, even when he fucked up. He trusted Nathan's words more than almost anyone.

Ilsa emerged from their room, a garment bag over her shoulder. Her blonde hair was up in some big poof at the top of her head, and she was wearing some draped contraption that would look ridiculous on almost anyone else, but it suited her. When she was the stylist for the band, she always made him look good for shows and photo shoots, but she had never warmed to him.

"Theo. It was a time seeing you."

"Just a time?" he asked.

Ilsa nodded at him." Yeah, let's go with that."

Nathan took the garment bag from Ilsa's hand. "Here, Petal, let me get that for you."

"It's two linen dresses, I can—" Nathan was already halfway down the hall with the bag.

"He can't help himself," Theo remarked.

"Don't I know it." Ilsa grabbed an apple out of the fruit bowl biting into it while staring Theo down. "You scare that nice neighbor away yet?"

Theo rolled his eyes at her. When he warned her off Nathan the year before, threatening her if she broke his heart, she was likely still nursing a grudge from it.

"You still don't like me, do you?"

Ilsa tilted her head to the side, studying him. "I'm warming up to you. Even you have to admit, your past behavior has never been endearing."

"I can be tremendously charming to certain people," he grumbled.

"Yeah, chicks you want to sleep with and fans who fawn over you. I've never been either."

Theo said nothing; in all honesty, Ilsa always scared him a little. She once pulled his hair when he called a pack of groupies "hoes" back at the start of their tour. He had a bald spot for months—not that he admitted it to anyone. He touched the spot and Ilsa's mouth ticked up with a small smile. "Though, you seem like you're trying to get better, so there's that."

"People can change, you didn't meet me under the best circumstances." Ilsa had joined the band on their Hellions tour a few years before. He spent most of that tour drinking, picking fights with his bandmates, arguing with Safiya, and then when Safiya dumped him in New York, sleeping with multiple groupies at each stop.

"I sure hope this isn't supposed to be your best." She motioned at him. "Last year, when Nathan and I got together, you told me you and I are similar. So, I'm going to tell you the same thing you told me. You are a lot like me. Get your head out of your ass and figure out what you want with that woman."

"That is not at all what I said to you." Theo narrowed his eyes.

"I paraphrased." Ilsa finished the apple, tossing the rind in the garbage can. "I don't know Mattie enough to give specific thoughts, aside from knowing she is way too good for you, but most women are."

"How did a nice guy like Nathan end up with such a mean girl?" Theo asked. The question wasn't with venom; he knew she wouldn't be offended.

"Trust me when I say, I'm plenty nice to the right people."

Nathan returned, clapping a beefy hand on Theo's shoulder. "I've got to get my bride back to L.A. I'll see you in a few weeks?"

Theo nodded. "Yeah, I'll see you."

In the shower, he tried to rub one out, but his conversation with Ilsa was a guaranteed boner killer. It didn't mean she was wrong, though. He hadn't thought of specifics with Mattie yet. He knew he wanted her back, that seeing her again and having this second chance was an opportunity he couldn't pass up. But it was proving more difficult than he imagined. He already knew Mattie mattered more than any other woman to him. He had always known that. But the idea that it didn't matter how much he cared for her, that he could still lose out on her, was frightening.

He hated to admit how easy it had become for him to get women. He couldn't remember the last time he had to put any genuine effort into finding a woman. In the beginning of their fame, he was surprised by it, the way beautiful women would come up to him after the shows, stroking his arm and whispering come-ons in his ear. He never had that in Cape Rose. Sure, he looked the same, but where he grew up, people knew him and his family. It didn't matter if he was attractive or not; he was the nephew of the town drunk, the son of the girl who got pregnant at fifteen. He worked for hours in the diner and reeked of old oil and sausage. Not a good way to get a girl. So, when he asked Mattie out, he was shocked she agreed. Mattie made it easy. Then. Nothing about this was easy now.

Ten minutes out of the shower, he walked downstairs to find Mattie standing in the foyer beside a bewildered Keller, a phone in her hand and some sort of walkie-talkie on her hip. "What the hell is this?"

Theo stepped closer to see the same article he read earlier. He knew there was a chance she would see it eventually, but he hoped he had more time. At least he got her on his side before she saw it.

His time was running out. "I can explain."

Chapter Thirteen

Mattie

With Kamari back to sleep, Mattie retired to the bathroom, grabbing her phone to turn on a show while she did her nightly skin care. Her head in the sink as she rinsed, she heard the chime of messages coming through. With blurry eyes, she glanced at the screen to see a string of texts from Shea.

Call me now.

Check AllCeleb

That's you right?

This is bad, Mats.

Wiping her face with a towel, Mattie clicked on the link Shea sent.

The Pickup Artist

Two lines in, Mattie had to steady herself on the bathroom counter as she sank onto the toilet, her legs jelly beneath her. She read the article twice before looking at the picture. Her skirt was so high on her legs that her underwear was practically in view. Her face was on the other side of Theo, but anyone who knew her would recognize the small birthmark on the back of her left knee.

How could Theo put her in this position? He was careless with the press, and he was being careless with her. Hurrying out of the room, she grabbed the baby monitor out of the junk drawer, fumbling to put new batteries in it. She never took the other unit out of Kamari's room from her baby days.

Clicking on the parent unit, she heard the familiar sounds of the children's audiobook, and nothing else. As she stomped over to the mansion, she clipped the monitor to the waist of her pajamas. Knocking with the side of her fist, she waited until Keller opened the door.

"Mattie, hey, what"—"

"Where is he?" she demanded.

Keller's eyes darted behind him to see Theo walking down the stairs, wearing only a pair of sweatpants and his hair wet. Brandishing the phone in the air, she demanded, "What the hell is this?"

He glanced at her phone, then back at her, his face pained. "I can explain."

"That's my ass, on display in a tabloid."

Beside her, she saw Keller grimace before shooting Theo a head shake and slinking away, leaving them alone.

"I was going to mention it, but I didn't want to worry you. It's really…"

With both hands in front of her, she shoved him in the chest, causing him to stumble back into the wall. She was stronger than she appeared. "Don't you dare. You think you can come back into my life, my daughter's life and fuck me over like this?"

"What. No. I didn't think—"

"Exactly, you don't think. You never think about the impact your actions have on other people. How I have a career and a reputation to maintain. How are people supposed to respect me when there is a picture of me looking like an alcoholic sorority girl splashed around the news?"

"It wasn't like that. You can't even tell it's you in the picture."

Shaking her head at him, a look of disgust came over her face. "You think I'm an idiot, don't you? Damnit, I was so foolish. I thought maybe you had changed, maybe you could take a little responsibility for your actions, but of course not."

"I'm sorry. Okay? I'll call my manager, and I'll ask her to get some PR spin on it and—"

His manager? PR?

Her vision grew red, and she tried to make sense of his words. He didn't live in the real world if he thought a few phone calls could get this cleared up.

"And say what? How are you going to protect me from one of the partners at my work seeing this? Or a client? Patrice probably told half the island about our little conversation at the coffee shop the other day. You think people can't put all this together?"

"It's one picture, I've had way worse said about me."

"I'm not you, Theodore. I never signed up to be written about in the tabloids." In the early days, she had thought about him being famous in a vague way that held no actual weight. It was parties and going to award shows and fancy dresses. Growing up, she had no concept of what fame was. As for her life now, it wasn't the life of a famous person. She might have been okay with the attention if only she had a chance to prepare, but this blindsided article? The impact it could have on her.

"I'm sorry, Mattie. I didn't think it would get this much press. It must have been a slow news day. It will blow over."

"For you. This will blow over *for you*. Not me. I have to live here. See people who now will only think about this picture when they see me. How am I going to earn any respect?"

"I'll take care of it, okay? I'm sorry."

She sneered at him. "Sorry? It's going to take a lot more than sorry to fix this. You come crashing back into my life and now I might have to explain to the partners at my firm why half my ass is on display on countless videos online. Not to mention the sideways looks I'll get in the school line from the other moms. This is a small community, Theo. This isn't Hollywood. Rumors live on forever here. People are still talking about when the owner of the hardware store dumped his wife for one of his employees, and that was ten years ago. People around here don't forget something like this. I will not have Kamari's life be messed up for one of your publicity stunts."

"Publicity stunt? Do you think I wanted this kind of press?"

Mattie huffed out a puff of air, attempting to slow her raging heartbeat. "I don't know what you want. All I know is, I have to protect myself and Mari."

Theo nodded at her words, taking the sharp barbs with a grimace. "Give me a few days, I'll fix this for you."

There was no fixing things for them. Even if he was able to get the story squashed, the picture scrubbed from the Internet. The fact remained, when she was around Theo, she made terrible decisions. She thought he had ruined her at eighteen, but this man in front of her today, he had the power to destroy her whole life and if he stepped any closer, if he held her face in his hands, she would let him. It was a dark and dangerous place that held onto this love for him. She couldn't fall for him again.

Mattie glared at him. "Better yet, why don't you leave me alone?"

With her arms wrapped around herself, she made it out the front door before the tears began to well.

HAVING HIM STAY AWAY was simpler. That way, she could tell herself she didn't miss him, didn't need him anymore. When she returned that night after yelling at him, her bed smelled of his soap, the clean freshness that lingered on his skin. Even though she was angry at him, even though he had sent shock waves into her life, she still buried her face into the pillow, breathing him in.

If he stayed away, she didn't have to resist him, didn't have to lose her self-control the way his presence made her do.

Shea didn't bother her about going to their weekly hot yoga, instead taking her to lunch at the local Vietnamese restaurant where she could focus on her pho and not have to interact with the gossips in town. Mattie had told her everything that was said. Shea called her harsh but said that Theo deserved it a bit. Luckily, her bosses were not the type to be reading an online gossip story. So far, no other news outlets had picked it up. She typed in Theo's name, but all the articles were older. Maybe she had overreacted a bit. So far, no one aside from Shea had come out and asked her about it, though Patrice was giving her an odd look in the kombucha and artisan salsa aisle of Manzanita Market.

For almost a week, he hadn't contacted her. He stayed away for days after that. She saw him running on the streets as she took Kamari to school, but he didn't come over to apologize again or offer an explanation. And what could he say? She knew her words were harsh, but he needed to hear them. Falling into his trap again would be a mistake, she knew that from the moment she saw him at Eloise and Keller's that first night. She had been fighting against her best judgment for a week, but the article only reinforced what she already knew.

Every night when she returned home, she would glance over at her neighbors. Whether she wanted to see Theo walking through the path in the trees, she wasn't sure. She was still excruciatingly angry at him, but most of the anger could only be placed on herself. From the first day she saw Theo she knew the sway he held over her. She knew, and still she allowed him in.

Days later, Jay dropped Mari off after her Wednesday ballet class. Jay asked Kamari to go watch television upstairs, a surprising move, since Jay had strict screen time rules at his own house. Mattie followed him through the house, watching as Jay bundled up the dirty dance clothes in his hands, stuffing them in the washing machine, starting it with a few beeps. "I have to head over to Eastern Washington on Saturday. I know it's my time with Mari, but I was hoping we could switch weekends? Suze has never taken the trip on Highway Two, I thought we'd make a long adventure of it. Stop in Leavenworth for beer and pretzels, all that."

"Sure thing. As long as you bring me back a bottle of that Shameless Hussy Red from that winery with Burt Reynolds on the wall."

"Of course, can't miss it. We'll be back on Thursday at the latest, hopefully Tuesday if everything goes well."

Dragging her towels out of the dryer, she threw them in the laundry basket where they would most likely sit until she ran out of clean towels in the closet, and then the cycle would start all over again.

After years with Jay, she could tell his travel plans weren't the main topic.

"Patrice cornered me at dance class today."

"She's a busybody," Mattie said, feigning confidence. Already she knew where this was going.

"I saw the picture, and while I don't care what you do when you don't have Mari, but—" He sighed loudly.

Jay folded his hands in his lap, snapping and unsnapping the watch on his wrist, a nervous habit that was always his tell. "I don't know how to ask this, so I'll come out and say it." He straightened up, staring Mattie down. "Should I be worried about Mari being around your new boyfriend?"

Mattie sunk into the seat across from him, shaking her head. "He's not my boyfriend, Jay."

"He's something, though, isn't he?"

They had always been honest with each other. That was one of the reasons she was with him for so long. That was one of the tenants of their co-parenting, that they would be upfront about anything that would affect their daughter. "Yes."

Jay's gaze grew far away for a minute. "He's the ex you never wanted to talk about, right? Teddy? Your sister told me once he was a musician."

Nodding, Mattie struggled for the words. "It was a long time ago and I never thought I'd see him again. Why would I? He never came back to Cape Rose and then his family moved away. I tried to put it all behind me."

"But now he's back. And he's interested in what?"

Mattie laughed a low, humorous thing. "We haven't exactly talked about what it is he wants. Teddy's always been a bit cryptic. When we were young, I thought it was romantic, but now—" She scrubbed a hand over her face. "I don't know what we're doing."

"Well, he couldn't be more different from me, could he? If I didn't know any better, I'd think he was a reaction to me." He paused, assessing her. "But he came first. I guess that would make me the overcorrection, wouldn't it?"

Mattie hesitated. "Jay—"

He put a hand up. "You don't have to explain yourself. I have no room to talk. We all have our baggage, and obviously, with me being engaged, I can't lecture you about moving on."

"Thank you," Mattie whispered.

"You are a great mom. And you and I are a team. So, I'll ask you one time and we can leave it at that." He sighed, gaining the strength to ask. "When it comes to Mari, is there anything about your relationship with Theo, I need to be worried about?"

Mattie shook her head quickly. "No. Our daughter will always be my priority. Nothing will change that." She left out that while there wouldn't be any risk to Kamari, her own heart was perilously close to disaster.

Jay studied her, his gaze steady and careful, and she realized that must be how witnesses he cross-examined felt. He must have believed her because his shoulder sagged and he gave her a small smile. "Okay, that's that, then."

Offering him a shaky smile, she grabbed a pillow off the couch, fluffing it.

"Are you okay?" Jay's straight black brows furrowed. "I don't have to be your husband anymore to care about you, you know that, right?"

"I know." Nodding, Mattie smoothed a hand over her lap. "I appreciate you saying that. I'll be okay. Teddy—" She sighed. She needed to stop calling him that. He wasn't Teddy, not anymore. He was a different man, just as she was a different woman. "Theo. I don't think he's going to be coming around anymore. The night I saw the article, I went over there and yelled at him. Said some pretty terrible things."

"The way he looked at you, that's not a man who's going to let go easily. I wouldn't be surprised if he comes back around."

"And if I don't want him around?" she asked.

Jay considered her for a moment. "Is that true?"

Blinking a few times, Mattie tried to will the lie, but it couldn't come with Jay. "No."

He raised a brow but didn't ask anything further. He knew her well enough not to. She had always been a terrible liar, and to lie to herself at this point was a fool's errand. The truth of how she felt didn't negate the consequences of her and Theo's actions. She only hoped he would have the control to stay away from her so she didn't have to.

CHAPTER FOURTEEN

THEO

H E WOULD HAVE THOUGHT after being away from Mattie for over a decade, giving her a few days to cool off would be easy. But after getting so close to having her back, the distance felt excruciating. How did his bandmates do long distance with their partners? Knowing she was right there, mere feet away most days, was horrible.

Setting his guitar down, he jotted a few lines in his notebook of a song he was working on. The band wasn't going in to record a new album for a few months, but he couldn't turn off the part of his brain that was writing music.

It was the only thing that distracted him from the longing to see her. He hadn't missed someone this much since, well, Mattie. With a start, the memory of those days came back to him. Long nights sleeping in a sleeping bag on the floor of someone's living room. The cracks in his hands from the cleaning chemicals used at his job. A tiredness in his bones every night of auditioning and getting nowhere. For months he would go to sleep with the single thought that maybe he had made a mistake, leaving Cape Rose, leaving Mattie. And then he let her go, because he knew he could ruin his own life, but he could never ruin hers.

He told himself for years, if he got a little more stable, he'd find her again. One more song on the radio, one more hit on TV. One more gold album or tour or appearance and he'd achieved enough to be worthy of Mattie. In all this self-talk, he never envisioned a world in which Mattie wasn't there to take him back. Using a fake account, he followed Mattie on social media, looking at the rare photos she would post, of food, or nature, occasionally of herself with a friend. On the eve of their second album release, he looked up her name, the way he always did, and saw her tagged in a picture. A tall man with short dark hair had his arm wrapped around her. He gazed down at her with such adoration as she held her left hand up for the camera. Even in the small, grainy picture, he could see the diamond engagement ring on her finger. The happiness on her face.

She had moved on.

For years, he held on to this idea that Mattie was once and would forever be his. But that wasn't true, not anymore. He had known in theory this could happen, but it wasn't until he saw that photo, he realized his time to get her back was gone. He should have spent that night celebrating the album release with his bandmates; instead, he spent it at a hole-in-the-wall bar, drinking cheap beer and doing a deep dive into who exactly this Jay West of Manzanita, Washington, was.

When a young woman recognized him, he let her buy him a drink, and then another. And when she asked him to take her home, he did. That night, as he was inside that woman, he couldn't see her. All he could see was Mattie's dark hair that should be strewn over his pillow, Mattie's soft tan skin under his hands, instead of this woman's pale skin. The sounds were wrong, screeching and shrill, and even when he came, a crack formed in his chest at how terribly he had used this woman.

He knew he was an asshole; she'd probably tell a reporter, but when he kicked her out of his house, shoes in one hand, and a fifty for cab fare in the other, he didn't look back as she slammed his door.

Before that night, he didn't sleep around much, maybe a few girls here and there he would take on a few dates, but never one-night stands. Never fast hookups in the back of a club or blow jobs in the green room. But after seeing that news, he changed. A place deep in his chest hardened. From the day he met Mattie he knew he could never love another woman, so what was the point of trying? They became holes to fill, a need to be quenched. It was all physical because he could never allow someone else to take the sacred space, Mattie held inside him.

Even when he tried with Safiya, one of the most beautiful women in the world according to magazines, pop songs, and fashion shows, he couldn't do it. Being with her, he knew she was the closest he could find to a replacement for Mattie but it was never enough.

When Aria called him in the middle of his workout, he thought about not picking up. But he knew she was tenacious, and if he let it go, she'd send him a wall of text messages.

"You love being photographed, don't you?" Aria asked, without a hello. In the background were the sounds of people shouting and machines.

Setting down the hand weight, he lay back on the weight bench. "It wasn't like I planned it. I wasn't thinking about the people at the concert. And where are you? I thought you wrapped a few days ago?"

Aria sighed. "After some consideration, they have decided, that this will be Breslin's last season." There was a murmuring of someone talking to Aria, and then her muffled voice. "Thank you, Tamir, extra sprouts would be wonderful." Her voice came back louder. "Sorry, lunch order time."

"Last season? Are they firing you?" Theo sat up, the phone gripped in his hand.

"They are choosing not to renew my contract." She sighed loudly. "Travis is getting the boot, too. It's just as well, how much longer could I play an immortal who stopped aging at seventeen? I'm getting an awesome death scene, sacrificing myself to bring down the Infernal Obscuria."

Theo really should have watched Aria's show. He had no idea what she was talking about. "Wicked."

"Anyway, tell me about her."

"How do you know there's a 'her?' It could be some random fan?"

Aria snorted on the other end. "Paa-leeze." She drug out the word. "You think I'm an idiot. When have you ever rescued a woman from a creepy guy?"

"It wasn't like that." He stared up at the ceiling, counting the lines on the exposed beams. "She was supposed to stay backstage, and when I went to find her, some guy was trying to pick her up. It wasn't that big a deal."

"Sure it wasn't. You stopped being a total asshole suddenly?"

"Why is everyone calling me an asshole to my face lately?" he grumbled.

On the other end, Aria laughed. "Maybe because you deserve it. Real talk,

Theo. We went to how many events together, countless guys flirted with me in front of you, and you never batted an eye. And don't give me any of that '*we weren't really together like that*' bullshit, because you know it's deeper than that. I saw you with Safiya, too and you didn't care who she talked to. And then suddenly you're picking up some random girl from Seattle and *carrying* her through a crowd? Make it make sense."

"She's not some random girl. I've known her since we were kids." There was a long pause on Aria's side. "From back home, before I moved away."

On the other end, a clambering of dull noises and shouts sounded, but Aria was slow to respond. "So, she's the one who got away. The reason you're all messed up."

"I'm not messed up."

"You, Mr. Blake, are a dumpster fire on top of a toxic waste center, next door to a cockroach zoo."

"Fuck off," he grumbled.

"I mean it. There has always been something holding you back from people. I could see it. Your bandmates know it. Eloise, Safiya—"

"How do you know how Safiya feels?"

"Oh, we talk. It's the Brokenhearted By Theo Blake Support Group. We meet twice a month at the Y. Membership is booming."

"Hanging up now. I don't know why I called you."

"I called you," she corrected him.

"So get to the point." He had bigger things to worry about than his friend heckling him in-between takes.

"My publicist thought it would be a good idea for us to both be at Brenton Michael's *I'm Nobody's Father's Day* party. Not go together or anything, just a few photos of us talking, to show people we're friendly and no hard feelings for the breakup."

The pop star had established the party five years before. It was an event to see and be seen. He had been a few years before with some up-and-coming singer, February Dickens, who got too drunk and lost one of her stilettos.

"Sure, let Beatriz know and I'll be there."

"Great. And you should bring Mattie. I want to meet her."

"After you called me a trash panda. No way."

"I called you a dumpster fire, and I stand by that statement. Bring her. Give her the VIP treatment; spa sessions, fancy dinners, show her how nice it is being with a rich man. Women love that."

"I'm hanging up now," Theo demanded, disconnecting the call before she could insult him again. Tossing the phone to the side, he picked up the weight at his feet. Curling it to his chest, he tried to focus on the burn in his muscles and not the nagging sensation Aria's call had created. He knew he had been an asshole in his previous relationships. He never cheated on Safiya...kind of; there were a few instances where he would flirt shamelessly with a groupie in front of her. Or go into a locked bathroom where he would sign a woman's bare breast. It wasn't full-on cheating, but he knew if he had a chance with Mattie, that behavior wouldn't happen again. His actions with Aria were worse. While they weren't really together, he had several dalliances with random women. He rarely turned down a beautiful woman in a low-cut top. Safiya-and Aria for that matter-deserved better than a man like him, but he could never conjure enough morality to give it to them. He never promised fidelity to either of them, no matter if they deserved it.

With a towel wrapped around his shoulders, he walked into the kitchen to refill his water bottle. Back in L.A., he couldn't drink water from the tap, but up here, the water was almost sweet. Chugging the icy liquid, his eyes caught on Eloise's phone left on its charging dock, beside canisters of flour and sugar. In the reflection of the overhead light on the screen, he could see the pattern of her fingers. Eloise really should clean her screen; the lock code was visible for anyone to see. Glancing behind him, he saw Eloise and Keller down by the water, pointing at the dock.

Studying the numbers on the screen, it was easy to see the code was Keller's birthday. Tapping in the numbers, her wallpaper lit up with a picture of her and Keller at her album release party the year before. One more glance at the window assured him they were still outside. He scrolled through her contacts but didn't see Mattie in them. Never had he invaded his friend's privacy like this, but he was desperate. Closing out her contacts, he went to Eloise's text messages.

Halfway down, between a GIF of a crying man from an early-aughts teen show and a reminder for an upcoming appointment was a message.

Neighbor Mattie: Here's the name of that tea I told you about. It helped me when I was nauseated with Mari.

Bingo.

Quickly he sent himself her contact info then deleted the message. As he was about to set Eloise's phone down, he heard a noise.

"I don't know why you're all worried. It's not jet-skiing."

"I don't want you out in the water at all. What if you fell?"

Fumbling, he set the phone down on the charger and twisted to see Eloise and Keller enter the kitchen. "From a paddle-board? I'd go in the water. These are the waters I was raised in. I know how to swim, Kel, and—" She stopped talking, her brows furrowing as she narrowed her eyes at Theo. "Why do you look guilty?"

Crossing his arms over his chest, Theo feigned confusion. "Me? What are you talking about?"

She pointed a finger at him with narrowed eyes. "That is the same stupid expression you gave me when you forgot your guitar at that show in Carmel and we had to drive two hours back to get it."

"That was nine years ago!"

Eloise approached him, glancing around. "Did you eat all my salt and vinegar chips again, Theo? It's the only thing I can keep down and if you ate them—"

Theo raised his hands up, in surrender. "Nope, didn't touch your chips. I'm going to finish my workout."

As he left, he heard the hushed whispers of his friends. "—Totally losing it. I'm about ready to send him back to L.A. with his moping."

He ignored them, escaping to their home gym. He should finish his workout with some cardio, but his energy was suddenly drained. It was days later and he hadn't figured out a solution to getting Mattie to forgive him for the terrible tabloid article. He picked up his phone again, rereading the article, but avoiding the comments; those were 90 percent vitriol and borderline pornographic words. Scrolling back to his contacts, he added Mattie to his phone, with a pink flower emoji beside her name. He wanted to call her so badly, but he couldn't do that until he had something to offer. Instead, he called their manager, Tamara, hoping she had a solution.

CHAPTER FIFTEEN

Mattie

WALKING OUT OF HER Seattle meeting, she fished her buzzing phone out of her bag to see it was Kamari's school calling.

"Mrs. West? This is Marla, from Agate Elementary. We have Kamari in the office. She started vomiting in the middle of music class."

She didn't correct the receptionist for calling her by the wrong name. "I'm in Seattle. I'll try to catch the next boat, but it might be a while."

The receptionist huffed, "She's already vomited twice in the last half-hour. We'll need Kamari picked up within the hour. Should I start calling other people on the list for you? I see her father Jay West and a Lynn West are next on the list?"

She knew Jay was at that conference in Spokane that week, and his Aunt Lynn didn't drive.

"No. I'll find someone. Give me ten minutes, and I'll call you back with the name of the person picking her up."

"You do that," the snide voice said.

Hanging up, Mattie cursed herself for taking this appointment in Seattle. She so rarely left the island while Mari was at school and the first time in six months she did had to be the day her daughter catches a stomach bug.

Scrolling through her contacts, she hesitated between calling Shea, who was still at work or Patrice, who would add it to her list of little barbs to zing at Mattie. Patrice was still annoyed about the time Kamari smuggled ten packets of fruit snacks in her lunch at preschool, handing them all out to her classmates.

Then an unfamiliar number flashed on her screen.

"Mattie?" the voice on the other end said, hesitantly.

"Theo?" She glanced at her phone. "How did you get my number?"

"Eloise's phone. Don't be mad at her, I broke into her phone after memorizing her passcode."

"That's a bit disturbing." She fished in her bag for her car keys.

"Well, I needed to talk to you."

Mattie groaned. "It's not a good time."

"I had my people fix the article. There's no reason anyone should tie the article to you anymore."

She doubted this, but now her concern wasn't on a silly article, but her daughter.

"I'll have to look it up later. Mari started barfing at school and I need to find someone to pick her up and..."

"I can get her."

Mattie snorted as she unlocked her car and climbed in. "Don't joke around with me right now. I'm not in the mood."

"It's not a joke. I can get her; I'll bring her home until you get there."

"Theodore—"

"Matilda," he interrupted. "Do you have someone else who can leave right now and be at the school in five minutes?"

Swallowing hard, she admitted she didn't.

"Then it's solved. I'll get her for you."

"She's thrown up twice already. Do you even know what to do about that?"

"I've been around enough celebrities partying their brains out to know what to do when someone's vomiting."

"She's a five-year-old girl, not a rock star."

"Can't be that different—fluids, rest, don't give them more cocaine, turn them on their sides, hold their hair back."

Pursing her lips, she made a low humming noise. He wasn't entirely wrong.

"What about a car seat? There's no way you have one of those?"

"Let me worry about that."

Letting out a loud huff, she thumped her head against the headrest. She didn't like this, but what were her other options?

"Fine, but you call me if anything is weird."

"Aye-aye, Captain."

Hanging up, she made a quick call to Marla at the front desk about Theo picking up. If the woman knew who he was, she didn't react.

After missing the boat by two cars, Mattie had to sit in her car in line for another fifty minutes until the next sailing. Theo sent her a picture of Mari in the back seat of an unfamiliar car, which she assumed was Eloise's. Her daughter was sitting in an unfamiliar car seat. Where he got the seat, she had no clue, but he was true to his word.

Stuck in her car, she had nothing more to do but pull up the article Theo had sent her.

Pickup Artist
Article Correction
Representatives from Blake's team identified the woman as a friend of the singer, Eloise Dunning Grant, Addison Sullivan. Research into Sullivan is pending.

The rest of the article was basically the same. Looking at the photo closer, she realized her skirt wasn't as high up her legs as she thought and the picture was far too grainy to truly recognize her. It wasn't a complete disaster; only a minor one. Still, her argument stood. It could have been bad. If they would have featured her face. If the tech-bro guy she had been talking to could have remembered her name right. It was a close call and his blatant disregard for how that would impact her was damning.

She was waved onto the ferry, following the deck crew's instructions to park. Turning her car off, she pondered going up to the cabin above but decided it wasn't worth it for the thirty-five-minute sailing. Her phone chimed again, this time with another picture of Kamari on a white leather couch, a plastic trash can beside her, a wet washcloth on her head, and a stuffed penguin clutched in her arms.

Teddy: Some singing princess movie is on and she is quietly watching that.

A swell of tenderness bloomed in her chest, but she tamped it down. Nope, she was not going to let him off that easy. No matter how kind it was for him to take her daughter.

Arriving at Eloise and Keller's house she thought about knocking, but after her busting through the door the previous time, she felt like it was probably okay to walk in. In the living room, Eloise was curled up in a chair, writing in a small notebook. A princess water bottle, some crackers, and a full bowl of broth sat on the table in front of the heap of blankets, and Kamari was on the couch. Joining her on the couch, Eloise picked up the blanket that was over Kamari while Mattie scooped her arms around her daughter. She was getting bigger, and the weight of sleep and sickness made her feel heavier.

"Thanks for helping with Mari." Mattie shifted her sleeping daughter on her chest.

Eloise shook her head. "I didn't do a thing. She was already sleeping when I got here. Theo asked me to watch her as he took a shower."

"A shower?"

Chuckling, Eloise gathered up the blanket from the couch, folding it a few times. "Yeah, Kamari threw up on him."

"That's embarrassing," Mattie said, gritting her teeth.

Shaking her head, Eloise gave her a knowing grin. "After that stunt he pulled the other day, it's no more than he deserves. Plus, it's a rite of passage with kids, isn't it? It's good for him to get used to."

"Why would he need to get used to kids?"

Eloise glanced from Mattie to someone behind her. "Um, no reason. How was your shower, Theo?"

"Good. Short." He approached Mattie, putting out his arms. "Here, let me carry her back to your house."

Shifting her closer, her arms already burned from the weight. "Are you sure? She's heavy, and you already—"

Theo motioned with his hands. It wasn't that far of a walk but she knew it would take twice as long if she carried her daughter. Kamari barely stirred as they did the handoff. He hoisted her up on his chest, holding her tight. Her cheek rested against his collarbone, and her arms wrapped around his shoulders.

It doesn't mean anything.

It can't.

She led the way to her home, waving goodbye to Eloise as they left. The short walk was silent and Theo held Kamari still as they moved. When they got to the house, he insisted on taking her up the stairs and laying her in her own bed instead of Mattie. Once her daughter was in bed, Theo left them alone.

"Mommy, where is Rosy?" Kamari mumbled.

"Who, darling?" Mattie brushed a dark curl from her daughter's forehead.

"Rosy, my new penguin from Theo. He said it would help me feel better." Mattie racked her brain before realizing it was the small stuffed penguin she was holding on the couch at Eloise's.

"I'll go get it soon."

Kamari nodded. "She's Pennyworth's wife. They're going to get married."

"Your stuffed penguins are getting married?"

Kamari nodded. "Daddy and Suze are getting married, and my penguins are, too. Are you going to get married?"

Mattie laughed, pulling the turquoise comforter over her daughter's chest. "I'm not planning on it anytime soon."

Kamari opened one eye. "What about Theo? He likes you. He got you flowers."

"That's a marvelous idea for another day." Mattie ran a hand over her daughter's hair. "Go back to sleep. I'll bring you some juice when you wake up."

"Watermelon juice?"

"Watermelon juice, it is."

When she came down the stairs, he found Theo in the laundry room, stuffing dirty clothes into the washer.

"I saw the article correction." Mattie crossed her arms against her chest. "Addison?"

Theo wiped his hands on his pants. Despite the precarious position he was in with her, he dared a smile. "Yeah. It was that douchebag at the bar who called you that in the first place."

"So, you made up a person? No one will believe that."

Tossing a towel in a laundry basket in the corner, he faced her. "Sure they will. That's the thing about stories like that. They move on to the next juicy topic in ten minutes. A friend of Eloise's, that's boring. And now, there's no one who can definitely say that's you in the picture."

"But it was me."

"Prove it. It was dark, the footage is terrible. And Eloise and Keller are going public with the pregnancy announcement soon. All the focus will be on them." He pushed past her, into the kitchen where he opened the cabinet and pulled out a mug, and then opened a drawer to pull out a tea bag, plopping it into her mug then filling it with hot water from the kettle. "I know I screwed up. I shouldn't have put you in that position."

"Thank you for trying to fix it." Her voice soft. "And for getting Mari."

Mattie settled onto the stool opposite him. When he handed her a mug of tea, she took it. The warmth from the mug radiated on her palms.

He leaned against the counter, crossing one ankle over the other. "I was happy to. She's a great kid."

Mattie wiped a hand over her face. She didn't need him there, saying kind words about her daughter, making her second guess her sense of self-preservation. "You don't have to stay here, having a sick kid is incredibly boring. It's mostly waiting around while they sleep and feeding them. And laundry. Lots of laundry."

"I can do laundry." He motioned to the room. "It's already half done, now."

Pursing her lips, the words failed her. She couldn't ask him to leave. Everything about him standing in her kitchen felt right, and it was aching inside her, how much she loved the scene.

"Teddy," her voice was a whisper. She wished she could be the type of woman who didn't cry, but that was never her. When she was angry, she cried. When a sad commercial came on, she cried. When she was overwhelmed, she cried. The tears came, unbidden but hot and stinging on her face. "Don't be kind to me. Please, can't you be the asshole I was promised rock stars were? You're making this so hard for me to hate you."

"I think I've hit my asshole limit with you, don't you think?" He cocked his head to the side to watch her. "Is that what you want? For me to be an asshole, to treat you the way I treat other women? Because I can't do that."

She threw her hands up in frustration. "Why? Why did you have to come back here and upset everything? I was perfectly happy, and now..."

"Were you? Do you truly think you could be happy without me, Matilda? Can you say there was been a single day since we parted that you felt complete? Because I can't."

"I was fine. I was content." With her face tilted at the ceiling, she urged the tears to go away. "It was enough."

He rounded the corner, taking the mug from her hands and setting it beside her. With a hand on her knee, he swiveled her on the stool until she was wedged between his legs. Staring up at him, her chest was tight with exhaustion, and something else she couldn't face.

"It's never been enough for me. You have to know that. The fame, the women. None of it."

"I don't want to hear about the other women you've had." Scoffing she tried to pull away, but he held her face tight in his hands.

"Why not? They don't matter. Who cares if they're on the cover of every magazine or starring on the most popular TV show? They're never going to be enough for me. Do you know why?"

Mattie shook her head.

"Because they're not you. Matilda Lewis, it's only ever been you."

She didn't stop the tears this time. A guttural sob escaped at his words.

"What do you want me to say, Teddy? I don't know why you're here, or why you won't leave me alone."

His thumb traced a line on her cheekbone. "Do you want me to leave you alone, Matilda? Is that really what you want? Or are you scared about how much you like having me around?"

Mattie didn't respond. She couldn't. For all the jokes people make about lawyers and lying, she never could be convincing.

"Why would you want me to leave?"

Mattie shook her head, the words failing her.

"Why?" he asked again.

"Because you broke my heart, okay? Because I spent years getting over you, crying myself to sleep over the very idea of you."

"Because you care for me."

"I *cared* for you. Past tense. I don't know this man you are today."

"Of course you do. You know exactly who I am. You are the only person who ever has."

Steeling herself, she shook her head at his words. "Maybe I could deal with it if you broke my heart again, but it's not only me I have to worry about anymore. I don't have the luxury of falling to pieces over some man."

"Some man? I refuse to be some man to you."

Mattie laughed a cold and sad thing. "Your actions made that choice for you, Theo. I have a child, and I have to be there for her. You talk of sacrifice, but you have no idea what it takes day after day to be there for someone else."

"I want to learn. You can teach me."

"Teach you?" She shook her head. "It's not my job to teach you how to be a good man. You need to figure that out for yourself."

"You want me to get on my knees and beg you for another chance? I will. Gladly. I will do anything for you." When she didn't say anything back, he dropped to his knees, wrapping his arms around her middle and gazing up at her. "Tell me you'll let me try."

Her hands found his hair, brushing the golden locks from his forehead. His hair, skin, and the gleam in his eyes was the same as twelve years before. In his embrace, she felt like she was the same girl.

"There is no world where you are not the only one for me. My heart only has room enough for one woman. You have to know that."

She did. For all her bluster, for all her shame and self-doubt, she knew his words were true. But she didn't know if it was enough.

CHAPTER SIXTEEN

THEO

BEING A SCREW-UP WASN'T a novel concept to Theo. He was all too familiar with self-loathing. But the emotions he had after Mattie left him were new. When he screwed up before, he knew he was the one with the consequences. When he kissed Eloise, when he drank too much at a show and fell off the stage, when he got arrested for peeing on a wall in Charlotte.

No one cared about him having a mystery girlfriend. It was all make-believe fodder for the tabloids. If it was Aria or Safiya or any of the other women, he could brush it off. They knew the score; they had their own teams to spin a story. But Mattie. His Matilda. He had truly fucked things up. Eloise was right, he had no clue how to take care of someone else. To put their needs before his.

He had been nothing but a selfish bastard for thirty-two years. But with his arms wrapped around her body, he felt her softening, the anger and fear melting from her. He could do this; she would forgive him eventually. He had made the call for the article to be changed, he had taken care of Kamari when she asked. This could show her he was serious.

Mattie pulled away, using her hand on the counter to steady herself.

"I have some things to say, and you need to listen. Over there." She pointed at the couch. "Sit down, I need to not touch you."

His finger brushed a lock of hair from her face, a smile crooking up on his face. "Because I drive you wild?" She stepped back and took a steadying breath. "Because you make me forget myself. You say you want me back; you need to listen."

He settled onto the couch, leaving room for her to sit on the other end. Electing to take the small armchair, she tucked her feet up beneath her.

"Twelve years ago, you left me." When Theo opened his mouth to refute her, she put up a hand. "I keep hearing the way you talk about what happened as if we were torn apart, but that wasn't what happened, Theo. We both know that. Don't act as if you're the one who had their heartbroken that day. You made the choice to leave me."

"I had to leave you, Mattie. You don't understand...if you'd give me a chance to explain how I was feeling..."

"Explain what? How I trusted you and you threw that away? The way I spent years trying to get over you? Or maybe how I have to block your name and your band's name on the Internet because everywhere I look, I see you? Do you have any idea how hard it is to get over a man who's plastered on billboards?"

"Well, I've never tried to get over a man so..."

"This isn't a joke, Theodore." Matilda clenched her hands into fists. "There were so many nights I wondered why; why was I easy to leave? What was it about me that made you go? I wished there could have been another woman, because at least she has a face. At least that can be hated. But your music? When I told you I'd go with you. I told you I'd be there every step of the way. But I wasn't good enough for you then. I would have done anything, gone anywhere for you, Teddy. But you didn't trust in us enough to let me."

"Trust? It had nothing to do with trust. I was saving you. What was I supposed to do Mattie, have you sleep on the floor of dirty studio apartments I was crashing in? Have you be the lookout for when I was using gas station hand soap to shave? Have you sit next to me on the sidewalk while I busked for hours to only get a dollar-fifty? I never thought you weren't enough. Everything I have done, all my music, all this fame, was so I could be good enough to deserve you."

His declarations took the air out of her words.

Theo cleared his throat. "You want me to tell you, I regret leaving you? I don't. I will never regret leaving that town. But that doesn't mean I don't feel shame about the way I left. It doesn't mean I haven't missed you these past twelve years. I should have talked to you. Reached out sooner. But I was ashamed. For years, I told myself I'd find you once I was successful, but by then I was too late. You were married, and I was alone, and I only had myself to blame. I know I fucked up with you, Mattie. But I was a dumb kid who didn't know what he was doing. I had nothing to offer you back then. I would have only caused you pain. Back then, leaving you was the best thing I could have done for you. "

"But that was my choice to make. To go with you, or be left behind. You never let me decide what I wanted. You left me, and I was alone."

"I was trying to protect you."

"You left to protect yourself. You were a scared boy who didn't know what he wanted. If you truly cared for me, you would have told me to my face."

He nodded at her. She was right; he knew this. "I wouldn't have let you go. If you would have come down, I wouldn't have said those things to you. Don't you see what me leaving you allowed for you? If I hadn't left, you wouldn't be a lawyer, you wouldn't have Kamari."

Swallowing, tears shone in her eyes as she looked away from him.

"You gave yourself a life I never could. I won't regret that. I can't."

Her words were a hiccuping sob. "You were my life then. And now you want to come back, and I don't know what to do with you. With how I feel. Because I am someone's mother. I have a life. It's not that simple anymore."

He was up from the couch, crouching before her. With her face in his hands, he leaned his forehead against hers. "Can't we try? There is nothing that can take back those years. But I won't let that happen again."

Her eyes were squeezed shut. "How different our lives could have been if you made a different choice then. We're both new people now. I don't even know you, really."

"Ask me. Let's start over right now, tonight. We'll put all the hurt in the past."

With his hands on her cheeks, she nodded. "Okay."

"Yeah?"

With a big sigh, she looked up at him, her words soft but powerful. "As the rain."

His kiss was tentative, as if their agreement was tenuous enough, it may break if he rushed it.

"Come to L.A. with me next week."

She pulled back, her brow furrowed. "I was thinking of a date in town or something, not jetting off to California on a whim."

He rocked back on his heels. "It's not a whim. I promised Aria I'd make an appearance at this one party. A show of solidarity and PR stuff. It'll be fun. You can dress up, we'll take a nice car, I'll pamper you the whole time. Free drinks."

"Free drinks?"

"My favorite kind. You can take the broke, starving artist out of Cape Rose—"

"This is crazy. We're rushing into this."

"Is that a yes?"

Pursing her lips, he could see the debate behind her eyes, then her face lit up with a smile. "Only you make me this wild."

"I like you wild."

Pulling his face to hers, she whispered against his lips, "Please don't break me again."

Chapter Seventeen

Mattie

"**I**'M SORRY, YOU'RE DOING what this weekend?" Shea set her glass of wine down on the rustic hewn wood table of the downtown winery tasting room.

Taking a small sip of her rosé, she tried to come up with an explanation that made her sound semi-rational. Floundering, she shrugged her shoulders. Shea heard her fine.

"Look I know this guy has you all mixed up, but to fly to L.A. with him? You guys barely know each other anymore."

"We've been getting reacquainted these past few weeks," Mattie said coyly.

With narrowed eyes, Shea leaned back and crossed her legs. "That's not what I'm talking about, and you know it. I mean, what do you even know about his life now? This guy you're seeing, that's him on vacation mode. His life is completely different from yours. He's a celebrity. Do you know the first thing about the entertainment industry?"

"Well, no, but..."

Shea interrupted her with, "I worry you're getting yourself in too deep with someone who doesn't have your best interests at heart."

"He would never try to hurt me."

With a head shake, Shea let her know how silly that comment was. They both knew people got hurt all the time, despite their best intentions. Mattie tried to lighten the mood. "I thought you liked Theo?"

"Yeah, sure, in theory. Not as the man who's turning my good friend's life upside down in the span of a few weeks. You're really going to jump back into a relationship with a man you haven't seen in over a decade because he dicked you down?"

"Can you not phrase it that way?" Mattie hissed, glancing over at the table beside them, where a group of middle-aged women stopped their conversation about the price of free-range halibut to eavesdrop. She mouthed *'sorry'* to the ladies before turning back at Shea. "It's more than that for us. You know me. I would never do something like this if it was just—" She dropped her voice. "Sex."

The way her friend was looking at her, made her want to squirm. "The Mattie I knew wouldn't do something like this, period. I mean, if I thought you were having a little fling, I'd say go for it. But we both know you are incapable of that, or else you would have gone out with that guy from Tinder."

"He was a child," Mattie grumbled, popping a cashew into her mouth.

"All I'm saying is, there is no casual with you. You're not built for it. And a guy like Theo Blake? He's spent the last decade being a musician. I've read the articles about him. Not only about his famous exes, but the other women he's been linked to."

"Are you saying, because I'm not supermodel beautiful, I can't be with him?" Mattie would have to be a blind idiot not to have the thought cross her mind. It didn't matter how much she'd worked on her own self-worth; seeing the flawless skin of his exes online was an ego hit.

Shea snorted at the comment. "Of course not. All I'm saying is, can he even be serious about someone?"

Mattie wanted to assure herself she was different from Theo. But an itch of self-doubt trickled in.

"Have you seen what people say about him? The women he's been linked to? His brushes with the law?"

Matti shook her head. "Theo said all the stuff they print is a bunch of BS."

"All of it? Really? You're a smart woman, Mats. We both know how libel works. It can't all be made up." Frowning, she cocked her head to the side. "Have you guys talked at all about the logistics of this relationship? He doesn't live here; you do. He probably has to tour and jet off to random places all the time; you get annoyed when you have to catch a thirty-minute ferry to Seattle. Not to mention Kamari. You're going to uproot her from her home over this man?"

"I would never do that to Mari." Of all the things Shea was saying, this one stung. Call her a fool for a man, or irrational, sure. But a careless mother? No.

"I know you wouldn't," Shea soothed. "So how is it supposed to work?"

"We'll have to figure that out later." Mattie couldn't drudge up the fortitude to argue anymore. "It will be fine. I'm a grown woman I can handle it."

Tapping her finger on the stem of her wine glass, Shea nodded. "All right, I hope you're right."

J AY WAS SLIGHTLY MORE understanding, if not a little perplexed by her announcement.

"I thought you hated flying?" he asked.

She didn't have the heart to tell him it was Jay who hated flying, and she long ago told him she didn't like it either, so he'd feel better about taking long road trips instead. Shifting from one foot to the other, the June air was cool around her ankles. She had opted to wear a sundress that had been hanging in the back of her closet for too long. It was slightly musty when she pulled it out, but a quick spin in the dryer with a wrinkled sheet sorted it out enough.

"We'll see how I do." She handed Kamari's school bag over to her ex-husband. "Mari's Father's Day gift for you is in there. She picked it herself this year."

Mattie wasn't sure when she was supposed to stop getting Jay a Father's Day gift...was there some protocol for divorced parents she didn't see? For the second spring in a row since they'd split, Jay made sure she had a Mother's Day gift, so Mattie followed suit.

"Thanks." He opened his mouth to say something, then closed it.

"I'll be careful, J-bird," she joked, using his detested nickname from high school.

He narrowed his eyes at her, ignoring the dig.

Jay hoisted the bag over his shoulder, the small purple strap comical on his body. "I meant what I said the other week. Even though we're not married anymore and I don't have to look out for you anymore, remember, if you need anything, you'll call? I can get you on the next flight to SeaTac in hours."

Fiddling with the small plastic key chain that held Kamari's baby picture, Mattie nodded. "I appreciate that. And I have my credit card to buy a plane ticket. I know how to travel on my own, you know."

He sighed. "I don't trust those L.A. people."

Biting her lip to force down the smile, Mattie fought the urge to ask him exactly how many L.A. people he knew. "I'm a big girl. I'll be fine."

"True story?"

"True story," she assured him. "I'll let you know when I've landed, and call tonight to say goodnight to Mari."

Jay called their daughter over to say goodbye. With one last kiss goodbye to Kamari, Mattie hurried down the steps into the waiting car, where Theo had been sitting. Climbing in beside him, she took in the new car smell of the luxury sedan. Her car, while only a few years old, smelled of crayon wax, wet leaves, and stale cereal. The kinds of parents who could keep food out of their cars were a total mystery to her. Most mornings, it was the choice of being twenty minutes later than she already was or granola bar crumbles smooshed under Kamari's car seat.

"Everything good?" Theo asked, his gaze at Jay's closed door.

"Yeah, fine."

"Your ex doesn't like me much," Theo commented.

Mattie caught sight of Jay at the living room window. Theo put the car into reverse, and she waved out the window. "He's protective. You have to admit this situation is unorthodox."

Theo shook his head. "He doesn't need to be protective."

"I'm the mother of his child. He's looking out for Mari."

Theo glanced in his rear-view mirror at the house one last time. "If you say so. All I'm saying is, you're not his to protect anymore. You're mine."

How terribly she desired to have the whole of her, to belong to him alone. Mattie wanted to tell him it was more complicated than that but stopped herself. It would do no good to start this trip off on unsteady ground. Instead, she leaned over as they waited in line for the ferry, pulling his face to her. His lips soft against her own, her tongue traced the seam of his mouth. He was surprised by her kiss, for a moment, before rushing his mouth to hers, his hand gripping the back of her neck to hold her closer. A horn sounded behind them, and they jolted apart.

Her mouth tingled from the kiss, and her whole body buzzed with excitement for what this trip would be.

INSTEAD OF DRIVING INTO the general parking area, Theo took them to a different gate, where he was waved into a small fenced-in area. From there they went into a small building, where they were screened by a security guard, who then helped them to the plane. She tried to carry her own suitcase, but Theo refused to let her.

Theo told her to pack light, that he'd get her anything she needed. It was just as well; aside from her suits for work, she hardly dressed up, more than sundresses. There was little point when her life consisted of work, gardening, baking, and kid-related activities. She didn't even know what was in fashion anymore. Her style hadn't changed too much from her high school and college days. In fact, many of the dresses in her closet were from those days.

Climbing the stairs into the small plane, she glanced around it. A flight attendant welcomed them, motioning Mattie into the plane. She counted six seats in the cabin, with a curtain that separated the back seat from the front.

Theo lounged in a seat and motioned to the one opposite him. Setting her purse down, she ran a hand over the soft leather seats. Aside from the flight attendants and pilots, they were the only ones on the plane.

"Where are the other passengers? Are they going to miss the flight?"

Theo held up two fingers to the flight attendant at the front. "There are no other passengers."

Mattie's hand stopped rubbing the soft seat, her eyes snapping to his face. "Is this a..." She lowered her voice. "Private plane? Do you own this?"

He laughed as he accepted a proffered glass of champagne. Mattie took the other one.

"Yes and no. I chartered it, or my assistant did it for me. You'll meet her in L.A., Beatriz is great."

Outside the window, she saw the tarmac, the plane picking up speed as it barreled fast to lift off. Faintly, she heard the pilot speaking about cruising altitude and the approximate time they'd be landing. She couldn't absorb any of it. "This is too much. You really shouldn't have."

Theo raised a challenging brow. "Don't tell me I can't spoil you. You'll ruin all my fun."

"But the cost of this..."

He shrugged. "I don't think it's that much more than a first class ticket."

Snorting, she took a sip of the champagne, the bubbles tickling her nose. "I've never flown first class either. Hell, I've only been on a plane twice. Both times on my honeymoon."

Holding out his champagne flute, he waited for her to tap her glass on his. "Glad to pop your cherry, then."

Heat flamed on her cheeks, and she ducked her head down. "Teddy."

"I love it when you call me that. Makes me feel the way I did when I was twenty." The plane bumped in the air a few times before leveling out. She downed the rest of her drink. Outside the windows, the blue-gray water of Puget Sound grew smaller on the right and the Cascade Mountains faded on the left and they were above the clouds.

Plucking her empty glass out of her hand, he set both on the small table beside him and leaned forward, placing a hand on each of her armrests. His face buried in her hair as he nipped at her neck, kissing and biting the tender flesh there. Heat pulsed between her legs, and she clenched her thighs together, rocking against the seat at the sensation.

His mouth on her ear was pure warmth. "When I get you home, I'm going to lay you out and lick that pussy until you can't speak for a week."

She groaned at his words, her clit pulsing at his dirty words. His finger traced up her bare arm to encircle his hand around her throat, his thumb tightening. "Do you have any idea how long I've waited to have you again? To feel this skin." His hand tightened again, not so hard as to keep her from breathing, but enough to sting. She had never been treated with anything but tenderness before, and this ferocity should have scared her; instead, it excited her more. Pushing out her chest, she leaned forward, nipping at his lower lip.

His hand still around her throat, he pulled back, a fire behind his eyes. "You have no idea what I'm going to do to you. I'm going to fuck that sweet pussy. You'll be begging to come, but I won't let you. Not until you say you're mine. Not until you cry for it."

"We can't do that here," she urged. "The flight attendants are right there."

With a wicked glint in his eye, he got up, pulling the curtain shut between where they were seated and the rest of the crew. Returning to her, he tipped up her chin. "If you don't want them to know what we're doing, then you better be completely." He pulled her mouth in for a kiss. "Wholly." He kissed her again. "Quiet."

Her core pulsed with a need for him as all her reason fell away with one last try. "We can't have sex on a plane."

"Not unless you're silent."

Theo's kisses rained down her neck, his teeth scraping against her skin. His hands pushed up her dress, lopping his fingers around the side of her underwear and pulling them off. She let out a low moan as he exposed her to the air.

"Shh," he chided, a knowing smile on his face. "Silent, or I have to stop."

On the other side of the curtain, she could hear the flight attendants gossiping in low tones about someone.

He slid a finger over her entrance, teasing her. "God, you are drenched for me. You want my cock, don't you? You want to be filled up."

Writhing on her seat, she nodded at him. Easing a single finger in, his thumb brushed against her clit. "I'll give you my cock, but first you need to come all over my hand."

He eased a second finger inside her, putting pressure on the spot that shot pleasure sparks through her body. With his fingers moving inside her and his thumb circling her clit, she edged closer to release. The low roar of the engine and sporadic laugh from the other side of the curtain made the sensation of Theo touching her all the more thrilling. With his free hand, he pulled down the front of her dress, freeing her breasts. Taking one in his mouth, his tongue circled her bare nipple. Then his teeth bit down, stinging her before he licked her again, before repeating the motion over and over, the sting of his teeth and tease of his tongue.

"I'm going to make you come so hard, and you can't make a sound."

With the sensation of his fingers inside of her and scrape of his teeth against her nipples, the crest came over her, electricity sparking all over her body.

"That's it. Let me see it." His voice was low, hushed, as he watched her fall apart.

"Teddy—" she hissed, grinding against his hand as she came. Her breathing hitched, and she held his face to her breast, needing more, to the point of pain.

He pulled out his hand, the absence of him filling her, causing an ache. "I told you; you can't make a sound."

Bringing his forefinger up to his mouth, he licked it clean, his eyes on hers. "You taste so good on my tongue. Here." His middle finger tapped her lower lip, her juices wet on it. "Taste yourself."

She opened her mouth, sucking his fingers clean. She could taste herself, the smooth flavor of her arousal. Hollowing out her cheeks, she sucked harder, watching as his eyes lit up at
the sight.

"You like that, don't you?"

She hummed around his fingers, nodding her head. Reaching between them, she grasped at the front of his jeans, unzipping him and pulling out his cock.

The tip was swollen, a single drop of wetness glistening in the overhead light. She had never really enjoyed giving oral before, seeing it as a necessary part of a sex life, but nothing that gave her any pleasure. And she had never done it unprompted.

Placing both hands on his chest, she pushed him back until he was seated. Taking his cock fully out of his pants, she pumped her fist down the length of it. He hissed as her tongue swirled around the tip. The salt tang of him on her tongue was incredible. Sucking him into her mouth, she savored the feel of his hard length on her tongue.

"Look at you taking my cock, like a good girl."

His hand rested on the top of her hair, pushing her to take him deeper.

His cock hit the back of her throat, and she gagged a little. Through teary eyes, she watched as his face screwed up and he cursed. The top of her dress was still down, and his fingers found her nipples. Even though she came a few minutes before, she knew if he kept going, she might come again from his fingers alone.

His hip moved with her head as he fucked her face. She had never felt so wild. Staring up at him through blurry eyes, she was in complete control of this man's pleasure, taking him exactly where she wanted him to go. She sucked harder, breathing deep through her nose.

Then he was pushing her shoulder, pulling himself out of her mouth. "The only place I'm coming is inside you." Before she could blink, he had her on her back on the floor. The carpet of the plane was thick on her bare back as he lined himself up at her entrance and drove himself into her. She let out a quick shriek as he filled her up. The bare feel of him inside her. The scrape of the luxury carpet on her back and sweat beading at her hairline.

"Fuck, your cunt feels so good. See how you take me?" On his knees, he leaned back, watching as his cock slid in and out of her. "See how you fit me? No one else."

His grunts as he thrust into her were getting louder. There was no way they didn't know what was going on the other side of the curtain.

At that moment, she didn't care if the flight attendants heard her; she came around him, her cry shuttering and high. She felt him come a moment later, filling her up. Her dress still bunched around her middle, he collapsed on top of her.

"So much for quiet," he joked, pressing a kiss to her bare shoulder.

Chapter Eighteen

Theo

Once they were able to pick themselves up from the floor to put their clothes back on, Mattie fell asleep somewhere over Northern California. Arriving in Los Angeles, a pressure formed in the middle of his chest at the knowledge that he was back. He had called L.A. home for over a decade; the city had been good to him in a way that was a rarity. He knew every day, people showed up in the city, looking for fame; he was a lucky man to find it. When he first moved to the city, he loved the heat, the way the salty air by the ocean felt so different from the sharpness of Cape Rose. He loved the sounds of the city bustle, the shouts of people, and the roar of cars. He didn't even mind the traffic, though he complained about it as much as any other Angeleno, he had made the area his home, but walking onto the tarmac with Mattie didn't have the same sense of anticipation it once held.

To have Mattie appreciate his world would help her understand his life now. Having her come at all was a big step, but he had a sense she was holding back. He watched from the car as her ex-husband glanced at him when they left. Theo knew he had some gains to make with Mattie still, but that was between him and Mattie. Sure, Jay seemed like a nice enough guy, Mattie never said a bad word about him; in fact, the adulation was annoying. Jay was a good father, Jay gave her the house when they divorced, Jay this, Jay that.

The man was everything Theo was not. He had no idea how to be domestic. Mowing the lawn or making lunches. Going to an office and sitting behind a desk. He never wanted that life for himself, but it was Mattie's. The little goodwill he got from taking Kamari wouldn't last long. He was going to prove himself again to compete with her ex. So, he would use what he had, which Jay didn't.

His fame, his money, and yes, his sexual prowess. Their time on the plane was by far the hottest thing he had experienced. He had been racking up miles on the Mile High Club for years, but never like that. Normally it was a quickie in the bathroom, never on the floor like an animal, only a thin curtain between them and the crew. He intended on waiting until they got to his place, but seeing her across from him, her thin cotton dress and sensible sandals, her curls wild around her head...he was overcome.

Making sure to tip all the crew generously when they landed, for what was going to be an eventful trip...he knew this company was discreet, so he wasn't concerned about their exploits getting out; nevertheless, no one wants to hear someone having sex.

Bleary-eyed, Mattie followed him off the plane and into the waiting car Beatriz had left for them. A brow raised, Mattie eyed his sports car with trepidation. "Will our luggage even fit in this?"

Theo took the keys from the concierge, sliding him a hundred.

"Should. Normally, the women I have in this car are packing lighter than you." Mattie narrowed her eyes at him. "I don't know if I want that explained."

Beating the concierge to the passenger side door, Theo held it open, holding a hand out for Mattie to get in. She slid into the leather seat, holding her purse in her hands, and looked around. "Where do I put this? There's no room."

Theo slid into the driver's seat, grabbing her purse from her hands and setting it in the small space behind her seat. "Most girls who get in this car aren't coming over for an overnight trip."

Frowning, Mattie turned away from him. "Charming, Theodore."

He started the car, listening to the telltale roar of high horsepower. A different rumble sounded inside the car, and Mattie grimaced. "Hungry?"

Though it was in the wrong direction from his condo, he drove her to the best place he knew. He had asked Beatriz to stock his fridge up with groceries for his return, but he wasn't sure what she bought, or how to cook them.

When he sent the list, his assistant sent him a string of GIFs of confused people. It had been a long time since he cooked for himself.

Upon parking, Theo went to the passenger's side of the car and opened the door for Mattie, extending his hand to help her out of the low vehicle. Standing beside him, she raised her hand to her forehead, scanning the old building.

"This is not at all what I was expecting when you said you wanted to take me to the best breakfast place."

Dot's diner was a hole-in-the-wall place that sat on a pier. He had been coming to Dot's for years, before he got famous, before the tours and fans. He introduced the diner to Nathan and Keller, who said Dot reminded him a little too much of his Avó, begging off. Theo never had the chance to meet Keller's grandmother, but if she was anything like Dot, he could see his apprehension. Nathan, on the other hand, loved the place. They didn't have to worry about getting spotted—the food was cheap when they were broke and the atmosphere anonymous when they weren't. The sea-ravaged sign beside the door showed it had been repainted at least a dozen times. Stepping over a pile of empty beer cans, he held open the old wood door. "What's the matter with this place? I like it. It reminds me of my uncle's place."

Mattie's face softened as she glanced around. "I can see it. Same metal creamer pitchers and everything."

Dot, the owner, poked her head out from the kitchen and narrowed her eyes at Theo, barking, "You know where to sit."

In the corner beside the window, Theo pulled out a chair for Mattie before taking the one opposite her. There was only one other table occupied in the place, held by two older men. A young woman hurried out from the back, carrying two menus, her curly black hair held back with a big clip. "Hi, Theo, coffee?"

Theo looked at the young woman and smiled big. "Absolutely, Lola, I'd love some." He motioned to Mattie.

Mattie scanned the laminated menu before nodding at Lola. "Yes, coffee would be great."

When the young woman left, Mattie looked around, and Theo watched as she took it all in. "Your uncle's place didn't have this view."

"Not unless you count the front of the auto dealership a view, no."

The young woman returned with a gold coffee pot and turned over each of their ceramic coffee mugs to fill. After she finished, she pulled an envelope out of her apron pocket. "Hey, I showed my grandma, but since you're here, I wanted to show you, too."

The girl handed the paper over to Theo, whose eyes darted over the words.

"Caltech. That's amazing, Lola. Congratulations. You should be proud of yourself."

The girl beamed at Theo. "I am. It's nice, because it's not so far from Grandma if she really needs me."

"What did I tell you?"

"Focus on school and my education, and forget about dumb boys."

"That's right. They're not worth it."

Dot came out from the back, a plate in each hand. "Dolores, what did I tell you about bothering the customers?"

"It's just Theo, Gran." She turned back to them, smiling. "I'll let you get back to your menus. I wanted to tell you, since you've been so encouraging."

The girl left, and Matilda looked over at Theo with an inscrutable gaze.

"What was that?"

Theo took a sip of his coffee. "What? Lola?"

Matilda raised a brow. "Yeah. You out here giving advice to underaged waitresses now?"

Theo shrugged. "I like her, she reminds me of someone I know. Someone who for a long time I hoped had focused on her school and her future. Although I'll admit, a part of me hoped she didn't forget about one dumb boy."

Mattie's cheeks colored as she stirred her coffee. "I didn't forget a thing."

The older woman came by, her hands on her hips. "Where's your trouble-maker friend?"

Theo grinned up at her. "Nathan is traveling with his wife right now."

"Breaking chairs and breaking hearts," she grumbled. "That boy is lucky he didn't hurt himself worse the last time you two were here."

Theo laughed. A few months before, they got their routine breakfast after a run on the beach. Like every time before, Nathan was tipping himself back in his chair, and Dot was yelling from across the restaurant for him to quit it. Then the chair leg splintered and Nathan toppled over.

Dot had thrown him a dishcloth and told him to clean up the mess he made. Nathan replaced every chair in the restaurant after that.

"I think his ego was the broken one." Tho smiled.

Dot sniffed at the comment, then looked at Mattie. "Who's the beauty?"

"Dolores, my darling, this is my Matilda."

"Your Matilda?" Dot looked Mattie up and down speculatively. "You a singer or what-not, too?"

"No, I'm a lawyer."

Dot snorted. "Not sure that's any better."

"I'm sure many would agree with you. But we all have to earn our keep somehow, right?"

Theo watched the exchange with glee. Mattie didn't seem intimidated by the stout proprietress. They ordered their food and were left alone. This was the side of him he wanted her to see, the part that was still down to Earth, the part that helped others. He knew he had a long way to go to be on the same level as her ex, but it could be a start.

They chatted about their lives, Mattie telling him stories about her college days, of parties and sleepless nights studying. He told her about his years of traveling in a van with the guys and Eloise, making barely enough to pay for the gas before they got their big break. He told her about the thrill of performing in front of people, the way the heat from the lights energized him, the joy of hearing your words sung back to you by thousands of people.

When the check came, he paid quickly, leaving a hundred-dollar tip. With a last glance at the small diner he adored, he walked Mattie to his car, helping lower her into the seat. His phone rang as he approached the driver's side door.

"Hey, Tamara."

As was her style, his manager got straight to the point. "I heard you're back in town, I had Beatriz add a thing at the Piedmont. Cocktails and ego-stroking industry thing, which you're so good at."

"I can't. I'm busy."

"None of your bandmates are playing ball with appearances right now, in their lovesick daze. I need you to pick up the slack. You're in town, and it'll be two hours out of your night. Take a break from the clubs and the groupies to shake some hands."

Through the window, he saw Mattie cross her legs, the tanned length he wanted to touch the moment he got to his condo.

"I have plans tonight."

"Plans?" she barked into the phone. "What plans? I checked with Beatriz, and you have nothing on your schedule."

"Maybe because I don't need to tell my assistant every detail of my love life."

On the other end, his manager barked a laugh. "That's rich. You are the least discreet person I've ever known when it comes to your escapades."

Grimacing, he switched the phone from one ear to the other. Being with Mattie made him want more than the same one-night stands and vapid conversations. "I can't make it."

Tamara's voice took on a firm tone. "Look, I wasn't going to say anything until we knew more, but Anton Dzik had been shopping around for collaborators for a rock musical. And he's going to be there tonight. If you went and made a good impression, it might seal the deal."

Anton Dzik was a legend on stage. He had countless Tonys under his belt and was responsible for transforming a self-help book into a commercial and critical hit. Gripping the phone, he thought about what this could mean for them. Having a musical based on their songs would mean not only an added level of financial security but a legacy.

His finger tapped a rhythm on the roof of his car. The party the next night would be more relaxed, people cutting loose and having fun. This was a work party, glad-handing and schmoozing. Mattie would hate it.

"One hour. That's all I can commit to. As I said, I have other plans tonight."

"Knew I could count on you." Tamara hung up without a goodbye. He cursed under his breath. This was exactly the sort of stuff he had to do for the band. As the face of it, he was the one being asked to these events, the meat offered up for deals. It was exhausting. Jerking his head to the side, his neck cracked. Only in L.A. for three hours and he was already getting a stress crick.

The ride was silent as they drove toward his condo. His mind was on the party that night, planning how to optimize his time with Mattie and still make the event.

Mattie was playing with the hem of her dress, her forehead wrinkled. "So, we have to go to this party tomorrow night, and they'll be a bunch of celebrities?"

Theo nodded. "Yeah, not A-list or anything, but a few B, mostly C."

"They'll be photographers?"

Switching lanes, Theo went around a sedan that was taking up the left lane. "A few. BMP always plans a good one."

"BMP?" Mattie wrinkled her brow.

"Yeah, Brenton Michael Phillips."

"The pop star. The one who sings 'Ride You All Night.'"

Theo wasn't a fan of the man's music, cringing at the name. Where was the poetry in songs like that? "The same."

"Teddy!" She slapped his legs softly. "You didn't tell me it was a party like that. I can't go to a party with Brenton Michael Phillips."

She started rooting around in her small purse for something before pulling out her phone.

"Of course you can. Are you worried he'll hit on you? Because yeah, that might happen, but it's no big deal. I won't let him corner you or anything. He's not that bad of a guy..."

"Hit on me?! Look at me, Theo," she huffed loudly, scrolling through her phone.

"What are you doing?" Out of the corner of his eye, he saw her pull up a travel website.

"Put that down. What's your deal?"

She tapped on—something, then began typing. "I need to go home, this was a mistake. I can't go to a party with a pop star."

"Why? You're sleeping with a rock star." He grabbed the phone out of her hand, tossing it into the back of the car. "I don't understand why you're freaking out. I told you I had a party to go to."

"Yeah, a party. I was picturing—God, I don't know what I was picturing. Not that."

He shot a sideways glance at her. "What do you think parties look like in

L.A.? Or my life, for that matter?"

Crossing her arms against her chest, she glowered. "I don't know. I tried not to think about it."

Flicking his turn signal, he took the exit ramp to get to his condo. "It's part of my job to go to these events. To be seen by the right people."

Mattie raised a brow. "And me? What am I supposed to wear to something like that?"

He pulled into the parking garage below his building, pulling up to the valet stand. "I told you; I'll take care of it. Someone is coming tomorrow before the party, to help you get ready."

Before they left, he had asked Ilsa for the name of someone who could help Mattie. Since Ilsa was a designer, she would know all the right people in the industry. Ilsa sent over a text that said, *I'm not doing this for you. I like Mattie too much to have her show up looking like a clown.* Then a moment later a second message. *No more than she already looks sticking with you.* With a middle finger emoji and contact for a Deja Gateaux. Nice to see his relationship with his friend's wife was making progress.

Mattie took a deep breath. "Maybe coming down here was a mistake."

Theo turned to face her, taking her chin in his hand. "I won't let anything happen to you. It's just a party."

"With celebrities."

"Yes, which I am. This is my life here, and I'd like you to experience it with me." *Forever.* He left that last part out but meant it the same. Getting out of his car, he handed the keys to the young valet driver.

Mattie climbed out of the car before he could get to her door, her arms crossed against her chest. "I don't like this idea anymore. I've seen the shows, I know what these people look like."

Theo came around to her side, setting his hands on her forearms, rubbing them as if he was warming her. "Are you comparing yourself to others right now?"

Pouting, her eyes darted around. "No, maybe."

Where she would be insecure, he had no idea. His idea of a perfect woman was Mattie from the moment he saw her dancing on that talent show stage thirteen years before. It had never wavered.

"I don't care about any of them. You'll be the only one I see." He wrapped his arm around her shoulder, pulling her to his side. "Come on, let's get you settled."

CHAPTER NINETEEN

Mattie

THEO WAS DELUSIONAL. How could he not understand how out of her depth she was?

The entire walk through the stark lobby of his building, she should have been admiring the large abstract painting in shades of blues adorning the walls and an oversized metal chandelier hanging from the high ceiling. A small café sat in the corner, with all-white chairs. All she could think about was the party the next night. In the heat of being near Theo, she hadn't given it more than a passing thought. Sure, she knew he was a celebrity. In theory. He didn't act like it. None of the others did. He was still so much the same; she was able to pass off the tabloid article as a blip, instead of an integral part in his life.

But now that she was here in the sunshine, it was becoming even more real. She was going to a party with famous people. Tastemakers and cover models. If the flight showed her anything, it was that the world treated Theo the celebrity differently than Theo the man. She liked the teasing man from the diner, but more and more she got the feeling that wasn't the Theo of L.A. He had someone park his car at his own apartment. He had an assistant who kept his schedule. Did he even pump his own gas?

She had no idea how to be with that man. She moved from population five thousand town to a population six thousand island. There was no way she wasn't going to stick out compared to the other guests at the party. While not fitting in fashion-wise was a concern, it was more than that. She didn't know how to interact with famous people, what do they talk about? Before she knew she had begun, she was half-gone to Theo. It was too late to turn back now, no matter how much she pretended to look up flights.

Theo waved at an older Asian woman behind a small desk. "Hello Gloria. How's my favorite saxophonist?"

"I got a show coming up next week with Francisco." She pushed her long salt-and-pepper braid over her shoulder.

He winked at her. "I'll make sure to post it on my stories for you."

"That would be wonderful, Mr. Blake. Last time you did that, we were able to book four more shows. Just don't go showing up and taking all the attention like you did that first time."

Theo placed a hand over his chest. "I learned my lesson. Spotlight on you alone." Theo placed a hand on Mattie's back. "Gloria, I'd like you to meet Mattie."

The woman raised a thick block brow. "Well, hello. This is a first. Mr. Blake, you've never brought a lady home with you before."

Theo smiled. "I was waiting for the right one."

"You take care of this boy, you hear me?" she scolded Mattie lightly.

"I'll try," Mattie offered, unsure.

Theo bid Gloria goodbye and led Mattie to the elevator. As they stepped into the mirrored space, she turned to face him. "You can't leave me behind tomorrow."

"I won't leave you alone." He chuckled as he pressed the button for the top floor and then slid in a keycard to make the elevator move. "Though I might have to use the bathroom at some point."

"I mean it. I have no idea how to act at an event like that. What do I have in common with anyone there?"

Theo chuckled. "It's just a party. They're people, the same as you. Talk about your garden or baking or Kamari."

"Baking? Do these people even eat?"

"Some of them, yes." His words got lost in her hair. "You are worried about everyone else at this party, when to me, you are the only one who counts."

She stepped back, and he matched her until her back was pressed against the mirror. Over his shoulder, she could see the strong expanse of his back as he reached down between them, holding her chin in his hand. "Look at me and hear me." His pupils dilated as he stared down at her.

He pressed a kiss to her lips, then pulled away.

"Only."

Another kiss.

"You."

Another.

"Matter."

"How long will it take for you to understand this?"

She gave him a quick smirk. "A few more kisses worth?"

With that, his mouth descended on hers. Her tongue matched his. Heat flooded through her body at his embrace, straight to her core. Her clit pulsed with need.

His hand slid from her throat down her body, pulling up her dress. His finger slipped past her underwear to part her fold. "Fuck, you're so wet. Always so ready for me, aren't you?"

She was enthralled with him, nodding. He slid two fingers inside her, and she thrust her hips until the heel of his hand pressed against her clit. She was so close, and it was only a minute.

"You make me lose my mind," he whispered in her ear. "I could take my cock out right now, and you'd be ready to take it, wouldn't you?"

She nodded again. She had never been so wild before. Her previous encounters had been in the confines of a bedroom, or if she was feeling especially frisky in the kitchen. With Theo, it didn't matter where they were her body craved him. But the idea of having all of him, uninterrupted for hours on a bed was too tempting.

"Stop, I bet there's a camera in here," she mumbled.

His teeth scraped against her throat. "Didn't seem to bother you on the plane."

Melting into his touch, the cold wall seeping into her back as he pushed into her. She could feel his hard length against her stomach. "Let's keep our voyeurism to a once-a-day maximum."

He grumbled as he pulled away, slamming his fist against the button, and the elevator moved again.

The need for release ached between her legs. When the elevator shuttered to a stop and mirrored doors opened, Mattie grabbed the front of his shirt pulling his face to hers. They tumbled backward into the hallway. Her shoulder hit something with a sharp corner, but she kept moving with him. His body flattened her against the wall, his kisses raining down her neck as she was pulling down his pants. Pushing her underwear to the side, he picked her up, holding her against the wall where he slid into her in a single fluid motion. With her legs wrapped around his waist, he fucked her. Faintly, she heard the sound of the elevator descending. They hadn't even waited until the doors closed to start.

Theo drove into her. With every thrust, she cried out louder.

"I can't wait," he hissed. "You feel too good around my cock."

He emptied inside her, the movement of him coming in her, driving her over the edge. She was an animal, only existing in the moment with him buried deep within her and the feel of his skin on hers.

Panting, he pulled back to gaze at her. "I'll never tire of this. You've ruined me."

It wasn't a love declaration, but in a way, it was more. You can love someone and still hold on to yourself in the process. But how she felt—this ever-present fever to be near him, was ruining her too. She craved everything with him.

"We're in ruins together."

He helped her slide down the wall, adjusting himself back into his pants. Her dress fell over her legs as she steadied herself on shaky legs.

A low tap sounded down the hall, and they both looked at the same time to see a young Latina woman emerge from a room, her hair in a messy top knot and red cheeks.

With the hand holding a cell phone, she waved her hand. "Uh, Hi, Theo."

After awkward introductions, Beatriz showed them the groceries Theo had requested. While they were talking Mattie walked around the large open living room. She caught little snippets of words but was too distracted by Theo's place to follow the conversation. A floor-to-ceiling window opened onto an oversized patio. Stepping out, she was awed by the expensive view in three directions. Glad that she wasn't afraid of heights, she leaned over the railing to look at the rooftop pool several floors down. A thin white woman was sunning herself on a striped chair, while a tanned man swam in front of her. Even from multiple floors up, she could see how thin the woman was, the space between her thighs, and the way her breasts were unnaturally high on her chest. Mattie touched her own breastbone. She was lucky not to have to worry about sagging after having Kamari, but that also meant she was filling out bikinis in an eye-catching way. She had known the people there would be beautiful. Even Theo's assistant was gorgeous, with her flawless bronze skin, high cheekbones, and amber eyes.

Adjusting the straps of her sundress, she suddenly felt particularly dowdy. The dress had seemed soft and carefree when she put it on that morning, but now she wasn't sure why she picked it. Not that any other item in her closet would give her a flat stomach and great cleavage.

Heat from Theo soaked through her back as he came behind her, wrapping his arms around her waist.

"Nice views," she commented.

"Are they? I don't spend a lot of time out here."

Mattie turned her head to look up at him. "Are you serious? Then why buy the top floor condo, if you don't want the views?"

He shrugged. "I don't know. The location, it looked cool."

She didn't know too much about real estate, but a condo like this must cost a hell of a lot of money for something that looked 'cool.'

"You've come a long way from that twin mattress in a back room, haven't you?"

Holding her tighter, he rested his chin on the top of her head. "And you're the only one who truly knows that."

From the living room, Beatriz called out, "Theo, I've got to head out for soundcheck. You need anything else before I go?"

He turned to face her. "Nope, I'm good, I know you'll kill it tonight." Glancing down at Mattie, he explained, "Beatriz is a comedian."

Beatriz bit her lip. "I'm just starting out. Haven't booked anything real big yet."

"Matter of time, and we both know it. I'll have to find a new assistant soon."

Beatriz ignored Theo's compliment, turning to Mattie. "Oh, I almost forgot. Theo said you might like this, so I picked one up for each of you."

Mattie accepted the black-and-white marbled drink carefully. It looked almost too pretty to drink.

"It's a potion purity smoothie."

"It's black," Mattie said, turning the cup in her hand.

"The charcoal. It's not my thing, but people swear it's worth the price tag."

Mattie took a tentative sip, tasting bananas and raspberries. It wasn't bad. "How much is it?" She took another sip.

"Twenty-two dollars."

Mattie almost spit black smoothie on the floor, swallowing down her shock.

Beatriz shrugged. "Like I said, not my thing, but Theo thought you'd like it."

When she left, Mattie turned to Theo. "Why would you tell your assistant I wanted a twenty-two-dollar smoothie?"

"I thought you liked smoothies? And it has raspberries in it, I thought—"

"Yeah, but I don't need something that's the cost of a month's worth of coffee beans. You have lost it." Mattie took another sip. Now that she knew how much it cost, she wouldn't waste a single drop. Who knows when she'd get something like that again?

Theo seemed to ignore her annoyance. To him, something like this was nothing. Mattie didn't have to scrounge for money or anything, but she certainly wasn't this level of rich.

He pressed a kiss to the top of her head. "Why don't you take a bath, while I get through a few calls I've been putting off." Theo set his hand on the small of her back. "Come on, I'll show you where you can get cleaned up."

After getting out of an oversized tub that sat in front of another floor-to-ceiling window, Mattie wrapped herself up in one of Theo's huge white towels. They were fluffy and pristine. She doubted these towels had been used to clean oobleck off the floor. She wasn't sure what Theo's plans for their night were going to be, so she pulled on some leggings and a tee shirt, figuring if they were going out, she could change. Walking back into the living room, she caught sight of Theo on the phone. He was listening, nodding his head, and interjecting with "Okay" and "Uh huh."

Mattie walked to the long bookshelf on the wall. Most of the shelves were taken up by records, but half of one was books. Turning her head to read the titles, she stilled as her fingers landed on the worn spine of a familiar book. The paper cracked away from the glue that held it together, but she recognized the yellowing book. She pulled it from the shelf, the same musty smell to the pages as when she let him borrow it years before.

She heard him say goodbye and put the phone down on the coffee table before joining her at the shelf.

"You still have it," she murmured. Her gaze strayed from the book up to Theo's solemn blue eyes. "I can't believe you kept it."

"You gave it to me." He stepped forward, placing his fingers on the top of the book, centimeters from her own. "That and the brooch were the only things I took with me when I left. It was all I had of you."

She stared down at the orange and yellow sun on the cover. It was one of her father's books, one out of hundreds. "It's just a musty old book. Honestly, a bit pretentious and overwritten, if you ask me."

"To me, it was everything." His finger brushed the side of hers, heat laying a trail where he touched her. "I named the band after this book."

Her breath caught as she looked from where his warm hand touched her back up to his face. "I didn't know that."

He paused, withdrawing his hand to shove them in his front pocket, his face shutting down, as if he had said too much.

Mattie set the book down on the shelf between a biography of Elliott Smith and Big Mama Thornton. The rest of his place was sparse, decorated with an almost clinical sense of design that didn't fit Theo at all. Pointing at a black-and-white painting on the wall, she said, "Your art is so macabre."

He glanced up at the painting. "Is it? I wouldn't know anything about it. My interior designer said the artist is some up-and-coming gal. Apparently, Eric Clapton has one."

Mattie frowned up at the painting. "It doesn't fit you."

Theo shrugged. "I don't know enough about art to say what would."

Mattie glanced at him. She had the sense that he had been directed to become this other person for far too long. "I always pictured you in a big house with lots of plants or something, not this mausoleum. With landscapes or something."

"Like a Kinkade? That's pretty corny, isn't it?"

Mattie pursed her lips as she thought. "What's wrong with a little corny? Why does everything have to be so dreary to be artistic?" She paused, gaining steam. "Besides, maybe I like corny Theo. Maybe I missed that part of you. I'd rather have a genuinely corny man beside me than the kind of man with whatever this gruesome picture is on the wall."

Theo considered her for a moment before walking to the wall and pulling on the painting. She saw the muscles in his back working as he wrenched it from the wall. As it tumbled down, it brought with it a small chunk of the wall, pieces of plaster falling to the ground. "It's gone."

Working to shut her mouth in shock, she stepped forward. "Did you do that for me? Because I was only half-joking. I didn't want you to rip a hole in your wall because I don't like your picture."

He shrugged. "It's fine. I'm sure I can hang up a nice seascape instead. You know, the ones with the orcas and dolphins you buy at a mall kiosk?"

"Now you're making fun of me."

"I would never." He put a hand over his heart. She frowned at him, narrowing her eyes. "Okay, maybe a little I am."

Theo led her to the kitchen, where he had plated their dinner. A single tapered candle sat on the island. Mattie whistled low, surveying the romantic dinner. "Wow, you were busy while I was in the bath."

Scratching the side of his neck, Theo gave a sheepish smile. "It's takeout. I asked Beatriz to pick it up for us. All I did was reheat it."

Mattie touched the edge of the candlestick. "Still, Italian food, candlelight. It's pretty impressive to a girl like me."

As she sat in the chair, which Theo pulled out for her, he bent down and pressed his lips to the back of her neck, breathing in her scent.

They settled into their meal, chatting about their trip, Theo making jokes about the traumatized flight attendants and even more traumatized assistant. Theo assured her that Beatriz had seen far worse behavior from him, a tidbit Mattie didn't want him to expand on.

As she finished her meal, Theo glanced at the clock on the stove. "I have to run out for a quick errand. It shouldn't take too long."

Mattie sat upright, her brow furrowing. "Right now? We just finished dinner."

"Yeah, it's a quick thing my manager needs me to do. I'll be back as soon as I can." He got up, grabbed her plate, and dropped a kiss on the top of her head before leaving her alone.

Curled up on the couch, with her legs tucked up, she flipped through his channels. He had every streaming service there was, including one for exclusively romance movies. When he came by to tell her he was leaving, he was now in a suit.

"You're running a work errand in a suit?" she asked.

Nodding, he adjusted the button on his sleeve. "Yeah, a quick thing. I won't be long." He bent down to kiss her.

"Ah, I don't want to go," he whispered against her mouth.

"Then don't, stay here with me." She wrapped her arms around his middle, pulling him closer.

He grimaced, shaking his head. "I have to. I'm sorry, I promise, one hour max and we can spend the rest of the night doing whatever you want."

Dressed in her silkiest nightgown, she felt him slide into the king-sized bed beside her. Staying perfectly still, she opened one eye to glance at the small clock on the wall. He had been gone for six hours.

"You awake?" he asked, his voice slurring. She could smell liquor on him; it made her stomach churn with nausea.

When she didn't respond, he pressed a kiss to her bare shoulder, then turned the other way, his breathing turning to a light snore in a matter of minutes.

She wasn't sure she liked this version of Theo.

Chapter Twenty

Theo

AT SOME POINT BETWEEN the third canapé and his second rye, Theo was able to sit down beside Anton Dzik. From there it was foolish to leave before building a rapport with the producer. So, it was another canapé, and then Anton insisted on introducing Theo to a choreographer friend of his, and then another bottle was opened. Before he knew it, the hour was late, and his cheeks were hot, the way they always were when he had too much to drink. Anytime he would check his phone for the time and start planning a graceful exit, someone new would show up, shaking his hand and asking him questions. His cheek hurt from smiling, and the pants he picked out were a little too snug on his waist.

The condo was dark and quiet when he stumbled down the hall to his bedroom. He had hoped Mattie would stay up for him, but as his blurry vision showed him, it was the middle of the night. Coming to the edge of the bed, he shed his suit, tossing the clothes on the floor. He could make out Mattie's tawny bare shoulder and a thin silk strap in the moonlight.

"You awake?" He slowed his words down to sound as sober as possible. He watched as her breathing never changed. Their first night together, and she was already asleep. His lips brushed her skin then he rolled over onto his side, his mind whirling with the possibilities the party had offered him, before falling asleep.

THE MIDMORNING LIGHT WAS shining rudely on his face, and even without opening his eyes, he felt the headache scraping against his skull. He couldn't even remember the name of the liquor Anton brought out the night before, only that he had too much of it. Hangovers weren't a new thing for him; he spent almost every morning of every tour hungover, only getting back semi-human a few hours before he was needed for sound checks. But since he saw Mattie again, he hadn't drunk more than two drinks in a single night. His head fuzzy, he rolled over to scrape a hand over his face. His beard needed a trim, but that was the least of his worries.

He had no idea how Mattie would react to him being gone the night before. He wasn't used to being beholden to another person. While he had his wild nights with the guys in the band, they wouldn't give him a hard time. Only Eloise tried to get him to rein it in, and that was more to keep on schedule for their events than for his sake. Even with Aria, he didn't care if he was out late when he said he'd see her.

Beside him, Mattie was still sleeping, her long, dark hair covering her face. The strap of her nightgown had fallen over her shoulder, and her legs were curled up to her chest. As quietly as he could, he slid from the bed and padded out to the kitchen.

He had no idea if she would be upset with him; she didn't look happy when he left the night before, but they had never talked about what the expectations were between them. They did a surprisingly paltry amount of talking, in fact.

Grabbing as many ingredients as he could carry, he began to make breakfast. He slammed a painkiller down with a cup of coffee, the acidity churning in his empty stomach. He should have eaten a few more of those little bread and tomato things, and a little less of the whiskey.

As he was putting whipped cream on the raspberry pancake, Mattie walked into the kitchen. He opened his mouth to say something, and she shook her head at him, anger in her eyes. Skirting around him, she opened cabinets, rummaging around until she found a mug. She held it out to him. He took the mug and filled it the way she liked it. Gripping the mug in both hands, she walked away from him across the large marble island and sat on a stool.

Theo opened his mouth. "Mat—"

She put up a finger as she took a long sip of the coffee, her eyes shut. Biting his lips, he waited for her.

Once she had finished half her cup, she set it down on the counter. "Your *errand* ran late last night," Mattie said, venom in her voice.

Theo set her plate down in front of her. "Um, yeah. A bit longer than I was expecting."

Mattie sniffed, staring down at her food. She waited a long time to talk; when she did, her voice was firm. "Do you think I'm an idiot? I will not be made to look foolish, Theo."

"No! Of course not! I know, I would never—"

"So why would you tell me it was an errand, when you went to a party?" Before he could say anything, she slid her cell phone across the counter to him, the page opened on a news site.

Sit here by Me: The Internet's source for anonymous gossip and blind items
Out on the Town, all the nightlife worth talking about

Between a picture of action star Duke Edgar beside his much younger fiancée, Anastasia, and members of the girl pop group Infinnitee was a picture from the night before. Theo was wedged between Anton and the socialite and handbag designer Devlin Teague. While he knew nothing happened with Devlin, the papers could spin this if they wanted to. That was the way of celebrity. If two good-looking single people were seen talking once at a party, they could spark speculation for months. He didn't even remember there being a camera there, but it didn't matter. There he was, in his pink-cheeked glory, a glass of whiskey in hand - and all too close.

He slid the phone back to her face down, not wanting to see it.

"Those the kinds of errands you run around here? Because I have to say, mine look awfully different." She pushed the plate away from her and took another sip of her coffee.

"This was a work errand. That guy, Anton Dzik, he's interested in collaborating on an upcoming project. He was only in town for a few days."

Mattie scoffed. "So are we. Or I am. I don't know about you."

Theo set his coffee mug down, dread pooling in his stomach. "What do you mean you don't know about me?"

"What do you think I mean? Your life here, I don't understand how I could ever fit in with it. Late-night meetings over drinks, paparazzi, and socialites. I go to bed at nine-thirty on Saturdays. How could I ever fit in a life like that, with a man like this?" Picking up the phone she motioned to the picture. "I mean, I don't even know that man. He's not you."

Theo rounded the corner, taking her phone out of her hands and setting it on the counter. Cupping her face in his palms, he led her gaze up to his. "Hey, that picture, that stuff last night. It's just stupid BS I need to do sometimes. It's not who I am. You know me."

Her brows furrowed as she looked at him, he could see her resolve crumbling and the indecision behind her eyes. "Do I, though? I mean, the past month back home has been great, but Teddy, it isn't your real life. This is. Parties and celebrities and thin women in bikinis outside your balcony. I don't see how I can fit."

His mouth came over hers. He didn't always have the right words to get her to understand, but his touch knew her, could convince her that they were right, that he was the only one for her. Burying his hand in her hair his lips found hers. At first her arms hung down by her sides, unsure. But then she brought her hands up to rest on his back, pulling herself flush with his body. Her legs fell open and he stepped into her, kissing her harder. Pouring all his devotion into the kiss, he hoped it was enough.

Breathless, he pulled away to gaze down at her. "You fit because having you back is the only thing that matters to me. I'll make you fit." His hand on her cheeks, he rested his forehead against hers.

"I want that, too, but—"

He shook his head. "No buts. No nothing. I'm not losing you again, not over stupid parties or vapid socialites, or whatever that shit about girls in bikinis was." He pulled away, his hand going to the back of her neck, to hold her head steady to look at him. "I love you, you know that, right? I have never loved anyone but you."

Mattie's eyes filled with tears, her voice soft as she whispered, "I love you, too. I always have."

"Then we'll be okay. More than okay. I have you back, and I'm not letting anything change that." He motioned to her plate of raspberry pancakes. "Eat your breakfast. I made it special for you."

"I'm not that hungry." Mattie picked up her fork, scooped the whipped cream off the top, and set it to the side before taking a small bite of the pancake. "My stomach is in knots about tonight."

With a shake of the head, Theo took the fork out of her hand, scooping whipped cream on top of a large piece, holding it in front of her mouth.

"You're going to feed me, like some child?"

"There is nothing childlike about you. I need you strong for tonight. In fact, I need you strong to handle all the things I want to do to you in about..." He looked at his watch. "Fifteen minutes."

A quick swipe through the whipped cream, Mattie brought her finger up to her mouth, licking the digit clean. "Tell me about these things."

Settling in a chair beside her, he motioned to the plate. "I'll tell you one thing for every bite you take."

She complied, and he leaned forward. "First thing is, I'm going to push the strap of that nightgown down until I can kiss that little birthmark you have on your collarbone." His fingers moved above her skin but did not touch her.

"I'm going to mark you, right there, so everyone who sees it will know exactly who you belong to."

Mattie crossed her legs, straightening in her chair.

"By that time, you're going to want my hands on you, but I won't, not yet. Using my teeth, I'm going to take that nightgown off until you are bare before me."

A low sigh came from Mattie, her pupils large as she watched his hand move above her body.

"I still haven't decided which beautiful breast I'm going to lick first. The left or the right? The right one is slightly bigger, but the left one has that small freckle. I love them both so much."

Mattie watched him, her breathing quicker.

"You have to keep eating, darling."

Mattie scooped a large bite, little bits of whipped cream clinging to her upper lip. How badly he wanted to kiss that mouth, but not yet. Not until she was soaked for him.

"Once I've given both the attention they need, I'll move down your body. Kissing your skin until I reach the exact place you need me."

Matti was now fidgeting in her chair, her thighs rubbing together to his words.

"Then I'm going to reach my hand between your thighs, to see how wet you are. And then you'll get my tongue, licking you, fucking you until you're begging for my cock."

Mattie threw her fork down. "Fuck all this foreplay." Before he could do anything, she was astride him, her nightgown riding up on her thighs as she ground herself on his hard cock. Her mouth crashed against his, her kiss hard enough that their teeth knocked together. His hand grabbed her ass, pulling her closer to him. He could feel that she was bare under her nightgown, only a thin layer of cotton between them.

"I don't need all that. Just fuck me already." She was tugging on the front of his pants, trying to pull him out. Wrapping his arms around her waist, he picked her up, walking her into the living room. He set her down in front of the wide window overlooking downtown L.A. Pushing her against the glass, he pulled her nightgown off her shoulder, licking and sucking at the soft skin there until it began to bruise.

"Teddy, please, I need..." He came up, silencing her with his mouth, while his hands moved to her breasts. Flicking her nipples with one hand, he ground himself against her. Her groan was in their kiss as he tweaked and pulled to the point of almost pain. Her hands moved down his back, pushing his pants down to his ankles. He pulled away, a devious smile on his face.

"I'm going to fuck you, but I'm doing it my way." As promised, he kneeled before her, taking the silk between his teeth and pulling it down over her body, his nose skimming her soft skin. She watched him with large eyes. Cupping her left breast in his hand, he sucked her right one into his mouth, his tongue swirling around the areola, nipping slightly with his teeth.

Against him, Mattie began to murmur curses, her bare skin flushed. He moved to the other side, licking the soft skin there until she gasped.

His eyes on her face, he kneeled at her feet. Just as he knew it would be, her cunt was dripping. He dipped a finger inside her, bringing it to his mouth. "How are you even sweeter now?"

Her hands in his hair, she pushed herself against his face as he licked her seam. Sucking her clit into his mouth, his fingers worked inside her, to louder and louder gasps. He could feel her getting closer, see the familiar flush of her chest and tension in her face.

He knew if he kept up his pace, she would come, but he wanted to be inside her when she got there. Pulling away, he rose to his feet and turned her to face the window, pressing her against the glass. "Look down at this city. It's yours. If only everyone knew I'm fucking the most beautiful woman in the world."

"You're not fucking me yet." She thrust her ass back into him, a teasing smile playing on her lips.

Lining himself with her entrance, he slid inside her. One hand braced on the cool glass, the other on her hip, he drove into her, his balls slapping her clit as he moved faster. "Look out there, your beautiful tits smashed against the glass and my cock inside you. What would the people say?"

"Fuck me harder," she demanded.

Her dirty words, the chill of the glass against his fevered palm, and the tightness of her slick heat were driving him closer.

Wrapping a hand around her throat, he pulled her body up against his. "Tell me no one else," he demanded as he moved quicker, racing her to the peak. He slid in and out of her, her pussy slick. His balls clenched, he needed his release soon, but not before her. "Say it. No one."

"No one else," she gasped. "Never anyone but you."

In his hold, her head was tilted to face him, his hand still holding tight to her throat. "I love you."

Her hand moved from the window to hold the back of his neck, her lips finding his as he held her there. "I love you. I love you. I..." Her words fell as he drove himself deep, her pussy contracting around him as she came.

He came after her, with a groan, their bodies slackening. He caught her as her legs lost their strength. Turning her body around, he pressed her back against the window. Holding her tight around her waist, he buried his face in the nape of her neck. Her arms were wrapped around his shoulders.

"I love you so much," he whispered into her hair.

Holding his face in her hands, she pulled his gaze to hers. "As the rain?"

"As the rain."

Across the room, his phone chimed with a text. On jelly legs, they walked to the couch, where he sat Mattie down and covered her with a blanket before retrieving his phone. Glancing at the screen, he groaned. Time was getting away from him. He was going to need to get to the hotel in an hour if he didn't want to be late. Beatriz had arranged for the jeweler to meet him and Aria there at noon.

"I'm going to shower really quick. I do have another errand to run today, while you're getting ready."

Pushing herself up on her elbows, she narrowed her eyes. "Really? After all that?"

He stood up, pulling on his pants. "I promise this one is nothing like last night. You'll like this." He bent down to press a kiss to her head, ignoring the annoyed look on Mattie's face. She'd forgive him once she saw what he had planned.

CHAPTER TWENTY-ONE

MATTIE

WHILE THEO WAS IN the shower, Mattie considered joining him, but she was still annoyed. Once he stopped touching her, she could focus on how she felt. His leaving the night before stung; they had so little time together, and to be pushed aside for an industry party hurt.

She believed him when he said the event the night before was a work event; there were certainly networking events she'd attended through the years. But her experiences were maybe twice a year, not all the time. How much of Theo's life did these kinds of things take up?

Wrapped in a blanket, she padded into the bedroom, where she found her suitcase in disarray. Her nightgown was still lying on the floor of the living room. She wasn't sure what Theo's plans for her that day were. She pulled a sundress out of the suitcase. It wasn't fancy, but it would be comfortable. Pulling it over her head, she winced as it brushed against her boobs. Theo must have bruised her a bit with his touch. She looked down and didn't see any redness, but they were likely tender from their antics in the living room.

With the shower running in the other room, she grabbed her phone, calling Jay. He picked up after two rings and made quick small talk with Mattie before handing the phone off to Kamari, who liked to video call while playing with her toys.

In the grainy video call, she could see Kamari had built up a large wooden house that surrounded her small plastic horses. After asking how she slept and what she had for breakfast, Kamari told Mattie she went to a concert in the park the night before and that she danced so hard, she fell into someone's picnic blanket.

"I miss you, baby," Mattie said, touching the screen. While she had been away from Kamari for longer periods, she had never been in a different state than her daughter before.

"You, too, Mommy," she said absentmindedly before holding up a doll with close-cropped hair. "Look, I gave Apple Angie a new hairdo."

Mattie raised a brow. "Pretty." That doll was an expensive gift from Jay's aunt, but she wasn't going to meddle in that conversation. "Now, I'll be back in two more sleeps, okay? And you can call me if you need to."

"Okay, Mommy. I'll give you back to Daddy now." Kamari carried the phone to her father, who looked at the screen with a bemused face.

"How's Tinseltown?" Jay asked. "See any big celebrities yet?"

Mattie grinned. "I guess I will tonight. Theo is taking me to a party that Brenton Michael Phillips is hosting."

"Are you shitting me?" Jay asked. In the background, Suze called out *language*, and Jay waved her off sheepishly.

"No, I'm not. I had a bit of a crisis about it when I found out. I mean, me? At one of those parties?"

Jay cleared his throat. She could see him moving though the house and out the door to the front porch, where he closed the door behind him. "You had to know it was coming, though, right? I mean, I know you say you put up blinders about the guy, but you had to assume."

Mattie ran a hand over her face. "I know, in theory, sure. But to actually *go* to one is different. I'm scared I'm going to make an ass of myself. Plus, everyone here is unreal beautiful. The valet driver last night was prettier than me."

"Don't be insecure now, you never have been," Jay chided her.
"Well, that's because I was up there. Where everyone is normal looking. Here, it's unreal."

Pursing his lips, he shook his head at her. "Mats. Are you sure this guy is what you want? You've only been there for a day, and you're already having an anxiety attack about a party."

"It's one party, and then I'll be back in a few days."

"Is it? One party, I mean. What is this future going to look like for you?" His words sounded all too similar to Shea's. "I'm having fun. We're having fun."

"Fun," he repeated back, unsure.

She nodded. She wasn't about to tell her ex-husband they were already exchanging *I love you* or that being with Theo made her feel the way she did when she was eighteen.

In the bathroom, the water turned off. Mattie quickly said goodbye to Jay. She didn't feel anything she said was bad, but Theo didn't seem to understand Jay's role in her life.

Pulling her hair up in a messy bun on her head, she walked back to the kitchen, where she poured herself another cup of coffee. Opening the many cabinets, she was surprised to find most were empty. He had at least three times more storage space than her, but half of the kitchen items. It was surprising to see even a multi-million-dollar place could still be treated as a bachelor pad. The last time she saw a place with less than six forks was when she was in college. She took a sip of the coffee, but it soured on her tongue.

Sitting at the island, she rested her chin in her hand. It wasn't the lack of cutlery, or even him leaving the night before, that set her on edge. An overwhelming urge to cry clawed at her throat. Theo seemed to think all they needed to do was love each other, but she couldn't picture where she fit in this life. It was all so easy when she was in his arms, but the real world was so much more than that.

Freshly showered, Theo appeared in the kitchen, wearing a simple white tee shirt, pair of jeans, and black ball cap with "L.A." on it, pulled over still wet hair. He picked up her coffee mug, downing the rest.

She watched his Adam's apple bob up and down as he swallowed. Normally his beard was a shade darker than his hair, but with his wet hair, they were the same shade, the bit of red showing in the light of the morning. How many mornings like this could they have together? As much as she wanted to sit back and enjoy her time in the city, everything about this place was making her feel more disconnected.

The doorbell chimed through the condo, and Theo set the coffee mug down on the counter. "That must be Deja."

"Who, wha—" she started, but he left her.

When he came back into the room, he was trailed by a petite black woman with colorful locs. A rolling rack of garment bags pulled in behind her. Theo ushered her into the kitchen. "Thanks for coming on such short notice. Ilsa said you're one of the best. I didn't want to take her to a store, so—"

Deja put up a hand. "I get it. I appreciate the call, Ilsa's been good to me since I started my own business." Her amber eyes turned to Mattie. "You must be Matilda. I'm Deja Gateaux. Theo told me you two are going to a big party tonight? I'm here to help with getting ready."

Mattie nodded, glancing at the garment bags with trepidation. She hadn't been in town long, but if the woman by the poolside was any indication, she wasn't sure how well anything would fit her. "I have quite a few options, so let's get you situated and play dress up."

"Oh, I'm sure something I brought is—"

"No. It's not." Deja narrowed her eyes at her. "Trust me, let your man spoil you on this. You'll feel much better wearing something I brought." She turned to Theo, who was starting to follow them into the bedroom. "You stay out here. Finding the right piece can be a fraught time, so we don't need your commentary."

"I see Ilsa's been saying wonderful things about me," Theo muttered under his breath before giving Mattie a quick kiss and pinch on the butt. "I'll be back in an hour. Call me if she says anything rude about me."

Once behind the bedroom door, Deja laid the garment bags out on the bed, unzipping them. Inside were various fabrics in a dazzling array of colors. Deja touched an outfit, glanced at Mattie, then shook her head. "Nope, the Elie Saab isn't right."

"Are these going to fit me? I mean, I've heard about sample sizing and—"

Deja set a white, flowy dress down. "I would never bring anything over that wouldn't fit you properly. Now, as long as you don't mind off the rack, we'll have plenty to choose from."

"As opposed to what?" Mattie laughed.

She blinked at Mattie. "Made to order. I have a few couture pieces, of course. We don't have time for the special tailoring, is all, since the event is tonight."

The last item Mattie had tailored was her wedding dress, and it mostly was the hem being taken up.

"Off the rack is fine." She trained her voice to sound as nonchalant as Deja was.

"I looked you up a little on social media, to get your general vibe. Not a lot going on there, but I have a few ideas. I dig the Earth mother chic aesthetic you have; we can work with that."

"I don't know what half those words mean."

Deja pulled out a dress in cream, with flower embroidery. "Now, most people can't pull this color off, but with your complexion and that hair, I think it will look great on you."

Mattie held the dress out in front of her. It had a low-cut front, and the back was sheer material, the skirt fanned out full at the waist ending at her knees. Small embroidered flowers adorned the dress, as if growing from the material. "How am I supposed to wear a bra with this?"

"You aren't." Deja held up a roll of something taupe-colored. "Now go shower, the beauty team will be here in thirty."

Once the team was done with her beautification, Deja sent them out of the room to help her dress. The last time someone she wasn't sleeping with had seen her nipples was four years before, during a breastfeeding malfunction. This was decidedly more intense, though at least it wasn't in front of an olive sampler.

"Okay, we're going to get real up close and personal here, but don't worry, I've taped many a nipple; they all start looking the same to me. Now, arms up, to get the best lift."

Mattie put her arms up in the air as Deja applied the strips. True to her word, Deja was quick, but the tight application made her boobs ache. Not wanting to complain about the pain, Mattie kept her mouth shut. It felt a little strange as Deja was physically moving Mattie's boobs to smooth tape over them, but once everything was in place, she had to admit her breasts looked perkier than they had in high school.

"This is a miracle," Mattie remarked, staring down at her chest.

"Just be careful when you take them off, slather yourself with oil, and the adhesive should start breaking down and peel slowly. Don't hurt yourself."

It was decidedly not a sexy look, but the undergarments that make you look sexy with clothes were almost always different from the ones you wear by themselves. Shapewear and lingerie were two vastly different things.

Deja unzipped the dress, allowing Mattie to step into them. It was an odd feeling to be so intimate with a stranger, but Deja was so professional about the experience, she couldn't complain.

"How do you know Theo?" Mattie asked.

Deja pulled the dress over Mattie's shoulder, smoothing the fabric. "I don't, really. I used to work with Ilsa before I started doing this. She gave him my number. She's been my biggest supporter. I've gotten a few clients through her."

Mattie had only brief interactions with Ilsa, who seemed the epitome of icy blonde beauty, but Eloise seemed to adore her, so maybe there was more to her.

"Anyone I know?" Mattie asked, half-joking.

A mischievous gleam in Deja's eyes shone. "My lips are sealed."

"I hope people are as nice as you when I get to this party. I'm so out of my depths here. A few days ago, I was elbow-deep in my garden, pulling carrots, and now here I am, wearing a dress that cost more than I want to know and medical-grade tape on my boobs."

Laughing, Deja handed Mattie an earring. "I'm not going to lie; it will be a mix. People in the industry can be catty, sure, but from what Ilsa's told me, there are quite a few kind people, too. Everyone is insecure about something. And if they're rude, remember, you have something no woman in the industry ever had, no matter how much they tried."

"What's that?"

"Theo Blake completely wrapped around their finger."

Mattie felt her face get hot. While they had said the words, she couldn't help feeling like Theo was holding back from being completely committed to her. "You don't know that."

Deja stepped back, her hand dropping to her side. "I've spent a long time reading people; you have to for this work. Insecurities, wants, needs. Trust me, anyone can see it."

A wave of emotion came over Mattie, her eyes filling with tears. Taking a shuddering breath, she looked up at the ceiling, fanning her face. "What the hell? Why am I crying? What is going on?"

Deja was quick with tissues, dabbing them expertly under her eyes to maintain her makeup as best they could.

"It's okay, darling, I didn't mean to make you cry."

"It's not you. It's this town, or who Theo is here, and honestly, I don't even know him really. Like, I knew him before, but now I don't, and my daughter is back home, and I've never been this far from her before." Mattie took a long breath, inhaling in the way she had taught Kamari as a toddler when her temper ran loose. She could get through tonight. She had to, and then she could return to Manzanita and her life.

Chapter Twenty-Two

Theo

AS HE WALKED THROUGH the lobby of the upscale condo, he pulled his ball cap down over his eyes. The disguise wasn't the best, but it was the best he could do on such short notice. When Theo asked her for a favor, she had offered for the jeweler to come to her place instead.

Aria let the jeweler and a security guard into the room. The security guard took out a small key and unlocked the handcuff around his own wrist, and one on the suitcase. Theo watched as the jeweler set up his large velvet case on the coffee table.

The gleaming choices were astounding. Theo had never been a big jewelry guy, spending his money on instruments and old out-of-print records instead.

"What do you think?" Theo asked Aria. He knew nothing about engagement rings, and without Eloise there to help him, Aria was the next best option.

Aria glanced at the rings. "Oh, I've always been partial to an emerald cut, but they're all so beautiful."

"That one," Theo said, pointing out a single large solitaire on a delicate glittering band in the middle.

The jeweler glanced at the ring. "Ah, good choice. The stone is a seven carat F coloring and near colorless clarity, with an eternity band, with each diamond ethically sourced, as you requested."

Theo knew it was the right one. She deserved something large enough that there was no doubt how much he loved her; a reminder that he would take care of her for the rest of their lives. A message to anyone who doubted them.

"Does the lady want to try it on?" The man's eyes shot to Aria.

Aria laughed. "Oh, it's not for me. I'm moral support."

After signing some papers, the man placed the ring in a box and handed it to Theo with instructions to call the store after the proposal for a fitting. The security guard shut the case, handcuffing himself to it once again. Unlike his night with Anton Dzik, this took fifteen minutes. With absolution on his side, it was an easy choice.

Sitting back on the couch, Theo opened the small box to look at the ring. It was perfect for Mattie. He could already picture how it would fit on her finger.

"You're really done for over this one, aren't you?" Curling up beside him, Aria took the box out of his hand, snapping it open. "Holy shit this thing is huge. She's going to need to start pumping iron to carry this around on her finger."

"Don't get it dirty." Theo grabbed the ring back, closing it and shoving the box into his pocket. "And yeah, obviously I am."

"So, you're going to propose tonight?" Aria asked. "At this party?"

"Yeah, seems like the right time. Not in front of a bunch of people or anything, but after the party, I will."

"And if she says yes?"

"'If?'" Theo scowled. "Why wouldn't she say yes?"

Aria put her hands up in a defensive pose. "I don't know. It's a little fast, I haven't met her yet, so I'm guessing here."

"It's not fast. We've loved each other since we were kids."

Pursing her lips, she widened her eyes and shook her head. "Wow, okay. My whole point is, what's your plan after that? I mean, you live here, she doesn't. What about her work or her house? Didn't you say she has a kid?"

"Yeah, so?"

"So what's your big plan, big shot? Where will you live? Is she going to continue working? What about her kid?"

"I can take care of her and Kamari for the rest of our lives. She can do whatever she wants."

"And what is it you think she wants, Theo? A big diamond ring? A mansion in the hills?"

"She loves me."

Aria softened. "I don't doubt that. I've never seen you this lovesick...well ever, but all I'm saying is, I think you two need to have a real conversation before you start making plans for the future."

"You don't know anything about me or Mattie." Sitting up, he laid his hands on his knees, pushing against his legs. Why did everyone think they knew better about his relationship than him?

Aria sighed in resignation. "You're right. Maybe I'm a bitter single woman who knows nothing."

"You're twenty-five." He shot her an incredulous look.

"Yeah, a twenty-five-year-old who is now too old to play sixteen, and not sexy enough to play a twenty-five-year-old."

Theo wished he had platitudes to give Aria, but nothing came. What did he really know about being an aging teen star? He was in his twenties when they became popular, and while there was pressure for him to maintain his looks, he was only called again a handful of times. "You getting ready here?"

Aria shook her head. "No, I'm meeting Quinn at the Four Seasons." She checked her phone. "In fact, my car should be here in five. Walk me down?"

As they walked out the front door of the lobby, a photographer jumped out from behind a potted tree. "Aria! Theo, over here."

They both jumped before starting in the other direction. The photographer was closing in, the camera in their faces as they made their way to the street. A neighbor must have tipped him off that he and Aria were there.

"Are you two back together? What were you doing at Aria's? Can we expect to see you at Brenton Michael Phillips's party tonight? What do you have to say about the rumor..."

And so on, the questions blasted them as they tried to walk away. The photographer got closer, almost tripping Aria as she made it to her waiting car. Theo wrapped an arm around his friend, pulling her to his side.

His blood boiling, he wanted to turn around and punch the photog, but doing so would only lead to more press. Once Aria was secure in her car, he turned to face the photographer. "Back up."

The man snapped a few more pictures. "Hey man, I'm doing my job, the public loves you two."

Theo knocked on the roof of the car twice to let the driver know she was free to go. Once the car sped off, Theo sidestepped the photographer. "Hey man, can I get a comment? Just a few words."

"Fuck off," Theo said, hustling back into the lobby of the condos, where his car was in the parking garage. The photographer snapped a few pictures of him through the window but didn't pass the threshold of the private residences. Slapping the button to get to the underground garage. He hoped the paparazzi wouldn't chase him down; it had happened before.

Mattie was already skittish about the night, being trailed by paparazzi would only make things worse. Climbing into his car, he sent a quick text to Mattie that he was on his way back. It would be an hour and ten minutes before he got back to his place; not too bad with traffic.

After a quick change of clothes and brushing of his beard, he was sitting on the couch, waiting for Mattie to come out. When he got back, she was still in the guest room with Deja.

The door opened, and Deja walked out first, pushing the rack of garment bags. Then came a man carrying a leather square with a clasp on the front.

Finally, Mattie emerged. The cream-colored dress almost had a bridal feel to it, which suited him fine for the activities of the night. She wore sky-high heels, walking surprisingly well in the stilettos. Mattie looked to Theo, a small smile on her face.

"Well?"

"You look amazing." He reached her, cupping her cheek in his hands. He bent down to kiss her, and the man cleared his throat.

"No smudging the lips until she has been photographed, please."

Instead, his lips brushed the shell of her ear as he whispered, "you look so good; I don't want to leave. Want to strip you bare and sink into you right here on the floor."

She gave him a wicked smile. "As nice as that sounds, I did not get taped up like a children's birthday present to not go anywhere. You don't want to go to this party, that's fine, but you owe me a romantic night out."

He groaned. "You're right, I know. Plus, I promised Aria." He pulled away, the motion painful. "Okay, we'll make an appearance, two drinks max, then you and I are going somewhere special."

She worried at her lower lip, then seemed to remember what the make-up artist told her and stopped, pushing out her lips. "And you won't leave me alone, right? I don't know anyone, and this is my first time."

Guilt lanced through him. Leaving the night before had been a dumb mistake; now she was doubting his commitment to her. No longer. After tonight, she would know exactly how he felt.

"Of course."

"Promise?" she asked, her eyes heavy with doubt.

"As the rain."

Her face softened as she took his arm. In her heels, she was almost to his chin. Getting into the elevator, he placed a hand on her lower back. She clutched a small bag in her hands, so tiny he doubted it held more than her phone.

"I'm so nervous," she murmured. "What if your friends don't like me?"

He scoffed, "that's impossible. Everyone who knows you loves you."

"Tell that to Douglas and Wright," she mumbled. Catching his eye, she explained, "The last case I took to arbitration. It was ruled in my favor."

"See how smart you are? How can people not love you?" He pointed at their reflection in the mirrored wall of the elevator. "And look at you. You are beautiful in those little sun dresses, and you are beautiful in this—" He pulled at the hem of her dress; it was so tight, he could barely fit his hand up between her thighs. "In this, I want to rip it off you and have my way with you right here."

"Please don't. I can't imagine how much this dress costs."

"Who cares what it costs? I'll buy you ten more." He bent down, avoiding her mouth, his mouth finding her ear. "I want to give you everything you've ever dreamed of."

His fingers moved up her thighs, and her legs fell open for him. He reached up to find her completely bare.

"Nothing at all under here?"

His finger swept over her center, feeling the shiver in her body as he hit that sensitive area. "I bet I could get you to come before the elevator reaches the ground floor."

Her voice was a gasp. "I don't doubt that, since you didn't push the button to make the elevator move." Her hands on his chest, she pulled his face to hers. "As much as I would love that, we can't. This look took hours, and I won't mess it up before the party."

Pulling away, he slumped against the wall. "You are denying me so much."

She pushed the button with her finger, smirking at him. "You're the one who paid to have me all trussed up like this. So let me enjoy it. Who knows when I'll get to do this again."

"As much as you want. There's always a party or something to dress up for around here."

An uncertainty flashed in her eyes before she blinked at him. "Let's get through tonight first. And don't mess with the dress too much. This is only the second time I've worn something really nice in my life; the other time was for my wedding."

Theo laughed. "Not even prom?"

The smile on her face melted off. "Oh, I didn't go to that. Um..."

Internally, he kicked himself. Of course she wouldn't have gone to prom. That would have been only a few months after they broke up.

"It's no big deal, who needs sweaty slow dancing in a mid-rate hotel ballroom anyway."

"You did. You should have."

She smiled up at him, a little more nervous this time. "It doesn't matter anymore. I'm here with you now."

He pulled her close to him, tucking her under his arm. "And I'm not letting you go."

The elevator slid to a stop, and with his hand on the small of her back, he led her out to the waiting car.

Chapter Twenty-Three

Mattie

WHY DID SHE TELL him about prom? They had been having such a nice time in the elevator, and then she had to say that. She truly didn't hold her not going to prom against him. It wasn't his fault; she could have gone with friends, and it would have been fine. She was truly past all that now. Theo was back, and he loved her.

Only it made all those feelings creep into the back of her mind. Pulling up to the party, she saw a man who looked vaguely familiar walking into the building, to realize it was a sitcom star. A model she recognized from a national makeup brand was standing on the curb, gesticulating wildly to her friend and laughing.

This was Theo's life. Dread pooled in her stomach as the car parked at the curb. Theo got out, and she could see him walking around the car to let her out, waving away the driver to open her door. She was thankful for the moment of peace before the car door opened and she had to join the fete. Smoothing her sweaty hands on her skirt, she took a deep breath before walking beside him.

With his hand on the small of her back, he led her to the party. People they passed looked at them together, and she felt the way their eyes stopped at Theo, the admiring glances at his face, before looking to her as a shadow passed over them as they wrote her off.

She had never felt like she wasn't good enough to stand beside Theo. She liked the way she looked, from the swell of her hips to the little extra of her belly. Even her ears, which stuck out, only gave her personality. But here in this sea of people who looked stretched, polished, and plumped, she could see how much she stood out.

It wasn't his job to make these people think her beautiful and wanted. It was no one's but her own. With Theo's hand warm on her back, he bent down to whisper in her ear. "Don't you worry about a thing; I'll be right here the whole time."

That lasted through one and a half drinks. And really, Theo had kept his word; he introduced her to people, who gave little air kisses and had the smallest pores she had ever seen. The whole time, he kept his hand on the small of her back, bending down every few minutes to kiss her hair or whisper about how sexy she looked.

His eyes were light with drink and joy. He liked these parties, liked the people, the noise.

He leaned closer, his mouth finding her ear. "You look beautiful. I can't wait to take you home."

She began to relax. Taking tiny sips of her drink, she was surprised to find herself discussing the benefits of coconut oil versus sunflower oil in baking with the host of a reality show. Relaxing enough that when Theo excused himself to the restroom, she waved him away. She could handle five minutes on her own. She had negotiated contracts for years, stared down red-faced male lawyers who called her "Missy" in the courtroom, and studied for and passed the bar exam - all while juggling a newborn at home. These were people, albeit with smaller wrists and bigger boobs, but people nonetheless.

Beside the television host was a tall woman who looked vaguely familiar, but most of the people in the room did. She towered over her date, but that seemed to be more common to her than she was expecting.

"And where did you find that dress, your local JC Penney?" the woman asked, looking over at Mattie's dress.

Mattie glanced down at herself, recognizing the dig but not rising to it. "No, I think the designer is Zhivago or something. Have you heard of them?"

An almost line pinched at the corners of the woman's mouth. "Yes."

"I hadn't before, but I like it. I love gardening, so the flowers are a nice touch." Mattie motioned to the dress the woman was wearing. "I like your dress. An Ilsa Kruger?"

The woman sniffed, and the man beside her was stifling a laugh. "Yes."

"She's a good friend of mine, I recognized the design."

Calling Ilsa a friend was a stretch, but when Mattie was doing her research deep dive on her new neighbors, she looked up Ilsa's website.

The woman seemed to ignore Mattie's rambling. "Now, Mattie, where would we have seen you?" The woman looked down a perfectly sculpted nose at Mattie. Even with heels on, Mattie was short enough to see up the woman's nostrils to see zero nose hairs. She didn't even know that was something people did.

"Ah, unless you're looking into zoning laws in Washington State, then I doubt you've seen me before." Mattie laughed at her own joke, and the group around her gave single huffs of laughter, their smooth foreheads never moving. "Um, I'm a lawyer. Back home in Manzanita. That's outside Seattle...well, not outside, it's an island but..."

"A lawyer." The woman looked as if she was trying to arch a brow. Seriously, Mattie knew women who had Botox before, and they were still able to move their faces somewhat. What was this woman using? "How cute."

Mattie sipped at the sparkling water in her hand, her eyes darting around in the dark to find Theo. There was no way it took that long for him to use the bathroom. She was going to look for him. "Excuse me." She nodded at the woman and television host.

The room was massive, decorated to the hilt with fabric over flashing lights. A large gilded sign over the stage emblazoned with the words. "Happy I'm No One's Father's Day!" She had caught sight of the pop star, Breton Michael Phillips, earlier. He was thinner than she thought he'd be, almost gaunt looking, and shorter. Everyone aside from the women was much shorter than she expected. Walking through the crowd, she brushed past a couple who had recently been emblazoned on the front page of *Star* magazine, almost knocked into the last winner of a reality singing competition, and narrowly avoided stepping on the foot of a celebrity designer.

Theo stood at a small table, leaning toward a beautiful red-haired woman. As Mattie got closer, she realized the woman was Aria. His ex-girlfriend. He told her it was only a PR relationship, but still, the same cold tingle in her stomach wouldn't go away.

Aria Kingston was beautiful, somehow even more so in person than on television. She had never seen someone with wrists so dainty or eyes that bright a shade of blue. She matched Theo in every way.

Theo told her he was friends only with Aria, but what if he was wrong? If all those articles were to be believed, they dated off and on for years. How could Mattie compete with that? Aria didn't have stretch marks and student loan debt. She had seen the many photographs of them together. Theo's arm around Aria's petite waist, the way she leaned into Theo's body. The smile on both their faces as they looked at each other.

Even now, their heads leaned close as they talked, a level of comfort in their body language that conveyed trust. From a distance, Mattie watched as they stood together. While they didn't stop talking, their body language changed. Aria stood taller, and Theo angled his shoulders slightly, both their smiles growing larger. Mattie couldn't figure out what the change was until the bright light went off. A photographer walked by; catching sight of them, he stopped, bringing his camera up to take a picture of the two of them in conversation.

They were posing. When that picture was posted, it would look truly candid, like they were caught off guard, but they weren't.

Not only did they know exactly how to stand and pose for a picture, they made it look seamless. Mattie didn't even know what to do with her hands in pictures, and these two were posing effortlessly. A sick feeling rolled inside her.

She couldn't stand beside Theo in a place like this. Couture dress or not, she was a fraud.

Theo caught sight of her, his smile changing from a cocky photogenic one to a full grin that showed his gums a little too much. A genuine smile for her.

He pushed past the photographer, who was already moving away, looking for the next group of beautiful people to shoot. "Hey, I was about to come find you. Look who caught me on my way back to you."

With a hand on the small of her back, he led her over to Aria. "Aria, this is my Matilda."

Mattie put a hand out to Aria. "Hi, it's good to meet—oaf." Before she finished, Aria had wrapped Mattie up in a crushing hug.

Aria's face in Mattie's hair, she gushed. "It is so good to meet you finally. I wasn't sure you could be real."

Pulling away, Mattie gave a halfhearted chuckle, her eyes darting to Theo. "In the flesh."

Holding Mattie's hands tight, Aria kept talking. "Theo has told me so much about you, I thought he made you up in his head. I mean, who could be that perfect, right?" Aria laughed, a beautiful tinkly noise. How was her laugh gorgeous?

Aria looked Mattie up and down, her eyes stopping on the hem of Mattie's short dress, where her thighs were sticking together. Mattie suspected Aria never had to wear special lace thigh savers to keep from chafing. Aria's thighs might not even touch each other.

"That dress looks amazing on you. I bet half the women in here are spitting mad seeing you in it."

Pressing a kiss to her ear, Theo whispered, "See, told you. You look beautiful."

Aria kept talking as if Theo wasn't there. "I bet Theo has barely said a word about me, he's so besotted."

Mattie studied Aria's face for a sign of her being cutting and found only a genuine smile. It was an odd feeling having someone she had only seen on the screen in front of her, telling her she was the lucky one, the loved one. "He's said all sorts of nice things about you. My niece is a huge fan of the show. She was devastated when Keegan cheated on Breslin. She cried during your breakup scene."

Aria wrinkled her nose. "Ugh, that scene was the worst. It was freezing cold, in the rain, a night shoot. And Travis was being a total dick because his boyfriend broke up with him, like, four hours before. He can be so unprofessional. Like, I get it, you're all heartbroken, but if I had to wait another hour in the Vancouver cold for him to cry it out, I was going to lose my shit. Then they got back together a week later, so I almost caught hypothermia in those stupid little tank tops they put me in for nothing."

Mattie relaxed. Complaining about coworkers was a universal experience.

"That sounds tough."

Theo laced his arm around Mattie's waist, pulling her to his side. He pressed a quick kiss to the top of her head before looking back at Aria. "So, cookie. When do you audition for that Lian movie again?"

Cookie? What kind of pet name is Cookie? Mattie studied him as Aria answered, her answer not making much sense with the film terminology.

Cookie?

She fought back the sense of uncertainty inside her. It wasn't Aria, as beautiful as she was. The way Theo was holding her felt possessive; he wasn't trying to hide who he was there with. It was this party, with its showy people and the uncomfortable heels. She could feel the tape on her boob peeling from the heat of hundreds of people in a room. If she was home right now, she would be in her pajamas, a big mug of tea, rewatching the musical episode of her favorite show.

She knew how much bringing Mattie to this party meant to him, and being there, seeing it, only made the knowledge that she was miserable all the sadder. This was his world. His job.

Standing there in her thousand-dollar dress and mink eyelashes, Mattie felt a deep, crushing sense of losing Theo again.

"I—um—I'll be right back." She excused herself, heading to the bathroom. Shutting the stall door behind her, she sat on the toilet, careful not to drag the hem in the water.

Letting out a staggering breath, she stared up at the ceiling. She should have stayed home, she never should have opened herself up to love Theo again. The only way this could ever end was in heartbreak.

There was a small knock on the door, and she heard Aria on the other side.

"Mattie you, okay?"

"I, um..." On shaky legs, Mattie opened the door, facing Aria. "I'm fine, a little hot, is all."

Studying her, Aria rubbed a thin-fingered hand on Mattie's arm. "You could never be an actress. You're a terrible liar."

Despite herself, Mattie laughed. "Good to know."

"This is my fault." Aria frowned. "I asked him to come down for the party. Get a few amicable pictures, put out a statement that we're still on good terms, blah blah. And I wanted to meet you. But this party was the wrong choice."

"It's not the party." She paused, seeing the look of disbelief on Aria's face. Brushing past her, Mattie walked to the sink, washing her hands, letting the cool water flow over her hands, focusing on the sensation, and not the woman behind her. "It's not only the party. It's this town, these people, Teddy himself. I wanted so badly to understand what his life was like here, and now that I do—"

She stopped herself. Knowing this life Theo lived; not only was it not the life for her, to know this was the life he chose over her so many years before. Who was to say he wouldn't choose this over her again? She could never offer him all this.

"He really cares about you. I don't know you that well, but I hope you don't mind me telling you that."

"I know he does. He's like that. He has a big heart and—"

"Uh, no," Aria interrupted her, with a snort. "Sorry. How he was out there with you? All loving, arm around your waist, whispering in your ear, that's not the Theo I know. We spent years pretending in front of the cameras together. He can be a good guy sometimes, but he is not loving. I mean, even when he was with Safiya, it wasn't like that."

Another wave of nausea rolled through her stomach. She could write off Aria, as it was all pretend, but his relationship with Safiya was different. She was a model, she lived in this world. That was what Theo should want, someone who knew how to act at these parties, what to wear, and what to eat.

Mattie went to rub her face before realizing it was full of makeup and fake lashes. "No offense, but talking about his ex isn't helping me."

With a speculative glance, Aria pursed her lips. "You know, you kind of remind me of her."

"Of Safiya Khan? The supermodel; the face and body of luxury lingerie and makeup companies? The one who had her cheekbones insured for a million dollars?"

Aria waved away the comment. "Pretty sure that last one is a rumor. But yeah."

"I don't look a thing like her."

Mattie looked at herself in the mirror; she had never felt more beautiful than when she walked out to see Theo in the living room earlier. But to compare herself against a woman who was statistically proven to have one of the most symmetrical faces in entertainment was a fool's game.

"Maybe not right away, but there's something about you that reminds me of her. Maybe it's the hair or the eyes, though I guess yours are green, aren't they?"

Mattie flashed back to the conversation she had with Eloise about Theo rambling about a girl with green eyes.

"And we all know who had his heart first. And seeing Theo with you tonight, it's obvious we're all pale comparisons." Aria patted Mattie on the arm. "I'll let Theo know you'll be out in a few minutes."

Leaving her alone in the cavernous bathroom, Mattie waited for the door to click shut before pulling her phone out of her purse. The lock screen was a picture of Kamari at the community egg hunt. Her wild, dark curls in two pigtails, a wicker basket full of colorful eggs in one hand, and a smear of chocolate at the corner of her missing tooth grin. This was her life, that little girl back in Manzanita. She thought of calling Jay to check on Mari but decided against it. It would only make her feel worse.

Stepping out into the oversized room, she glanced over to where Theo and Aria were chatting with the nonbinary singer, Aerin, who was in a pink sequin tuxedo. A steady breath, then two, before she fumbled with the small clutch in her hand.

A shadow passed over her, and she looked to the side to find the host of the party, Brenton Michael Phillips staring down at her with a wide smile.

"Hey, I haven't met you yet." His teeth were impossibly white, and the green eyeliner around his eyes was smudged.

Mattie put out a shaking hand. Theo was one thing, but this man was famous-famous.

"Mattie. I'm here with Theo."

In what she assumed was a brow raise, the man glanced over at Theo, still talking to Aria, and back to her. His gaze swept over her, and she could read his thoughts as clear as can be. "Theo Blake? Theo Blake brought you to my party?"

Mattie nodded.

"Are you having a good time? I try to make all my guests comfortable, and you look like you could use some..." His eyes swept over her body again, stopping at her cleavage. "Comforts."

Swallowing, Mattie blinked up at him. Was this man hitting on her? There was no way, right?

"I'm comfortable."

"You don't look at all like the kind of women Theo is seen with."

Internally, Mattie groaned. Yet another reminder of how out of place she was in this sea of shiny gold perfection.

"And what kind of women would those be?"

Brenton Michael eyed her once more, a dangerous glint in his gaze.

"Don't get me wrong, I'm glad to see Theo is opening up to the pleasures that extra cushion can give. I know I want something to hold on to, if you know what I mean."

"I'd have to be an idiot not to." She glanced over to where Theo and Aria were standing and found the space empty.

Ignoring her crack, he leaned over, touching her collarbone, tracing a line to the hollow of her throat. She gulped, frozen in place.

His finger came back to show her a piece of gold confetti. "Sticky little things."

Her stomach rolled, and her eyes darted around the room. While she didn't think an international pop star would hit on her, being stuck talking to someone was her fear, and Theo was nowhere to be seen.

"I should go find—" she started, but he interrupted her.

"No, please stay. I was having a fun time talking with you." He reached over again, this time to tuck a stand of hair behind her ear. His finger brushed the shell of her ear before it was wrenched away.

Brenton Michael's wrist was held in the air by Theo, a murderous gaze on his face. "Get your fucking hands off her."

Brenton Michael laughed, trying to pull his hand out of Theo's grip. "Be cool, man, I was saying hi."

"You don't ever touch what is mine. Do you understand?" Theo's face screwed up; a harsh scowl carved his lips. The tendons in his hands were bulging from the grip he had.

Brenton Michael was able to free his wrist, rubbing it with a shake of his head. "Never seen you be jealous before."

Brenton Michael's eyes darted behind Theo, where Aria stood, a pinched look on her face. "Hey, Ari."

Aria glanced from Theo to Brenton Michael, with concern.

"You don't know me at all," Theo spat.

Laughing, Brenton Michael stepped back. "I know you didn't give a damn how many times Ari and I have fucked the past few years."

"Bren—" Aria hissed.

He put up his hands. "What? It's true, and you know it. We all do. Don't act like you give a damn about anyone else. We've shared women before, why should this one be any different?"

Stepping closer, Theo's shoes touched the tips of Brenton Michael's sequin loafers. "I'll tell you this one more time. You stay away from Mattie."

"Sure, okay." He chuckled. Glancing at Mattie, he smirked. "Call me when you want some good dick, I'll take care of you all night. In fact—" His words were cut off as Theo's fist slammed into Brenton Michael's nose. Blood spurted down the front of his all-white suit.

Clutching his face, Brenton Michael stumbled back. "What the fuck, man? I have a photo shoot in five days for Dior."

Around them, a crowd had formed, the flash of camera bulbs and murmurs of shock.

Theo stepped up, pushing his chest into Brenton Michael's. "I told you. You don't touch what's mine."

Before Mattie had time to process what happened, Theo had her hand in his, pulling her out of the party and onto the street.

"Teddy, wait, I can't run in these."

Theo slowed long enough to scoop her up and carry her to the waiting car. A little spot of blood was scattered on the front of his white dress shirt. Her arms wrapped around his neck; she could see the pulsing vein in his throat as he walked. Setting her down in front of the car, he opened the door and pointed inside.

"Get in."

"Teddy..." Chancing a glance at the party behind them, she saw no one was chasing them down. "You hit him."

"Get in the fucking car, Matilda."

"But you hit him..."

"Get in before I go back and kill that bastard for daring to touch you."

"Are you kidding me right now?" Gaping at him, she put up her hands.

"Do I look like I'm kidding?" His jaw feathered as he stared her down. "I mean it. If you don't get in, I will go back into the party and finish this."

Seeing no recourse, Mattie slid into the leather seat, Theo slamming the door shut. She had little time to process what he had done. No one had ever fought over her before. Fought for her. She wanted to be disgusted with this show of aggression and possessiveness, but damn if it wasn't a little thrilling.

As he slid in on the other side, he shouted at the driver to go. Shucking his coat, he tossed it on the floor of the car.

The party faded away as the dark street swallowed them up. Who was this man who partied and drank and punched pop stars?

"You just punched Brenton Michael Phillips."

Theo was running his hands up and down his pant leg, the muscles in his forearms standing out as he clenched his fist. "And I'd do it again. I can't believe that man thought he could lay a single pinky on you."

"Is that true what he said about Aria? He was sleeping with her when you were together?"

Theo glanced over at her. "Maybe. It's hard to say. We weren't keeping tabs on each other. She was free to sleep with whoever she wanted."

"And you?" Although he had told her his relationship with Aria was never real, she hadn't thought it would be that open.

With a grimace, he glanced away from her. "Do you really want me to answer that?"

There was her answer. "How many?"

A glance back at her, his gaze softened. Laying a hand on her cheek, his thumb traced her cheekbone. "It doesn't matter. They don't matter. You are the only one who does."

"So, you'll punch someone for touching me, but you didn't care if he slept with your ex-girlfriend?"

"Yeah, that about sums it up." He nodded, pleased. "I wasn't lying when I told you, you have always been, and will always be, the only woman I love. Why would I care who Aria is with when I'm not around? That's how things are around here. It's not a big deal."

"You mean that's how *you* are around here. You didn't act that way back home."

"L.A. is my home."

She didn't want to think about that. She wouldn't.

"Nathan and Keller don't seem like the type to sleep around on their wives."

He laughed. "Not now, but before they got together with Ilsa and Eloise? They were just as bad as me. Worse, even. The morning Eloise married Keller, she had to kick a groupie out of his hotel room. And the first time Ilsa met Nathan, he was getting rode hard by Shelby Waters."

Mattie tried to reconcile this information with the lovestruck men she met in Manzanita. "You shouldn't have punched him."

The car began to slow, and the buildings grew smaller and in worse repair. "He's lucky I didn't strangle him. That face of his has been asking for a good hit."

"It was a mild flirtation. A little creepy, sure. But nothing I haven't heard before."

With a frown, he turned to her, his hand on her chin as he brought her face level with his. The words were low but firm. "You have no idea what lengths I would go to for you. You are mine—do you understand? Those smiles, that coy glance. They belong to me. I am the only one who gets to kiss that mouth, who can see that ecstasy on your face when you come. The first and the last. I will bring this world to ruin before I let another man touch you."

His hand on her cheek, he brought her mouth to his in a punishing kiss.

Melting to him, his muscular arms wrapped around her waist as he pushed her onto the seat. The hard length of him pressed into the juncture of her thighs.

"Uh, sir. We'll be there in five minutes," the driver called out.

Theo groaned into her neck, bringing himself up to a seated position.

"Where are we going?" Mattie looked around. While she was familiar with the area, she had a good enough sense to tell they were nowhere near his condo.

"I have a surprise for you."

Mattie groaned. "It's not another party is it? Because I can't handle that tonight."

"Even before the incident with Brenton Michael, that party was overwhelming for you, wasn't it?"

Mattie opened her mouth to disagree, then decided against it. "Yeah. It was. I guess I didn't realize how different your life is now. The kind of parties and these people, it's so strange to me."

He seemed to ponder what she had to say. "It's not the same as a party back home, is it? I haven't given it much thought, but it's been the norm for years now, I don't see them as weird. But yeah, the contortionists might have been a little much. But Brenton enjoys going all out. It's not the party I'd throw, but still entertaining."

"What kind of party would you throw?" Mattie asked, not sure she wanted to hear the answer. Seeing this side of him had led her to doubts.

"Honestly, I love a good jam session. Where we're creating music because we love it, not because it needs to sell. It's been a long time since I've had something like that. The pressure to stay relevant, to stay marketable. I liked hanging out at Eloise and Keller's back in Manzanita way more. Not to say I don't have fun at these kinds of parties sometimes, but I can see how if you don't know these people, it could be a bit much."

Mattie let out a sigh of relief. He got it. He was more comfortable in Manzanita, too. This L.A. Theo was a fluke, not the real him. And he had been so loving at the party, rubbing her back, giving her small kisses. If Aria was to be believed, this was odd behavior for Theo, reserved for only her.

"Where to now?"

"It's a surprise." He leaned over, kissing her softly. When he pulled away, he gave her a mischievous wink.

Chapter Twenty-Four

Theo

BEATRIZ HAD ALREADY MADE the arrangements with Dan, the owner of Proper Bar. Pulling up to the nondescript building, he saw the sign on the door that the bar was closed for the night. People in their early twenties were milling around the sidewalk, going into the other restaurant beside the bar.

The driver took them around the back, parking beside the heavy metal door.

"This the place, Mr. Blake?" the driver asked, with a furrowed brow.

"It is, Tomas. Thank you."

Getting out, he saw that the dumpster was still in the same spot, cardboard boxes piled beside it for the recycling truck to take the next day. He wondered briefly if it was still on Monday mornings, the way it had been when he was a dishwasher here.

He held the door for Mattie, she climbed out, careful in her heels. Glancing around the alleyway, she frowned. "Where are we?"

"A special spot."

Using the side of his fist, he rapped against the metal door several times before a young man opened the door, his eyes getting big when he saw Theo. "Mr. Blake, wow. Dan said you were coming by, but I didn't think he was for real."

Theo put his hand out to the man. "I'm here. And you're..."

"Derrick."

Theo placed a hand on Mattie's lower back, her warmth seeping through the embroidered dress. "Derrick, lead the way for us, please."

The young man led them through the kitchen and into the empty bar. A stage was still set up in the corner, a small stool on it, with a single low light shining. Derrick rushed in behind them, pulling out one of the cheap seats the bar had at the table in front of the stage. Around the small table were vases of peonies, hundreds and hundreds surrounding the small table where a bucket of chilled champagne sat beside two long-stemmed glasses.

Once Derrick poured them each a glass of champagne, he left them alone to wander around the empty bar. It seemed much smaller than when he worked there years before. Not much had changed from his days working in the back, scrubbing dried ketchup off plates and mopping up spilled beer. The same chipped sign over the doorway to the bathrooms. The same metal condiment holders on each table beside the napkin dispenser. Even the neon beer sign behind the bar were still burned out on the "R," so it said "BEE."

"When I first moved down here, this was my first job. I worked my way up to bartender while I was trying to get my music off the ground. Played their open mic nights. Met Eloise here; she was underage but kept sneaking in to sing." He pointed to a wall of framed signed napkins on the wall. "When I left, the owner, Dan, had me sign a napkin in case I got famous one day. He made everyone do that."

Wandering over to the wall, she inspected the framed napkins. "Anyone else I would know up here?"

Shoving his hands in his pockets, he glanced over the wall. "Is mine not impressive enough?"

A smile brightened her face. "Truthfully, I don't want to think about you as famous. Complicates things for me."

"What should I be, then?" he teased, pulling her closer to him.

"Teddy. My Teddy." Her green eyes were earnest in the dim light of the bar. A line of lights bordered the ceiling, fading from white to blue to pink.

He loved this about her. From the moment they saw each other again, it clicked in place for him. This was the only woman who knew him, who could understand who he was and what he needed. "To you, I always will be."

Something dark flashed over her face quickly replaced by a smile. "I hope so." She turned away from the napkin wall to face the empty bar. "Not that I'm not happy to be here with you but where are the other people?"

"I rented the place for tonight. The owner closed it up for us."

Raising a brow, Mattie surveyed the place, as if she was doing math in her head. "Private planes, renting out bars, penthouse condos. You've come a long way."

"I wanted you to have the full experience. All the glamour of L.A."

Biting back a smile, her eyes shifted around the bar, taking the peeling pleather seats and dented baseboards.

"Okay, this place isn't glamorous. But it means something to me. I wanted you to see it, for you to know how it was for me back then."

"When you dumped me?" Her words were without malice, but it still stung.

"To show you how far I've come to be able to deserve you again. And I think I've done that."

Stepping closer, she laid a hand on his cheek, pulling him down to her. "Teddy, I never needed fancy parties or expensive dresses to see that." She glanced around the place again. "Honestly, I'm much more at home in a place like this than that other party."

Theo held out his hand. "It's not a senior prom, but can I have this dance?"

Accepting his hand, she let him lead her to the empty floor. A song from their early days of dating played. He had sent Beatriz a list of Mattie's favorite songs and asked her to have them played at the bar when they got there. He had never been a great dancer, that was more Mattie's skill, but they fit together, as they had in her kitchen a month before. Her back against his hand, her fingers were at the nape of his neck as they moved to the music.

The song changed, and Mattie's eyes softened.

"Our song."

Around them, the familiar guitar played its haunting refrain. Bending down to her ear as they swayed to the music, he sang the familiar lyrics in her ear. Her body melted into him, the lightness of their bodies as they moved together. This was exactly where she belonged. Holding her tight to him, they swayed to the music. All his years of sacrifice had led him to this moment, holding Mattie in his arms and knowing he would never let her go. He had spent his best years running from this feeling. Without Mattie in his life, he never felt he deserved them. Having her take him back, having her love him was all he needed.

His mouth found hers; coming together, their kiss was soft and reverent. The ethereal song was almost over, the last notes playing as he held her face in his hands to deepen the kiss. Her arms wrapped around the back of his neck, their bodies were flush. He felt himself growing hard at her nearness, but he couldn't give in yet. The song changed, and Theo stepped back from her arms, staring down at her. He loved her; this was the moment.

"There has never been a day since I met you, I didn't love you. Years spent trying to get back to the last time I was happy, only to find it was with you all along. I'm not a perfect man, you know that. I'm broken. But I'm fractured into pieces only you can fit together. You have given me a second chance, and now that I have you, I'm not letting you go. I want to take care of you for the rest of your life. I need you, forever."

Stepping back, he dropped to one knee. Mattie's mouth opened as she stared down at him, her eyes widening.

"Teddy, what—"

Pulling the small maroon box out of his pocket, his heart beating loudly in his ears, he opened it up. "Will you marry me?"

CHAPTER TWENTY-FIVE

Mattie

"**M**ARRY ME."

She stared down at the huge diamond, then back at Theo, his earnest face so bright. In the back of her mind, those doubts started to rush her, but staring at his beautiful face, there was only one answer. There was only the man who held her heart.

"Yes." She nodded her head so hard; the heavy earrings slapped the side of her jaw. "Yes, yes, yes."

He seemed to let out a large breath, standing and swooping her into his arms in a single motion. His mouth found hers, his kiss full of all the words.

Once they broke apart, he grabbed her left hand, sliding the ring on it. The oversized diamond glittered in the low lights of the bar. It was so large; it didn't look real.

"I don't know if I can even lift my hand, this thing is so huge."

He took her hand, kissing the knuckle above her ring. "It looks amazing on you. Exactly how I pictured it. It's seven carats, and I made sure it was ethically sourced."

Wiggling her fingers, she tested the unfamiliar weight of the heavy rock. She didn't get an engagement ring with Jay; only a thin wedding band. There was no romantic proposal, it was an agreement, a you're pregnant and we are in that stage of our lives so let's do this together type thing. This was an all-consuming, ruinous love she couldn't turn away from. Saying yes wasn't a decision she made. It simply was the only way.

In that moment when Theo asked, she couldn't remember any of her fears. Her "Yes" was immediate, it was a reflex from deep within her. She knew there would never be another man who would make her feel the way Theo did. Who loved her the way he did.

Bringing his face to hers, she kissed him again, her face wet with happy tears. "Take me home."

They didn't wait until they got to the penthouse. As the car left the alley behind Proper Bar, Theo had her skirt pulled up and brought her to orgasm before they had driven a few miles. She was thankful for discreet drivers and partitions. At least this one wasn't as flimsy as an airplane curtain.

As the elevator opened on the top story, Theo looped his arms under her knees, picking her up and carrying her bridal style over the threshold into his penthouse. Her shoes fell off her feet as they moved down the hall. Her mouth never left his as every kiss and dip of their embrace brought them closer to the bedroom. Once inside the room, his kiss turned fevered, his tongue dipping and meeting hers. Hands strayed from cupping the back of her neck to slide onto her shoulder, trying to push the dress off it. The structured dress held it tight. "How—"

Turning around, she pointed to the long row of small buttons down the sheer panel.

"If you want me naked, you'll need to unbutton me and help me with the tape."

He pulled back as he stared down at her. "Tape? You're taped?"

His fingers slid each button out as he moved down her spine, kissing each spot, a brush of his lips on her exposed skin. The dress slid down her arms, loosening enough to fall off completely. Standing away from him, she gasped as his mouth trailed down her back, sensual kisses that stopped as he reached the bottom of her spine.

"I can't believe you were bare for me this whole time."

Her dress fell to the floor, and she kicked it away from them.

"You sure made use of it in the car." She smirked.

Still on his knee, he touched her hip, turning her to face him. "That was nothing. A taster for you."

Rising to his feet, he pulled her hands away from where they had been cupping her breasts. The tape peeled slightly away at a corner, but they were still pulled up high.

"You were taped up. Let's free these beauties." Rustling through the side drawer, he came back with a large bottle of oil. She didn't want to think about why it was over there.

Squeezing a generous amount of oil on his hands, he rubbed them together before placing them on her breasts. They were still tender from being man-handled earlier in the day.

"I think you need more, but maybe we should move to the bathroom. You'll get oil all over your shirt."

"You think I care about my shirt?" He laughed before pouring oil over her skin. She could see the edges of the tape peeling up. Tenderly, his hands massaged the edges of the tape, little bits coming up as he rubbed her down. It was sensual, his eyes on hers as he worked over her breasts. He was meticulous as his motions triggered heat to build between her thighs. Once the last piece was removed, his thumbs brushed against her bare nipples, the sensitive peaks reacting to his touch. His hands descended her body until they gripped her hips, picking her up and tossing her onto the bed. She let out a gasp as she landed on the soft surface.

Standing over her, he slowly unbuttoned his dress shirt, glimpses of his hard chest emerging as he stared down at her. Her feet now bare, she slid them up until her legs were splayed open. Leaning on her elbows, she watched as his shirt fell off his shoulders and onto the floor. His eyes were on the place between her legs where she needed him the most.

"You're dripping for me, aren't you?" He licked his lips as he stared her down.

"Come here and love me," she beckoned.

Shedding his pants and boxers, he fisted his length as he looked her over. He was hard as he pumped his hand up and down his shaft. "I don't know what would feel better, your cunt on my tongue or it squeezing around my cock."

"Your cock, I want your cock."

His eyes darkened with her words, and he prowled catlike over her body.

She flattened against the bed, the heaviness of his strong body delicious on her.

"We have all night. I'm going to show you how good I'll make you feel for the rest of our lives."

"Yes," she breathed. Between them, she ran a hand over his stomach until it reached the tip of his hard cock. A little droplet of moisture clung to her finger, and she brought her finger up to her mouth to taste it.

With her lips around her finger, she hummed with appreciation. On each side of her head, the muscles in his forearms tensed. His mouth descended on hers, and he slid inside her in a single motion. She cried out at the intrusion, a sob escaping her as he filled her up. Half-kiss, half-gasp, he moved inside her. His hands reached beneath her, to drive himself deeper inside.

"I fucking love you," he gritted out as he pushed himself to the hilt, then drew back. Sitting up straight, he grabbed her legs, pinning them together and bending her knees until her feet were planted on his chest. The angle of him, hitting her in a spot, sending sparks through her. He sent her closer to orgasm, pushing and thrusting until her cries echoed around the room.

"I'm...I'm..." she gasped out. Pulling her legs apart, his body crushed down on hers, his tempo never ceasing.

"Look at me," he commanded. "Look me in the eye when you come."

Her eyes flung open, to find him staring down at her as he thrust deep and true. A wave of emotion flooded her. This was the bliss she had been chasing for years, the connection. No one could ever love her this way. With her hands on his back, she pulled him closer. Tears stung at her eyes as he fell apart around him, her climax a rolling sensation that crested in lightning through her body. "I love you."

"I love you. I love you," he cried out as he came inside her. As he pulled away, she saw the wetness clinging to his lower lashes. Blinking away her own tears, she brought his face to her chest, holding him there. Tangling her fingers in his hair, her short nails scratched at his scalp. There were no words between them.

Their heavy gasps were the only sound in the silent room. Playing with his hair, his body relaxed into hers. In mere moments, his breathing slowed, steadying out. In the moon's glow, her large diamond caught the light. Heavy on her finger, she closed her eyes.

CHAPTER TWENTY-SIX

THEO

WAKING WITH MORE VIGOR than he had in years, he rolled over to press a kiss to Mattie's shoulder. His fiancée. Soon enough, his wife. Buoyed by the thought he rushed through his morning tasks.

Beatriz answered on the second ring, her voice groggy on the other end. He didn't let her answer before he started talking. "I need you to call the best wedding planner in the city. Who's the guy that did Drew Kent's wedding to that heiress? That one."

"Good morning to you," Beatriz grumbled. Something rustled on the other end and there was the sound of running water. "So I take it she said yes."

"Of course she said yes." He threw a handful of spinach into his blender, along with some powder his dietitian insisted he use to maintain muscle mass.

"Anything else?" Beatriz's voice was clearer now, but she was still annoyed by the early hour.

"Yeah, I'll need a real estate agent too. This place is fine for me right now, but I'm sure Mattie will want something bigger, with a yard."

"So, you're planning a wedding and moving in the same day?"

"Not today, no. But soon, I want to take care of everything for Mattie." He hit the button on the blender, the roar of the blades drowning out whatever it was Beatriz said. With one hand, he scratched his stomach, which had gotten softer on his vacation. That wouldn't do for his wedding day. He needed to be perfect for her.

The blender shutting off, Beatriz repeated herself. "I'll have some contacts in a few hours." She hung up on him before he could ask her for anything more.

Green smoothie in hand, he walked out onto his balcony overlooking the city. He had only bought the place as a bachelor pad, and while it was decorated well, it wasn't home. Mattie would want something better. He'd miss the views, but a house with a yard made more sense for them as a family. Surely, they could expand that line soon, too. Already, he could picture Mattie's belly round with his baby. She would look beautiful pregnant. Soon after their wedding, they could start trying. Maybe their children would have his light hair and her green eyes. He hoped they had her ears. She was self-conscious about them as kids, but he loved the way they stuck out.

He texted Keller and Nathan a quick update that he proposed, then Aria a ring emoji. Then it was a joint message to his publicist and manager about putting out a press release. He wasn't sure how that worked—since he was often trying to squash stories—but they were the best for a reason.

Only thirty seconds after he sent the message, he got a call from Tamara.

"You twat-waffle. What's this I hear about you punching Brenton Michael Phillips at his party last night?"

"He deserved it."

"You're lucky you didn't break his nose."

"Wish I would have."

Tamara huffed loudly on the other end. "No, you don't. If he was in breach of his contract for the photo shoot, you know they could come after you for damages. BMP doesn't want to look like a wimp who gets punched at his own party, but corporate entities don't care who they bury in legal fees. I worked it out with his team, you're getting the medical bill."

"That's fine."

"Figure out how you're getting ahead of this story, and do it fast."

He glanced down the hall at his bedroom door, where Mattie was still sleeping. "I'm on it."

PULLING THE CHAIR OUT for Mattie, they sat on the terrace of one of the city's most exclusive restaurants. He rarely went here, as it always had at least three paparazzi camped outside during business hours. While the food was great, it was the place to go when you wanted to be seen. He and Aria had several "dates" there when they needed to drum up attention for her new season of the show, or Theo had an appearance he needed to promote.

It was the perfect spot for Mattie and him to be spotted to get the press out. He left his ball cap at home, donning a white tee and jeans. Mattie matched him in her white button-down shirt, tucked into a pair of shorts, and some big jewelry. In the light of the afternoon sun, her ring sparkled. It looked great on her finger, as he knew it would. He made sure to seat her with her left side facing the street, in case it could be caught in pictures.

They ordered their food and drinks. Mattie was in the middle of telling him about her call with Kamari that morning when a clicking sound distracted Mattie. She glanced at the street, where a woman was standing a few feet away, a camera trained on them.

She frowned and leaned forward, her voice dropping to a whisper. "Teddy, I think that lady took our picture."

Theo glanced at the woman. The paparazzi weren't allowed to ask them questions while they were dining, but they could take pictures, and once they walked out of the building, it was fair game.

"Yeah, they'll do that. I got papped leaving Aria's place yesterday, after getting the ring."

Water glass froze halfway to her mouth; Mattie blinked at him a few times in surprise. "I don't understand."

"What part?" He took a sip of his drink while waiting for her answer. The pap was now on her phone, likely calling some contacts.

"All of it. You not only going to your ex-girlfriend's house, but being photographed there?"

He grimaced. "Aria isn't really an ex—"

Mattie kept talking, ignoring him. "That I'm supposed to sit here and eat an overpriced lunch while someone is a few feet away, watching my every move."

"Oh, the paps can't bother us while we're eating. And it's a given that a few will hang out here; this place is popular with celebrities."

Mattie's face was full of doubt. "I didn't know I'd be photographed today."

"Part of the job. Plus, it's a good way to get this new narrative out there. Have people see you with me before the story breaks."

"Story. Narrative." She paused, as if rolling the words around in her mouth. "Is that really how you want to describe us?"

He sensed he was making a misstep and quickly corrected himself. "No, of course not. You and I, this is real. But like everything else in my work, it must be spun in a certain way. Trust me. If we play it this way, the tabloids will back off soon enough."

Uncertainty clouded her expression as she glanced over at the photographer. "Are you sure? It all feels so invasive."

With a steady hand, Theo reached over the table to grasp Mattie's left hand. "Last night, I promised you, and I mean it. I love you and want to take care of you for the rest of our lives. I won't let anything bad happen to you. This way is for the best."

Eyes still dark with concern, she frowned. "If you think so—"

"I know it." Taking her hand, he lifted her hand up to his mouth, opening her hand up to press a kiss to her palm. Her hand and his face, directed toward the street and paparazzi.

RETURNING TO THE PENTHOUSE, he was relieved to see Beatriz had already set out some information for them. She was a true asset. He was going to be devastated when she left him, but that was the way in L.A.

Beatriz set a binder down on the table in front of Mattie and Theo. "This is the name of a few wedding planners I found today. This woman had a recent cancellation, I suspect it was Chris and Bianca's, but you know..."

Theo nodded. "Yeah, Chrisca was going to be a good one. Bianca was looking particularly chummy with Brenton Michael last night."

Beatriz's eyes widened, but she kept to the task at hand. "I called Javier, who did Drew Kent's wedding, but he's booked until next year, and I'm assuming you two are thinking the sooner, the better?"

Theo waved the comment away. "That's fine, now that I think about it, I don't think he would be the right fit. That wedding was too modern art-esque. That isn't our style at all."

Beatriz pulled up another email. "This is probably the best fit for you two. Libby Cohen. Her weddings are always gorgeous, that perfect mix of charming and classy. And Mattie, Theo told me you're an avid gardener, I know Libby always has the best arrangements for her clients."

Mattie squinted at the screen, her mouth drawn. "I don't know. It's all so sudden. We got engaged last night and—"

Theo interrupted her. "She'll be great. Perfect for us. Call her and set up a meeting later this week."

Mattie blinked, her brow creasing. "This week? Teddy, I need to fly home tonight. I have work tomorrow."

Theo shot her a smirk. "Work? Don't worry about work, you don't need that job."

Mattie huffed loudly once, half-incredulous laugh, half-annoyance. "Are you serious? And what about Mari, I told Jay—"

"Bring her down here, of course. I'll have Beatriz get everything she needs in the spare room, excuse me, in her room ready." Across from them, Beatriz's lips formed a line, and she was shooting Theo a dangerous glance, shaking her head slightly. What was her deal?

"Her room? What?" Mattie asked, her voice slow and expression confused.

"Yeah, of course she'll have a room here. Until we find our own place, what do you think, a place by the beach or in the hills? I don't know much about schools, but I'm sure Beatriz can find someone to help us with that as well."

Blinking a few times, Mattie slowly turned to Beatriz. "Could you give us a minute?"

Chapter Twenty-Seven
Mattie

U PON WAKING, MATTIE HAD scratched herself on the truly outrageous rock on her finger. It was almost unwieldy, it was so large.

That was going to take some getting used to.

The late morning sun trickled over the bleached floorboards of the bedroom, and she padded to the bathroom. Her whole body was tender, but in a good way, the way a good workout would do. Not that she pushed herself hard while working out, but still. Maybe she should start working out more for the wedding.

Engaged. She was getting married.

Not just married, but married to Theo. A thrill ran up her spine at the thought. It was everything she had wanted since she was seventeen years old. Unlike some of her divorcee friends, she was never opposed to marriage again; she only needed to be pickier this time. Wiggling her finger, she watched as the light caught the bauble on her hand, refracting light around the room. Engaged, engaged, she rolled the word around on her tongue. My fiancé.

She heard the telltale sound of her phone ringing, and she hustled to catch Jay's call before it went to voicemail.

"Mommy!" Kamari called out. "Hi! I caught a fish at the derby today. Daddy says it's the biggest he's ever seen. I told him I want to eat it, but he said we have to put it back in the pond."

Mattie settled onto the edge of the bed, cradling her phone in her hand.

"That's amazing, darling. I'm sad I missed it."

"Me, too, but Daddy took a picture. I'll have him send it, so you can see. How's your trip? Have you seen any princesses yet? I told Gertrude where you were at school, and she said that's where Princess Anna lives. Have you seen her?"

Mattie laughed softly. "Not this time, but I'm sure I'll be able to bring you to Disneyland soon."

As she said the words, she realized she had no clue what the future was going to look like for them. Of course, Theo would have the work he needed to travel for a lot, but did he need to live in L.A. to be a musician? She glanced around the room; he would likely keep this condo as a home base here, but they'd have to be based out of Manzanita, right? Keller and Eloise lived there as well, not that big of a stretch.

"Really, Mommy?! And see the Harry Potter World, too?"

"Of course." She smoothed the sheets away from her. Her previous fears about Theo's commitment to her had vanished the night before. Yes, he had left her when they were foolish kids, but he had proposed. He wanted to marry her now, wanted to be a part of her life. "Does Daddy want to talk to me?"

There was a rustling, and then Kamari spoke. "No. I don't know where he is. I unlocked his phone; the password is my birthday. Zero two one eight."

Pursing her lips together to keep from smiling, Mattie said, "Yes, it is." She would have to tell Jay to change his code. The last time Kamari got on her phone without her knowing, Mari ordered one hundred bottles of bubbles. Mattie was still giving those away at every event with children.

"Oh! Daddy's calling me. I got to go. Bye Mommy." Kamari hung up on her, without waiting for a response. Chuckling to herself, Mattie set the phone down beside her. The heavy ring slid around on her finger, the large stone hitting the side of her pinky. Wiggling her fingers, she righted it. It was a lovely ring, truly. Obviously more expensive than anything she had ever seen before. She pictured herself typing up briefs with it on, appearing in front of a judge, baking in the kitchen, or pulling weeds in the garden. The image was incongruent with the ring.

It wasn't the kind of ring she would have picked out for herself, but Theo had bought it for her. He wanted her to have it, so that meant something. He was proud of the life he had built and wanted to share that with her. She could wear an ostentatious ring, if he loved it on her finger. She got up to see her new fiancé and spend the rest of her last day in L.A. with him.

DISCONCERTED. SHE DIDN'T ENJOY the sensation of being in front of those cameras. She wasn't a shy person, but the flashing bulbs of the photographer had set her on edge. Theo assured her it would calm down once the press figured out there wasn't much of a story between them. He assured her Keller and Eloise had the same level of press surrounding them when they first started dating, and now they were only featured when they wanted to be.

She wanted to believe Theo. He was so confident in playing this game in front of the camera. While she knew his feelings for her were real, there was a posturing quality of his action at the restaurant. The way he insisted she sit with her left side facing the street, how he kissed her hand, holding her ring out to the cameras. It was all a show for these people. Far away was the carefree and soft Theo in Manzanita. He even held himself differently here—with more swagger and a small smile on his face at all times—as if he could be photographed at any moment. It was a rendering of his onstage persona. Was this the man he would be in this town?

Upon entering the penthouse, she knew they would need to talk about what the future would look like before she flew back that night. Setting her bag down, she was surprised to see Beatriz at the dining room table, binders, and her laptop covering the large glass top. She didn't get more than a hello out before Beatriz and Theo were talking about wedding planners. She was ashamed of how long it took her to understand what was going on. Theo expected her to stay there. With no regard to what she wanted, he had begun making plans for their future.

Mentally kicking herself, she realized she had done the same thing that morning. She assumed when he proposed they would go back up to Washington. They didn't need to talk about it, because of course her life was there.

But he wasn't thinking about that. The opposite was his thinking. How could she be so foolish? Glancing down at that colossal rock on her hand, she closed her hands into a fist.

Was he going to make her choose? Surely, he had to understand why L.A. could not be their home?

And for him to ask her to bring Mari down. She had school and dance classes. They had a life up there she couldn't interrupt for a meeting with some celebrity wedding planner.

Beatriz likely realized there were many conversations they needed to have. Making an excuse that she needed to get something out of her car, she left them alone in the penthouse. Theo hunched over a wedding magazine featuring a spread on a famous baseball player and his new bride. "I think the venue should be the first thing we look at, don't you? There are so many places around here, but we could go anywhere. A lot of people like Italy, but I don't know—"

"Teddy. Stop." Mattie sunk into one of the high-back plush dining room chairs. Why did he have so many chairs around such a big table?

"Or France. I liked Paris, though I thought Nice was more my style and—"

"Please, hold on—" Her voice shook as she tried to stop his words.

With one hand, he shoved the magazine to the side, grabbing Beatriz's laptop. "Or New York would be cool. It's up to you."

"Theodore," Mattie yelled, slapping the glass top table. "Stop it."

Blinking up at her, his mouth dropped open at her outburst. "Oh. Sorry. I'm getting ahead of myself, aren't I? What do you think about these wedding planners?"

With a shattering breath, she squeezed her eyes shut. "I think we only got engaged twelve hours ago, and there are a lot of things we need to talk about before we discuss France vs. Italy."

"Oh." He shut the laptop, pushing it away. "Like what?"

On the wall was another one of those oversized black-and-white paintings, so morose and high art. This whole place was cold. "Where are we going to live?"

"Here, in L.A. I can put my condo up for sale, and I'll get us any house you want. Money is no object for you. Oceanfront, in the hills, wherever."

"And Kamari?" She knew his answer before he said a word. It was written all over his face, the nonchalant way he was scanning the screen. He had made this decision.

"What about Kamari? I'll take care of her as much as I will you."

"We're not moving to L.A, Theo. I can't." Tears clung to her lashes as she spoke.

"But I have to live here for work," Theo said plainly.

"And I have a daughter who lives in Manzanita."

"We'll get her into the best private school in the area. I have some friends who could give me some recommendations. She'll love L.A."

Mattie rubbed the spot on the inside of her palm. "I'm not moving Kamari. Her whole life is in that town. And if you think for a second Jay would let her move out of state, you have another thing coming."

"I can pay for the best lawyers in the country, don't worry about that."

"It's not..." She took a shaky sigh. He couldn't see how implausible his idea was. Since the day Kamari was born, Mattie's life was irrevocably changed. Every choice she made was for her daughter. "I'm not going to do that to Jay."

Theo sat back in his chair, a single loud scoff coming out of his mouth as he shook his head. "You'd choose what your ex-husband wants over marrying me?"

Her co-parenting relationship with Jay was hard-won. She swallowed down annoyances at parenting styles, and he did the same, as they battled to get to a place where they trusted the other would always take their daughter into consideration. It was never about Jay, but Kamari. It would be traumatic to uproot her daughter because Mattie wanted to spend her days with Theo. As much as she loved Theo, he had to understand that. It was more than her at stake here.

She thought about what he had said the morning before. *I'll make you fit.* That was his answer. Never that he would accommodate her life; her role would be to fit around his life, and never the reverse. How could the life she built work in his? And her daughter. If it was only her, it would be no question. But for Kamari. No. Mattie's teeth slammed together. "No, I'm choosing my daughter. I will never do anything to harm her. And moving out of state, putting her in a new school, taking her from her family, and her friends.

Her father. That would harm her. For what? For twenty-dollar smoothies and constant sunshine? So you can be closer to your industry buddies?"

"It's not only my industry buddies. I need to be here to..."

"To what, go to clubs? Parties? Drink whiskey with socialites and producers? Be seen by the paparazzi, be another cog in that machine you complain about?" She thought about the party the night before. The way he acted around all those people, the posturing, and his fake smile. The way everyone expected him to do more, to entertain them. "You say you want to have a real life with me; well, here it is. My life is my daughter."

"I know that."

"No, you don't. I'm not asking you to give up your career. But Keller and Eloise live up there, why couldn't we? I don't want to lose you, Theo. But you can't expect me to be the girl hanging off your arm at events, and not my own person. When you left me, you made sure I built my own life. So here it is. Do you want to be a part of it or not?"

"Of course I do. You're all I've ever wanted."

Her mouth fell open at his lie. "That's not true. We both know all you've ever wanted is exactly what you have. You wanted this." She waved her hand around the cold penthouse, with its beautiful furnishing and morose art. "You wanted all those fans chanting your name. To be on the cover of magazines, and to be on the radio. And you got it. I'm so proud of you, I am. But don't say I'm all you wanted, when you gave me away."

"When will you stop punishing me for what I did twelve years ago?"

"When will you actually show me you've changed?" She pursed her lips together, waiting for a response, only to watch him sputter. A heaviness pressed deep in her chest as she realized the futility of saying yes to him. She wanted to believe in Theo so badly, she let herself think he had changed. But a single good day with her daughter and passion-filled weekend was not a life. For any other man, she would have run long before, but with Theo, she was blinded to his faults. To her, he would always be that boy she loved many years before, but that was no longer enough for her. Lowering her voice, she tried to take the venom out of her words. "I am not a doll you set on a shelf twelve years ago you can pick up now that you've achieved everything else."

"I know, I don't want you to be." Theo struggled. "But can you see how I sacrificed everything when I left you?"

She thought back to those days when she was eighteen in her bedroom, lovesick over a boy. His harsh words as he told her not to come down to see him. Whether he thought he was doing the right thing, it didn't matter. She was hurt and from that hurt came scars. He could kiss her mouth. Love her body. But how she felt deep down, this heartache he caused by leaving her? He couldn't kiss it and make that better.

"No, you didn't. You have no idea what sacrifice is. What it looks like putting someone else first. To love someone unconditionally. Because if you did, you would never ask me to choose between you and my daughter."

"I'm not—"

Putting a hand up, she evened out her voice, her words slow and precise. "That is exactly what you are doing. To love someone else is to give them stability and love; it isn't leaving them when they are most vulnerable, it's not taking them from the only life they know."

Say you understand.

Tell me you'll do what it takes to build a life with me.

When he didn't say anything, she pushed off from the table. With blurry eyes, she stamped past him and into the bedroom. Hoisting her empty suitcase onto the bed, she grabbed her clothes out of the dresser, shoving them haphazardly into the bag.

"What are you doing?" Theo asked behind her. He stepped around her, grabbing her things and pulling them out of the bag. "You're not leaving me."

"Like hell, I'm not." She snagged a shirt from his hand, shoving it into her suitcase. More than likely she'd forget a few items, but getting out the door and away from him was her best option. "This is what leaving looks like, you should be familiar with the process."

"No. You stay here. You stay with me, and we talk this out."

"Talk what out? All today has proven is, you don't have the slightest idea what I need in a partner. I need someone I can trust will keep me and my child's best interests in mind, above their own selfish life."

This time his voice was hard, each word biting. "I gave up everything to get where I am today. Am I supposed to throw that all away now?"

The words stung, little slashes in her chest. This was what she still was, a distraction from his life. His career would always be more important than her. "You won't have to. Keep your precious career and your barely legal starlets and your parties. I'm done. For the past few years, I've known I wasn't good enough to make you stay. But I'll be damned if I make my children know that pain." She pushed past him. "I'll call you when we land."

Tugging her ring off her finger, she slapped it down on the table, the diamond sharp against her palm.

Following her, he grabbed the ring off the table. "You have to stay. Stay, and we'll fix this, I'll change. I'll do whatever it takes. You promised to marry me."

And you promised not to break me again.

Laying a hand on the side of his face, she willed the tears to stay away until the elevator door closed. "Teddy, if you can't see where this went wrong, I can't help you. I told you before we came down here, I can't teach you how to be a good man. And I can't marry you this way."

Theo blinked at her. "Of course you can. I love you, and you love me back."

Words, his beautiful words. The devastating song of his promises. His words couldn't keep her safe, they couldn't protect her daughter. The stark reality of it was this. For all his ballads and diamond rings and citywide views, she wasn't meant for this version of him. If he wanted to be Theo Blake, he could never be her Teddy.

"I will never stop loving you. But it's not enough." She stepped back, the mirrored elevator doors closing.

Chapter Twenty-Eight

THEO

IN THE DAYS WHEN he first broke things off with Mattie, he threw himself into his music. Writing sheets and sheets of terribly melodramatic songs where he rhymed "love" with "dove." He tried to fill that hole by drinking at Proper Bar after hours. He wrote songs, and he focused everything he could on either making music or getting drunk. It was a mistake the moment he hung up the phone, but the damage had been done. He had broken them both, and the best thing he knew he could do was allow Mattie to live her life free from his roach-infested apartment and stale sandwich days.

Losing her a second time was more acute, a sharper pain. Just as he had been sure twelve years before that he should break up with Mattie, this time around, he knew fate had brought them together. So why would she give back the ring, leaving him alone?

In all the years he had written songs, countless of them were about losing love. He thought he knew what those words meant, but now he realized they were foolish, childish lyrics. Seeing those elevator doors close on him, it was as if his chest was cleaved open. His breath came out shaky, and he needed to steady himself on the wall. He waited for far too many arduous minutes for that elevator to come back up to his floor. For Mattie to say she didn't mean it, that she loved him and all that mattered was that they were together.

But that never happened.

He had the crashing realization of how Mattie must have felt all those years before. Even in the haze of his pain, he recognized he had it easier. At least Mattie had given him a reason. He didn't agree with it, but it was there. Stumbling to the couch, he plopped down. Looking around his apartment, it all felt too large, the open space flowing from the living room to the kitchen from the hall to the balcony. The floor-to-ceiling window overlooked the hazy blue of the California sky. What was the point of this view, of this penthouse with its priceless art, if it couldn't make Mattie stay?

Since he left Cape Rose, all he ever wanted was to be on that stage, to play his songs, and be loved for his music. This fame and fortune were everything his young heart wanted, and yet it all was hollow without her.

He had never been so lonely. Always in the back of his mind was a refrain, a lyric, something to hold on to in the darkest days. But now, his mind was blank with the absence of her. He had nothing to heal himself. Nothing but a bottle of wine left over from their dinner. That would have to do.

His manager called several times, wanting him to do a few smaller appearances and interviews, but he turned her down. In the two years they had been working together, Theo had never turned down a job Tamara lined up for him. No work was too small for that paycheck. But now, he could barely get himself up to eat.

Beatriz brought him takeout, more booze, and a healthy lecture about taking a shower, but he ignored her. What could she know about the state of his broken heart? How many days passed, he couldn't tell. It might have been late afternoon or six in the morning, for all he knew, when he stumbled out of the bedroom. His eyes bloodshot, he found Eloise standing in the hallway, her eyes narrowed and arms resting on her small bump. "This story better be a load of bullshit."

"What are you doing here?" he asked, blinking at his friend as if she was an apparition. "Where did you come from? How did you even get in here?"

Waving a hand in the air, she brushed aside his comment. "I have a key, dumbass. We're doing a photo shoot to announce the pregnancy. That's not the point. This story, is it true?"

"What story?" He pushed past her and into the kitchen, where he opened his freezer to grab his backup bottle of whiskey. Despite being much shorter than him, her little pregnant body pushed him out of the way and snagged the liquor out of his hand. "Hey!"

Eloise shoved the bottle back in the freezer and slammed the door shut, resting her back on the door so he couldn't open it. "The article about you getting together with Aria?" She pulled her phone out of her little purse, shoving it at his face.

A Rekindling
By Trinity Flay

We have a tip that Theo Blake and Aria Kingston were seen leaving Kingston's home. Could it be he has seen the errors of his ways and is getting back in the good graces of a certain television star?

Reports of Aria Kingston and Theo Blake stated they were looking very chummy at the annual "No One's Father's Day" party held by Brenton Michael Phillips. An insider had this to say: "They were whispering and giggling together all night. If I had to wager, they're back together."

News of the couple's breakup rocked fans two months ago when Theo was spotted at a concert in Seattle with a still unverified woman. Rumors abound about this beautiful couple. Are wedding bells in the future?

This author hopes so!

If you have a celebrity sighting or a tip, email us at gotcha @allceleb.com

The paparazzi photo taken outside Aria's building appeared above the article. Theo's arm was over Aria's shoulder, and hers was tucked into his side. If he didn't know any better, he'd think they were back together again, too.

"That's old news." He grimaced. "And you know better than to trust anything you read in that rag."

"Good. Because I might not give you a hard time with some of your previous bullshit, but you can't do that to Mattie."

He walked to the living room, flopping himself on the couch with a groan. "What are you talking about? You guys always give me shit."

"Not enough, apparently." Eloise followed behind him, glancing around the messy room.

He scrubbed a hand over his beard. It was unkempt, in desperate need of brushing, but that involved looking himself in the mirror. "Mattie left me. I proposed to her, and I thought she wanted to be with me, but the next day she flipped out and left me."

Eloise wrinkled her nose at him. "I knew this was a bad idea."

Grimacing, he pulled himself up to a semi-seated position. "You did not."

"Tell me what happened." In one hand she had an empty bottle of whiskey, and in the other was what he could only assume used to be a shirt or a towel; it was so bunched up, he couldn't tell.

As much as he could, he recounted the weekend. He trusted Eloise more than almost anyone with the truth. He knew she would judge him a bit but still care for him.

Pursing her lips, she blew out a big breath through her nose. "Poor Mattie."

"Poor Mattie?! Poor me! I'm the one she left behind, dumped her engagement ring and everything."

Eloise glanced at the table. "Oh, is that what that thing is? I thought it was a paperweight."

"That ring cost four million dollars."

Eloise raised a brow. "That's a lot of money spent for a ring she can't wear half the time."

His eyes narrowed into slits. "What does that mean?"

With a passing hand, she gestured to the ring. "How is she able to garden with that thing, or bake, or do any of her interests? Does she even like diamonds? It's a beautiful ring, but it doesn't look like her style."

Picking up the ring between his fingers, he inspected the rock. He had selected it because it was the biggest. He had seen other celebrities with similar rings before. Safiya herself had been spotted with one even bigger since she got back together with her husband. He wanted Mattie to have the best, because she deserved the best.

"Who doesn't like diamonds?" he grumbled, his energy waning. "It was the best. Is it so wrong to get her the best?"

"The best for who? For you? Yeah, sure. That ring would have photographed beautifully for appearances, but is that the life she wants to live? Did you think about her when you bought this? When you planned your life?"

"All I think about is her," Theo snapped. "How can you say I'm not?"

"Because nothing about this feels like *her*. Taking her to Brenton Michael's party? Really? I hate that shit, and I'm used to the scene. But you thrust her into this with no preparation, and you were probably peacocking around in that pompous way you do."

He sneered at her. "What are you talking about? I do not."

Cocking her head to the side, she frowned at him. "For a born performer, you have the least amount of self-awareness. You act completely different at industry events."

Blinking, he considered himself at the lunch. Only thinking about how to frame the shot for the paparazzi, he hadn't been paying attention to Mattie's comfort at all. The night of the party was worse. God, had she been stuck talking to that terrible model girlfriend of television host Chad Rice? He hadn't thought much of it, but looking back, there was a tension to her all night that didn't go away until they left the party. Had she really been that unhappy?

"That industry stuff is part of my job."

"Why? Theo, do you even like doing all these jobs? The constant photo shoots, television appearances, and interviews? Keller and Nathan both have been cutting back for years, since the Hellions tour, but you keep going. Is it what makes you happy?"

"Of course it is. I love my work. It's everything I've worked to achieve."

Eloise raised a brow. "Is it? Being on stage and music, sure. But hocking cologne for fashion houses? Selling cars in Germany? Watches in South Korea? Going to club openings and constant parties? This is your idea of a great life?"

He frowned at her. "What's your point?"

Putting her hands up in mock surrender, she shrugged. "All I'm saying is, anyone who sees Mattie can tell that wouldn't make her happy. And she has a daughter to think about."

"And I told her I'd take care of Kamari."

Eloise snorted. "By what? Enrolling her in a private school? Away from her life? Hire a nanny to take care of her and be gone every single night for a different premiere or late-night party? She had a father, from the sound of it, a great one. I wish I could have had a mother who looked out for me. Instead, my mother, Dana was drinking her checks away and bringing home random guys, while my brother and I hid away in our room."

Theo scratched the side of his nose. Eloise rarely talked of her life before L.A.; they had that in common. "You turned out okay."

"Despite, not because. There is a difference. I have done years of therapy to process a childhood where what my mother wanted was more important than me. Who knows what my life could have been if I had a parent who put me first. Are you really asking Mattie to make the same choice? She's a good mother, and if you loved her the way you say you do, you wouldn't put her in the position to choose."

"I wanted to give her the best life, that's all I want for her and Mari."

"Did you stop and ask her what that life would look like? Because something tells me it has nothing to do with fancy parties held by douchebag pop stars and million-dollar rings."

A sinking sensation pooled in his stomach. It was the same thing Mattie had told him, but he didn't want to listen. He thought he had the right answers using his wealth. "But that's all that I've made of myself. I didn't have enough to offer her before, but now I do. I can give her anything. She deserves it."

"Is that really what you think?" Eloise's voice softened. "She deserves you. The real you. Do you think she cares about your money or your fame? I saw the way she looked at you when you were taking care of Kamari that day. How she looked when she saw you at our party that first night. How she feels for you has nothing to do with your status."

"You can't know that." Theo's voice faltered.

Eloise huffed out an incredulous laugh. "Yeah, I can. Or else she would have stayed for that monstrosity right there. If you want to, you can fix this, Theo."

"How could I possibly?"

Eloise sat across from him, her ankles crossed. "You need to think good and hard about what kind of life you want. Is it this?" She waved a hand around the room, the art on the walls and the view of downtown from his balcony. "Or is it a life with Mattie?"

"Why do I have to give up everything?"

"You wouldn't have to give up everything. There are planes for a reason. You need to come down here, you can. You know Keller isn't going to be working at the same breakneck speed anymore. And I doubt Nathan wants to either. So really, it's you alone, clinging to this rock and roll lifestyle."

"You don't understand, this is who I am."

"Is it?" she paused. "Or is it a front so you don't have to do the hard work it takes to be worthy of her?"

Crossing his arms over his chest, he grumbled at her, "I don't know if I like this new bossy Lou. You used to be nicer. I think Ilsa is rubbing off on you."

"Call it pregnancy hormones. We both know I'm right, though." With another glance around the room, she smiled. "I'll be calling Beatriz and telling her you're on detox from now on. I'm taking that whiskey. You don't need it if you're going to be working on cleaning yourself up."

"You are the worst."

Standing, she smoothed the front of her dress. "And please, for the love of all that's holy, take a fucking shower."

As she walked away, he yelled at her back, "That kind of language is bad for the baby."

O N HIS SEVENTH GLASS of champagne, he stopped feeling the way his shoes pinched his toes. Why were there so many people there, and more importantly, why had he agreed to this celebrity restaurant opening?

That's right, because showing up and being photographed was good for his image. He had hoped he would see at least Aria there, but no one he wanted to talk to had come. When he asked Keller, he had laughed, saying, "They couldn't pay me a million dollars to show up at that horse-and-pony show.

Those people are insufferable."

Nathan and Ilsa were at some art gallery opening somewhere. How had he lived in this city for so many years and never noticed how lonely it was? Before Mattie came back, he was content with the shallow conversation, expensive drinks, and banal company.

He knew she ruined him in relationships, but now he couldn't even enjoy a stupid party without thinking of her, and how much happier he would be to have her nearby.

With a dress that was so tight it might as well have been painted on her, the young woman sidled up to him, a delicate hand on his forearm as she leaned in. "Theo Blake, you are even more handsome in person."

He blinked down at the woman; she looked vaguely familiar, but with the trends in plastic surgery these days, women in the city all had the same upturned eyes, sunken cheeks, and overly filled lips. This one had blonde hair, so light it was almost white. From his angle above her, he could see the pinpricks of darkness on her scalp that let him know she wasn't a natural blonde.

A year before, someone asked him if he wanted to get the buccal fat removed from his face, to create a more angular look to his cheekbones. He was almost tempted until he thought about the shit his bandmates would give him. Staring down at this woman, he was glad he didn't get the procedure done.

"Have we met?" he asked coolly, sliding his arm out of her grasp.

Unfazed by his movement, the woman put her hand out to him, fingers down turned, as if he was to kiss the back of her hand. "Klaudia Dzik, Anton's daughter. I was at the dinner the other night, but I had another event to go to, so I was unable to fully introduce myself."

"Right." He racked his memory of the party, but the drinks had done their job, and it was all a fuzzy mess. "Good to see you again."

She leaned in, her voice low and sultry. "I was so disappointed to have left early the other night. I was hoping to get to know you better, since it sounds like my father was especially impressed with you. Something I'm sure I would share if I had the chance to be *better acquainted*."

Blinking at the woman a few times, he processed what she was saying.

Anton Dzik liked him, so this collaboration might go ahead. It was a huge goal, and he could achieve it. The *but* hung in the air as the woman eyed him appreciatively.

The woman was gorgeous; there was no doubt about that. All smooth skin, no hair out of place, her sky-high tits, and flat stomach were the kind of aesthetic that photographed beautifully beside him. He knew how they would look in pictures together, how the press would eat up a dalliance between the two of them—the rock star and nepotistic model. He could stay there and cling to this fame. The spotlights. Everything he had done, had sacrificed was all for that. What was it Eloise told him once? *All you love is the pretty lights, the white and yellow sea.* It was hollow without Mattie.

Why was he clinging to this lifestyle when it hadn't made him happy in years? He loved performing with the guys, making music, writing songs. He loved his fans and the other musicians he met through the years.

But this?

He glanced around the party—the slick smiles and the way everyone's eyes darted around the room, searching for a better person to talk to. Had he ever liked this? Or was it the way he was so easily lauded at these events? He could show up, flash his smile, and brush his hair off his forehead, and people loved him.

Beside him, the woman gave a small finger wave to an actress, her plumped-up lips taking on what Theo had to assume was supposed to be a smile. "Did you see what she wore to the Emmys? Green is not her color; she looked hideous."

How many times had he stood there listening to biting comments and felt lucky to be on the inside of this world? His mouth dried, a sour taste on his tongue.

Turning back to face him, Klaudia purred in what must have been her most seductive voice, "This party is boring; you want to join me for some real fun?"

He knew how the night would go; drugs and alcohol consumed, the photos taken, the lackluster sex, and the need to be always *on*. This woman seemed the kind who would welcome a seven-carat ring. How could he think the Mattie he loved would have wanted something like that?

With an audible *thunk*, Theo set his glass down on a small table. "I can't.

I have something I need to take care of."

Leaving the woman before she could engage him in any more conversation, he had his agent and manager on the line by the time he got into the back seat of his car.

Chapter Twenty-Nine

Mattie

T HE PAIN WAS TANGIBLE. Her emotions always were. The first time she held Kamari, she felt a piece of her chest click together, as if something that had always been loose had slid into place, completing her. The first time Theo had held her hand in his old truck, the bouquet of pilfered peonies between them on the seat, it was a warmth that flowed through her and burned her cheeks.

And when she left, it was as if her body was chipping away, little piece by little piece floating away as she rode the elevator down, got in the hailed cab, and headed to the airport, where she took the first available flight back to SeaTac.

In the years since she had Kamari, Mattie had phantom kicks in her stomach, the sensation of a nonexistent baby moving around. The sensation of holding someone inside you and being connected never went away.

Losing Theo again was full of phantom touches. On the plane, in the car, in her bed, as she lay down to sleep, she could still recall the pressure of his touch. It was a choice she never wanted to make. The entire ride back to Manzanita, she thought about turning around. More than almost anything, she wanted to be beside Theo. As much as she hated the party, and the paparazzi shooting them, and the silly boob tape, she would have stayed if she didn't have someone else counting on her. She alone would have given everything to that boy, twelve years before. But she was not alone.

He lived in a world she would have shaped herself to fit into. The lights, the glamour, the unmoving foreheads; it was the dream of a wayward teen girl.

She was not that girl. Moreover, she didn't want to be.

As much as she loved Theo, she couldn't live that life, and if this was the only version he could offer, they would never share it.

Still, as she rested her head on her pillow, she found herself reaching into the dark to grasp at the absence of the life they could have had.

There is no room for a broken heart when you have responsibilities. Her work was still there, the dishwasher needed loading, and the gymnastics classes needed to be attended.

Before, she had an anger that could sustain her. She was the one broken-hearted, the one thwarted by his leaving. She could hold on to the pain as a talisman that she was wronged. But she had been the one to leave this time. It was a mistake to have allowed it to go so far. From the moment he followed her on the garden path, this road would lead to ruin. Neither of them could stay away from each other. For someone who prided herself on her rationality, she was a fool for Theodore Blake.

It had only been two days, but she knew this void inside her would not heal. How could it? It was the same that had been carved years before. Theo told her he never had space for someone else. She should have told him, inside her they matched. It wasn't hubris, or being melodramatic, when she told herself she would never love a man the way she loved Theo. Before, she could have filed it away in childish dreaming, but now she knew the truth. And in that truth, she had broken her own heart in the process.

A FEW DAYS AFTER she had come home, a news report came up.

Two-Timing Teddy!!
By Trinity Flay

A day after reports and eyewitness accounts showed Prevalent Notion lead singer, Theodore Blake leaving on again off again girlfriend Aria's Kingston's home Friday afternoon, he was spotted kissing a dark-haired woman at Proper Bar.

Cell phone footage shows the singer and the now unnamed woman, dancing and kissing on an empty dance floor after the bar had closed for the night. Bartender and aspiring actor Derrick Worth told AllCeleb reporters: "They were definitely together, dancing, kissing, grabbing at each other. Honestly, I was surprised they didn't stay too long, if you know what I mean. I thought he was dating that hot actress from that witch school show, but I guess not."

Blake is no stranger to being seen with multiple women. He was spotted recently canoodling with an unknown woman, Addison Sullivan of Seattle.

Addison

Aria

Maybe this other woman is an Amy?

Will Aria take him back?

This story is evolving. If you have information regarding this story or have any other celebrity news, please email us at our tip line at gotcha@allceleb.com.

It was a day later when the pictures from their lunch at the restaurant popped up. They still hadn't found her name but were speculating about the large rock on her finger. Her stomach rolled at the picture. Even from a distance, the ring was visible. What should have been a happy day was clouded by her own doubts and his ego. She clicked out of the site and set up her trusty keyword blocker.

No more Prevalent Notion, no more rock stars, and no more Theo Blake.

The house next door sat dark and empty. She saw Eloise and Keller through the trees leaving a few days before, the house sitting quiet on the bay. It was just as well. While she liked talking with Eloise, she didn't want to explain herself to Theo's friends. How could they understand the situation?

No, it was better this way. She could go back to doing what she did well enough. Being a good mom, her job, and pulling up weeds.

A N UNSEASONABLY HOT DAY, Shea and her kids came over to swim in the bay. Set up in a low-slung chair beside her friend while the kids splashed in the cold salt water, Mattie broke down somewhere between her second spiked seltzer and half a bag of caramel popcorn.

Listening to the tale, Shea's smooth forehead moved in shock at different parts of the story, but she never interrupted.

With a focus on her feet on the beach, Mattie burrowed little holes in the beach with her toes. The sand's top layer was hot from the sun but beneath it was cool and damp. "Did I make a mistake?"

Shea leaned back, setting her drink in the mesh holder attached to her chair. "I can't say whether you made the wrong choice or not. It's a really difficult decision."

Mattie wiped under her eyes with her fingers. "I should have known it was a mistake to get involved with him. What did I expect? He's a rock star, and I'm some single mother from a small town. In what world would we make sense?"

Shea studied her friend. "He loves you, though. As crazy as I thought this whole trip was for you, I could see that."

Mattie's eyes filled with treacherous tears once again. "But that makes it all the worse. It doesn't matter how much he loves me, or I love him. If we can't be together the way he wants it, it won't happen."

Watching her daughter in the water, she knew she had made the impossibly hard choice, but it wasn't the wrong one. She only wished there was a world where she could have Theo, too.

Her face warming in the sun, Shea excused herself to get them new drinks before emerging a few minutes later, empty-handed. "Mats, you might want to get up to the house. You have a visitor."

"What? Who?"

Shea pushed her back. "Go see. I'll watch the kids."

Draining the can of lukewarm seltzer in her mouth, Mattie made her way up the rocky path to her lawn. As she rounded the side of the house, she scrunched the can to throw in her recycling bin.

Can in her hand, she stopped short to find a large black SUV parked behind her sedan. The windows were blacked out, but she could see the familiar set of his wide shoulders through the windshield. It looked like he was breathing deeply; his hands were gripping the steering wheel, and his eyes were closed.

The can fell from her hand and onto the gravel driveway as she watched Theo behind the wheel, mumbling to himself, as if he was psyching himself up.

No thoughts beyond getting closer, she walked to his door, pulling at the handle. It was locked, and she couldn't see but sensed him watching her through the blacked-out window of the driver's side.

The mechanical click of the door being unlocked, and she stepped back as he opened the door.

He climbed out, his eyes on Mattie.

A million things flew through her head.

I missed you so much. I love you. Say you love me back and we'll figure this out.

Instead, she motioned to the car. "That's a nice rental."

What kind of greeting is that?

Theo glanced at it. "I bought it. Consumer reports gave it the best score for a family SUV. I figured if I'm going to be driving Kamari around to ballet and gymnastics and stuff."

"You bought a car...for what?" Mattie said.

"For us."

Mattie blinked up at him. He took a step forward, and she stepped back in sync. Her hands came up, as if to protect herself; she couldn't get her hopes up.

"You were right. I was selfish. I don't need the rock star life, the parties, the booze, and the fanfare. You are what I need; a life with you. I told my team, from now on, this will be my home base. If you want, I'll get a place in town. As long as I'm closer to you."

Couldn't hope, wouldn't. But it was there. A brief spark of maybe. "What about work?"

He shrugged. "Keller lives next door half the year. I already talked to the guys; they agreed that slowing down was the best thing for all of us. My agent had a fit when I turned down the watch commercial in Singapore, but it's the week of your birthday. Nathan and Ilsa can come up. And there's always an airplane. It's a quick flight down to L.A. for meetings. We've put out five records. Keller's going to be a father soon enough. I think slowing down is a good idea for all of us."

"You're giving it all up for me?"

He laughed. "No, I'm rearranging my life until you and Kamari are in the center. I can make the other parts fit, as long as I have you."

Tears came now, unabashed. She didn't try to wipe them away as he stepped closer. This time she stayed in place, allowing him to cup her cheek in his hand.

"I said once, everything I've done is to be enough for you. But I realized that isn't enough. I can tell you the truth, that you're in every song I write, every note I play. You say I've ruined you for every other man? For me, there's never been someone else. I can never replace you." He swept her hair off her face, running a thumb over her cheek. "But all those are words. You deserve more than words. You deserve my actions, my commitment to you, and to the family we'll create together. Get it now. All those years ago, I thought I had to sacrifice you to get what I want, but I won't do that again. I make this vow; I will always take care of you the way you need it. I will fit myself into you."

Words wouldn't come. She threw her arms around his neck, pulling his face down to hers for a kiss. His arms swept her up, firm under her butt as he raised her to his level to kiss her thoroughly.

He didn't stay the night that night. Instead, he retired to Eloise and Keller's house. Every morning, he would come over first thing and help her make breakfast for Kamari. At night, he would make them dinner or take them out to eat. When Eloise and Keller returned two weeks later, they were surprised to find Theo sitting with his laptop at the kitchen counter. As best he could, he explained that he was giving her time to let him back in. He didn't have to wait long.

It was that night when Mattie told him to come over to stay the night. He wouldn't leave.

The proposal came three weeks later. After a quiet dinner at a French restaurant in town, he brought her out to the garden, where he got down on one knee and, with Kamari beside her, asked her to be his wife, then asked Kamari if he could be her stepfather. The last part was obviously rehearsed, as Kamari agreed in an English accent, the way she preferred when pretending with her toys.

On the thin white gold band, Mattie immediately recognized the emerald from her grandmother's brooch. That heirloom meant more to her than all seven carats of her previous ring did. A low summer drizzle started, misting the dahlias that grew tall and wild. The spray hit their hair as Theo held Mattie tight in his arms. At that moment, the rain was rare indeed.

Epilogue

Elio Francis Blake was born on a Sunday night in mid-July. With a shock of golden hair and green eyes, he was a terrible sleeper, but a wonderful cuddler. Kamari had taken to her role as a big sister with vigor. She already had some experience as Eloise and Keller's helper for their daughter, Selene Liliana, born in early January.

Theo offered to have a smaller wedding if Mattie wanted one, but she insisted they do it up big, the way he wanted. It was a grand affair, overlooking the Puget Sound, celebrity guests mingled with the small-town folks of Manzanita. Pictures of the wedding were sold and the proceeds donated to a charity that aimed at providing dance and music to at-risk teens in the area.

Theo turned down many appearances, though Mattie talked him into finally doing the watch campaign in Singapore, if only to get the free trip overseas for them. The ads paid for their new home in a single go. As much as Mattie loved the small bungalow, beside Keller and Eloise, with their new addition, the square footage was too cramped for four. Their new house was a mile down the road, still on the bay, boasting almost an acre of gardening plots for Mattie to cultivate.

The band recorded their sixth album in Seattle, to great critical acclaim. Mattie worked out a new custody agreement for Kamari. In the school year, they would stay close by in Manzanita, when at all possible, but in the summers when school was out, Mattie and Kamari would join the band as they toured. This tour was shorter than previous ones, with many stops and hotel rooms. The backstage rooms were complete with a nursery for Selene and Elio, with a special area for Kamari. They hired a full-time nanny, who helped with all three children while on the road, who all the kids loved to pieces. Gone were the days of the band traveling in a rusted old bus with a broken turn signal.

Twelve years before, Theo had driven away from Cape Rose with his guitar, an emerald brooch, and a beat-up copy of a paperback book in his passenger seat. In the days when he was hungry, or cold,he would take out that book and read about a war-torn world and looming death.
Of the prevalent notion of believing in something more outside ourselves. Of the futility in relying on a higher power to save us.

It was the nihilistic view of a boy who knew nothing of the golden ruin of loving someone.

It took mistakes, and sacrifices. Crowded stadiums filled with songs, and quiet sessions with only their voices. It was drunken marriages in Vegas chapels and dirty pickup lines. Pilfered peonies on the front seat of a truck and emerald brooches pinned to guitar straps.

It may have been a million last moments on the pages of the book, but now the only prevalent notion they cared about was the need to live in music and love.

Also By Linnea March

Faultless Notion

Waking up with the wrong man's ring on her finger never felt so right.

Eloise Dunning ran far from her small town in the Pacific Northwest to Los Angeles with little more than the clothes on her back and a dream of being a singer-songwriter. Now she is a personal assistant to the rock band, Prevalent Notion, and leaving her songbook in the bottom of her bag.

Keller Grant is everything a rock star should be. Sinfully attractive, an enigmatic artist with a dark past, and an immensely talented drummer. He loves the revolving door of women in each city, creating music with his bandmates in Prevalent Notion, and teasing an uptight Eloise.

The night before the band kicks off their American Tour, Eloise and Keller wake up in each other's arms with wedding bands on their fingers. Forced by the record label to maintain the marriage for the public, they face a hungry press, rabid fans, and jealousy from all sides.

As they get the world to believe in their facade, they find that, maybe, this marriage doesn't feel like a performance.

For fans of music, bungee jumping, steamy moments behind closed doors, and heartfelt moments on the wings of the stage. Here is your new favorite rock star romance.

Faultless Notion is a full-length contemporary standalone romance. It is book one in the Prevalent Notion Series

Treacherous Notion

It's treacherous to picture your best friend naked.

Nathan Ayers prides himself on being likable. He's the sweetheart bassist of the world's hottest rock band. He has millions of fans who love his talent, kind smile, and old-fashioned Southern charm. He is everyone's friend, so why can't Nathan stop thinking about Ilsa in a not-so-friendly way?

Ilsa Kruger is determined. Determined to launch her fashion line. Determined to be as successful as she was as a teenage beauty queen. Most of all she is determined not to let her growing attraction to her friend, Nathan, distract her from her goals.

As they find themselves growing closer, darkness from their past threatens their happiness.

Can they stay together? Or will the perils of fame tear them apart?

For fans of sweet wine, dirty pick-up lines, lingering looks in crowded rooms, and passionate embraces where no one can see. Here is your new favorite friends-to-lovers book.

Treacherous Notion is Book Two in the Prevalent Notion Series.

Also by Linnea March

Reckless Liar

The One You Chose: A Holiday Novella

About the Author

Linnea March is a contemporary romance author who writes steamy stories about self-confident women and the rugged men who love them. She lives somewhere in the wilds of the Pacific Northwest with her husband, their two boys, and a plump dog. After fifteen years of teaching early childhood education, she put down the googly eyes and picked up a pen. When not writing, she can be found reading her way through an ever-growing pile of books while drinking copious amounts of coffee. She proudly refuses to use umbrellas.

Acknowledgements

My overwhelming thanks to the following people.

My editor, Emma Jane of EJL Editing, and Karen and Amber of the Word Slayers for helping me make his book into the best version of itself.

To Laura, Brenda, and Emma for taking that final read-through with me.

To my RAWR girls for always having a funny picture/GIF, encouragement, and telling me what is wrong with my original cover. Aperol Spritzes and bear cuddles all around.

To the readers who have been there through this journey, with special love to the advance readers who took a chance on Faultless Notion years ago and stuck beside me since. You are the reason I do this.

My family for not always reading my books but always encouraging me to write them. My boys, who can never read these books. I love you all.

Heidi for being my go-to for all things baking and sustainable gardening.

Cassidy and Kate for being my first readers.

My husband for being my biggest supporter and most ardent fan. If I can write love it's because of you.

www.ingramcontent.com/pod-product-compliance
Lightning Source LLC
Chambersburg PA
CBHW020151310726

48970CB00006B/2096